A DEADLY COMPLOT

Tom Walsingham Mysteries
Book Four

C. P. Giuliani

SAPERE
BOOKS

A DEADLY
COMPLOT

Published by Sapere Books.

24 Trafalgar Road, Ilkley, LS29 8HH,
United Kingdom

saperebooks.com

ISBN: 978-0-85495-255-7

To the memory of my uncle Luciano, who would chuckle to himself —
and, I hope, be proud of me.

ACKNOWLEDGEMENTS

It is in the nature of a series that more and more new characters will walk onstage with each book, and new knowledge will be needed — not just about them, but for them to possess and use. Not-quite-yet physician Ambrose Lopes is one such "new entry" — and, for discussing Ambrose's medical knowledge, as well as the gruesome details of the behaviour of dead bodies, I give heartfelt thanks to Adolfo Vaini — a truly great stage actor with a medical degree and a sense of humour.

Many, many thanks also go to Chas Jones, who saw how things were bound to stand between Tom and Frances well before I did.

And Almo Dalporto — a whiz at all things technical, and Excel among them — has my deepest gratitude for creating the "Characters, Characters…" database for me. It's a most useful tool, and one day I'm going to write something about Alfredo Statico, assassin for hire.

Last but not least, thank you Mother and Milla (Hello, Echelon!): your patience and good cheer in the face of endless Tom talk is always much appreciated.

PROLOGUE

Elizabeth Tudor, by God's grace Queen of England and Defender of the Faith, was in a foul mood.

The glistening of the Thames, almost blue for once under the sky's summer glory, the soft breeze, the smooth rhythm of the rowers, the sweet strains from the lute-player sitting in the prow — none of it changed the fact that the Queen had a toothache, nor the gist of her Principal Secretary's tidings.

Sir Francis Walsingham sat straight in his black velvet robe, as though he were sitting in Council, and was so damnably unfathomable in his evenness of voice and mien.

"And still you leave this Babington free to plot our murder!" Elizabeth found it a feat to keep to a muted snarl. She would have roared — being very much her father's daughter — but the royal shallop was small, and voices carried on water.

Sir Francis tilted his head. "Young Babington is only the figurehead of this conspiracy, Your Highness. A well-born, well-moneyed one — but a figurehead nonetheless. The true danger lies with Ballard."

Father John Ballard, of course — Catholic priest out of Rheims, friend to Spain, traitor and intriguer.

"Who is, we believe, also free," Elizabeth retorted.

And the man had the gall to bow his head like one receiving praise!

"For now, yes," Sir Francis said. "And believing himself safe, under the alias of Captain Fortescue."

A twinge of the cursed tooth made the Queen loosen her jaw. "And still you don't seize them! What is it that you lack? Proof?"

"In fact, we have much evidence — the last piece being a letter of a most damning nature…"

Oh, the way he let it trail, like an angling hook drifting in the water! There were those who said Walsingham could play his sovereign like a fiddle. Well, by God, this sovereign flattered herself that she could read her spymaster like a hornbook.

"A letter." She kept her gaze on the glittering drops that trickled from the oars with each stroke.

"A cyphered letter, commending Babington's zeal in the endeavour of overthrowing the State and restoring Catholicism. And —" there was the shortest pause — "in that of murdering Your Highness."

"And who wrote this missive?"

The Queen had long learnt that little in this world ever eluded Sir Francis's notice — most surely not the danger quivering in her words. And yet he waited until she turned, and held her glare before answering, "The Queen of Scots, Your Highness."

"God's wounds!" There were times when Elizabeth Tudor swore for the sake of rattling her Puritan Secretary, but not this time. She had cause to swear, surely? The Queen of Scots — the dethroned Mary Stuart, Elizabeth's own cousin, a Papist, the fond hope of every Catholic in the realm, and a tireless, malicious intriguer! "Nigh on twenty years our prisoner, and still she plots!" She hit a palm on her silk-covered lap. "And still you haven't learnt to keep her from it?"

Not that she believed it, not even when Sir Francis gave a rueful frown and said, "She has adherents, Your Highness, and friends. Somehow she smuggled this letter out of Chartley

Castle. It is only through much work and vigilance that my men came to be in possession of it."

Just the one letter? And how did Mary elude her keepers? The Queen bit down the sour questions. She didn't want to know. She didn't want to hear that, as long as she lived, Mary Stuart would be a beacon for all the enemies of Protestant England, even imprisoned as she was at Chartley Castle in Staffordshire. She didn't want to even contemplate the notion of ordering the death of a sovereign. She leant forward to shout, "Enough! Bring us back!"

Jesu — how shrill she sounded! In the prow the music stuttered to a halt, the bargemaster barked an order, and the watermen bent their scarlet-liveried backs on their oars. It was a weighty affair, to alter course.

"This letter..." A dull pain pulsed in Elizabeth's tooth, sharpening as she squinted against the glare of the river. She turned to scrutinise Walsingham. Even in the red shade of the heavy silk awning, he looked wan. "You've no doubt of it?"

He didn't hesitate. "So far, only the deciphered copy was brought to me, but I never doubt the work of my men, Your Highness — or their loyalty." And then, as though he'd been asked, he went on, "The Queen of Scots entrusts Babington's efforts to God's protection, and to the help of the Spanish Ambassador in Paris."

Spain — the Pope's great vulture, hungrily poised to descend on England with fire and sword, and the Inquisition marching in the wake of those savage troops, the *tercios*, ready to raise Mary Stuart to the empty throne. And they all knew from the Low Countries what Spanish rule was like.

"Enough!" Elizabeth took an angry gulp of river air. "Scheming a queen's death is one thing; effecting those schemes is another." *Let Walsingham think well on this!* "Keep these traitors from murdering us, Mr. Secretary, and there will be no vacant throne to covet."

There was no expression on Sir Francis's face as he bowed low. "Your Highness must be assured that this will be my foremost concern." Not the only one, though. "My men in London have the firmest grip on this conspiracy."

CHAPTER 1

That evening, Tom Walsingham — Sir Francis's kinsman and protégé — was pacing the length of his small writing room in the spymaster's house in Seething Lane.

"'Tis like holding onto a bucketful of eels!" Tom broke his pacing and threw himself into a chair with enough vehemence to make the candle's flame dance in the stifling night air. "Curse the man to Hell!"

Across the narrow writing table, Frank Mylls, secretary to Sir Francis, bunched his brows into one grey bush — for he shared with his master a deep dislike of swearing. "It seems to me you're letting your dislike of Gifford sway you, Mr. Thomas."

"My dislike...!" Tom threw up both hands. "Our tame turncoat vanishes into thin air, he may or may not have warned Babington and the rest — and I *dislike* him?"

Mylls hummed. Near on fifty years, he was twice Tom's age — but Tom was a Walsingham. "He did devise the means to seize Mary Stuart's letters at Chartley Castle —"

"He and Phelippes, ay — and it will count for nothing, if he's given us away to Mary Stuart's friends!"

And here was a preoccupation not even Mylls could dismiss — but still he pursed his lips, raking a hand through his grey mane. "I'm not saying we should set great store by Gifford's loyalty — but then, 'tis with men's disloyalty that we work, rather than otherwise."

"But that of our own men?" Tom scoffed — and at once felt the colour rush to his face.

Was it a sneer playing on Mylls's face? Small blame to him, if it was. "Mr. Thomas, Bernard Maude started in life by blackmailing a bishop, and there's no worse knave than Poley, and Gifford…"

Why, Gilbert Gifford wasn't even one of theirs. A Catholic traitor, spying on his fellows out of deathly fear … to expect loyalty from such a man!

Before Mylls could rub more salt on it, voices rose in the next room — and Fates be thanked! Tom was at the door in a trice, peering into the gloomy passage furnished with nothing but two benches and a cupboard. On one of these benches two young men slouched side by side, with a half-empty trencher between them, watching a third who stood just out of the halo of one candle.

"Is that you, Berden?" Tom called, squinting from the threshold. "Have you found Gifford — or Savage?"

Nicholas Berden stepped into the light, a spare fellow of thirty with a dark, angular face and a sweaty air of having walked all over London. "Not a whiff of either," he said. "I hoped Rouse had…"

Sitting straighter on the bench, Rouse Casey shook his fiery red head and struggled to gulp down his cheese. "Gifford always turns up…"

"Ay, pity Mr. Tom wants 'im now," the third fellow groused through a full mouth. Being Tom's servant for near on a year now — and Sir Francis's before that — hadn't improved Nick Skeres's manners or speech a whit.

"He never liked being set to watch Savage," Mylls said, coming to join Tom at the door.

As though they were to mind what Gilbert Gifford liked! Tom bit his tongue and counted to ten in Latin. What was he going to write to Sir Francis — that whenever they had good certainty of one plotter, three more slipped out of their grasp? And, worst of all, there was so little that Tom himself could do.

Nor anyone else, at this time of night, for fretful Gifford wasn't one to roam the streets so long past curfew that the Watch would look askance at him — which Berden knew, no matter the show of hound-pup-eyed readiness.

"Do I go out again, Mr. Thomas?"

Tom sighed. What was the use? "Have them give you some supper, Berden, and then go home."

When Berden dithered, Tom, having a fair notion of what was coming, retreated into the writing room and closed the door in the fellow's face.

"*I'm not after gain, but...*" he murmured — one of Berden's habitual phrases — drawing a small snort out of Mylls.

"A leech, Berden is — but no fool. And more trustworthy than most."

Which wasn't saying much, was it? Tom perched on the windowsill. "I'm putting him after Ballard again, tomorrow," he said, earning a glum nod.

"Ballard! That one I'd like to see in gaol."

Oh, wouldn't they all! "Well, we have the letter of the Queen of Scots, now. Perhaps..."

Perhaps. Because the plain truth of the matter was, they knew all there was to know about Ballard's complot. They'd long known, and let the traitors weave enough rope to hang themselves a dozen times, and could have arrested them all at any time this past month, only waiting for the imprisoned Mary Stuart to compromise herself in treason and murder. She hadn't so far — but this time perhaps...

Mylls braced himself upright, both palms on the table. "I pray that, while we wait, they don't grow bold and act."

A shiver ran down Tom's back, for all the warmth of the summer night, for all that it seemed disloyal to question. What if this rope-walking ended in mayhem and regicide — and, on the tail of it, a Spanish invasion? Weren't they losing sight of one traitor or the other half the time? Weren't they misdoubting their own men?

There was nothing for it but to straighten his back and strive for that even certainty, so reassuring when it came from Sir Francis. "Let's hope this letter is what we need, then. And if it is... You still have the pursuivant at your house?"

"Two of them." Mylls grimaced. "'Tis like having two wolfhounds on the leash. Just let the order come soon."

All the way to the gloomy hall, Mylls grumbled of warrants, and the untrustworthiness of city men, and the barring of doors at night. It was good to see him out with his linkboy at last. The fellow was tireless, sharp-witted, and trusted by Sir Francis — but, Jupiter above, such a nay-sayer!

Tom took a deep breath of the damp night air before the servant shut the door. Could he go and stroll a while in the garden? He'd heard all his reports — he did little else, these days.

"Mr. Thomas?"

But no, of course — no such blessing. By the staircase, coming from the kitchen, Berden stood together with another man carrying a candle — a beardless man with a grey jerkin and a head of flat yellow hair... Oh Lord!

"Rob Poley — what are you doing here? If you've lost Babington, I swear —"

Poley smiled — and why it should set Tom's teeth on edge, he didn't know. Poley was discreet, and a smooth talker, and Tom was inclined to trust him a little better than Mylls did — but like him? That was a horse of another colour.

16

"Lost him? Bless you, Master — no," Poley said. "But I'm supposed to see to her Ladyship's preparations, now and then. I thought I'd run and hear if you want anything with me."

Of course. Poley was, at least in name, a servant to Tom's cousin Frances — Sir Francis's only daughter, and Lady Sidney this past year. She was to leave and join her husband in Flushing — and even a gudgeon like young Babington was bound to wonder if his zealous new friend never attended to his work.

"There's nothing new," Tom said, dearly wishing there could be. "I won't ask if you took care not to be followed."

Poley smiled a little wider, as though Tom had been jesting, and Berden took it as a sign that his turn had come.

"Mr. Thomas…" He stepped forward, lips pursed and eyes wide — a hound-pup dealt most unfairly.

"'Tis back to Father Ballard for you, Berden," said Tom. "Rouse will find Gifford."

"Ay — but…" Berden took hold of Tom's sleeve. "Mr. Thomas, I'm not after gain, and it grieves me to have to draw on His Honour's treasure —"

"Especially since you drew on it just last week, I'm sure."

Behind Berden's back, there was no mistaking the amusement in Poley's manner. Berden himself looked aggrieved.

"But is it my fault that I go to so many expenses?" he moaned. "Is it my fault that these traitors eat and drink like earls? You know how it is. You think I relish to burden you and His Honour? 'Tis an odious calling, being a spy —"

Tom had used to laugh at Berden's oratory gift — back when he'd not been stuck in Seething Lane to deal with the man and his fellows. He was instructing Berden to leave a note with young Tobias Chandler, grown from apprentice to scrivener proper, and in training as a cypherer — when there was fierce knocking on the door, and Poley hastened to open it.

What now?

A thin hope that it could be word of Gifford was stifled when a squat, bony fellow burst inside, half knocking Poley off his feet.

"Let me in, you sluggard!" the newcomer growled. "Sitting here all snug, while a fellow has to —"

"And a good e'en to you, Isaac Finch," Tom greeted, as cuttingly as he knew.

Finch stopped short, but his glare didn't soften a whit as he tore a soft hat from his head, as though both Tom and the hat had done him grievous injustice.

"'Tis you, Mr. Thomas," he growled. "Ay, well — but you don't know the life I have of it. They wouldn't let me through at the gate. At dawn, they said — the whoresons! The papers, it took, before they bothered — and then ... ah, then they jumped..."

And all the time he rummaged inside his doublet. If a man had ever been fashioned for discontent, it was Isaac Finch — all made of angles, from his knobby, greying head, down to his big-boned knees, with a louring, pockmarked face to scare small children, and a harsh voice to match. At last, from the depths of his rumpled clothes, he wrenched out a battered letter and thrust it at Tom. Even his hands were riddled with deep, ugly pox-scars.

Poley was at Tom's elbow with the candle without having to be told — quiet as a cat, eager as a dog. Tom broke the seal and had hardly read past the hasty salutation, when Skeres appeared at a half run, with his own hissing light and Rouse Casey on his heels.

Skeres stopped as he caught sight of Finch, and sneered. "Cuds-me, Mr. Tom — but we thought it was the Spaniards!"

Which had Rouse Casey and Berden chuckling, and set Finch a-bristle.

"You brats, kicking your heels all day. I'd like to see you galloping from Greenwich at night, and before that, sweating under the sun all the way from Lichfield —"

"Enough!" Devil tie Isaac Finch's tongue in knots! Tom turned his hardest glare on the small group — five Service men, and not all of them supposed to know of Chartley Castle, and the trafficking of letters that was going on between there and close-by Lichfield. "Squabbling like urchins in the street — and you all Mr. Secretary's men!"

They had the grace to fall quiet where they stood on the white and black floor, like pieces on a chessboard. Skeres alone made to speak — but even he swallowed his words under another glare. Casey and Berden were abashed enough, Finch worked his mouth, and Poley looked at his feet with the virtuous air of one who hadn't been squabbling. How many of them did know where Lichfield was?

In this awkward silence Tom read the message from Greenwich: that they should keep a close watch on Babington and his cronies — Father Ballard first among them; that they should be ready to act; that warrants of arrest would be procured; that they should do nothing yet to frighten the plotters into action; and had they found Gifford and John Savage?

Again! Hadn't Sir Francis written much the same just yesterday? Did he fear they may forget? What was the hurry of sending Finch after curfew like this?

Tom caught himself short. He had questioned his great kinsman's reasoning sometimes — but grown impatient with him? The very thought felt like betrayal — or at least like a great impertinence.

His little audience eyed him warily, shuffling their feet.

Never let those who depend on you see you doubt or waver, Thomas — lest they doubt you. It was an irony that, of all of Sir Francis's maxims, this one should echo inside Tom's mind right now. Tom shoved the irony aside.

"Berden, Poley, Rouse — you have your orders, you may go. Finch, you wait. I've a message for Mr. Mylls."

And, before Finch could think to grumble, Tom sent him to the kitchen and repaired to his office.

There wasn't much to tell Mylls, in truth — but perhaps the man would sleep better for knowing Mr. Secretary was considering warrants and arrests? And there was of course Gifford — Jove rain on the fellow.

Tom swore aloud when he dropped a glob of molten wax on a finger in his haste, and sucked at the small burn. Tartarus take it all! Tartarus take Ballard and his complots, and Mary Stuart at Chartley — reckless all her life, now must she learn wariness? — and these long, hot days of doing naught but waiting, and hearing what other men did. Had Cicero of old felt like this, while he waited for the traitor Catiline to make his move? But Cicero, at least, could do his own work!

And, as though it weren't all enough to give a fellow the megrims, he could hear the damn pack of fools, still bickering in the hall. Oh, but this time they were going to hear it!

Tom strode back to the hall to find that Poley alone had obeyed the dismissal, while Finch groused at the sneering Casey and Skeres, while Berden sat on the stairs like one watching a bear baited.

"What's this?" Tom snapped — and see if, instead of showing guilt, they didn't try to draw him into the argument!

"Let them laugh," Finch said, waving a chunk of bread at the others. "But I told the man to his face, and I'll tell you, Mr. Thomas — and I'd tell His Honour himself: a knave, is that Poley, and there's no trusting him! And sink me if he didn't thank me, and smile — he had that gall —"

"Enough!" Tom roared.

The lowered gazes were no great consolation. Oh, but this whole matter was making them all fretful and quarrelsome!

"We meant nothing by it, Master." Berden rose from his perch. "'Tis that Finch is always at it: if it isn't Poley, then 'tis someone else."

"All knaves to him, we are," Casey piped up. "All knaves, but for one Isaac Finch."

Which was true enough, for the man was a pest, and ever talking ill of each and all. He was also ticklish as a wasp.

"At least I'm no blunderkin!" Finch turned on the lad and gave him a shove. "A blunderkin — or worse, like some who make themselves known to the traitors!"

Oh this, now — this! Tom silenced the sudden chaos of exclamations.

"What's this?" he demanded. "And mind what accusations you make, Finch."

Finch chewed his lip. "I make no accusations. I tell what I saw. Last I was in London, Mr. Mylls sends me to the Exchange to find this young nit." He jerked his chin at the scowling Casey. "Like a messenger boy, he sends me — but never you mind. I find him watching a clutch of fine young gentlemen, and as I tell him what's what, I hear calling aloud, and it's his father: *Idling about, Rouse?* says he, loud as you please. *And what I've done to deserve a do-naught for a son...* Loud as a bell, and every soul in the Exchange ogling. What if they took

21

suspicion, your fine gentlemen?" And, as punctuation to his harangue, he chewed off a big bite from his bread.

Young Casey, like many of his complexion do, had grown scarlet in his anger.

"Is that true, Rouse?" Tom asked.

"'Tis true that… Oh, rat it!" The lad shook his red mane. "I can't help my fool of a father."

Tom gave a snort: was it Roman Lucretius saying how something could be true and of no use at once? "And you never thought to let us know — so I won't ask if you were discovered."

"No — they…" As pale of a sudden as he'd been flushed, Casey turned to Berden, and Berden came to the rescue.

"There's always such noise at the Exchange, our crows never spared it a thought."

Indeed, if such a mishap had to happen, the Royal Exchange wasn't the worst place: a huge flagged square with galleries and shops all around, half market and half idling grounds, crowded any day of the week. Babington and his friends were fond of it for that very delusion of safety. Still, it being a delusion…

"You'll tell your father he's not to accost you like that."

Casey gave a mirthless huff. "I'll try, Master — but I told you: my father is a fool, he thinks aldermen only heed the Queen and God himself — never his son, for sure."

"And why should he, poor man?" Finch snarled. "A Cain-headed runagate like you! Thank God you ain't my son, Rouse Casey — and never will be."

Again! Tom took a breath, and it was enough that they all fell silent. "A penance — that's what you are! Off with you, Berden. Rouse, you'll talk to your father, and find Gifford, I don't care how." He thrust the letter at the messenger. "This goes to Mr. Mylls, Finch — now. And I want you here tomorrow at cockcrow."

Contrary as he was, Finch knew better than to answer back. Lips twisted, he clutched the sealed note in a badly pockmarked hand. There was a pit the size of a three-farthing coin between finger and thumb, so deep that, in the flickering yellow light, it made the hand into a talon. Had there been harpies in this world, had there been a male of the species, this fellow would be one!

"At cockcrow, mind," Tom insisted, which was a whit unfair, because, in his years of couriering, Isaac Finch had never been but prompt and precise — but Tom was out of charity with the man, and with everyone else. And, to be honest, with himself.

He slammed the door behind his departing men, drew the bolts, and leant against the jamb, rubbing at his brow.

Oh, let this one tangle be solved soon, and this bunch of traitors disbanded, and…

A sound dragged him out of his bleak musings. The sound of chewing. Nick Skeres, of course. Nick Skeres, sitting at the foot of the staircase, munching like a contented minotaur.

"I forgot to throw you out with the others," Tom groaned. "Do you ever stop eating?"

Skeres held up a piece of sausage. "Poley's never 'ungry… Waste not, want not, I say. D'you want me gone?"

Tom waved him quieter — more out of habit than any hope of obtaining softer speech. "Won't Tichborne wonder where you are?"

Attaching himself to one of Babington's friends hadn't made the lad admire the conspirators… "Bless ye, Mr. Tom!" He half choked on a mouthful in his merriment. "'Tis you who worries where folks are. Those gudgeons … it never crosses

23

their nowls. They think servants are kept in presses, when we're not serving." This was said with perfect cheerfulness, and with the transparent expectation of earning a laugh from Tom.

When the laugh didn't come, not even a chuckle — that was when the Minotaur's countenance knotted in concern.

"Can't be that bad, can it, Master?" He squinted over both shoulders like a villain at the play as he rose and tiptoed close to boom in Tom's ear for discretion's sake. "They lack an 'are's brain among them. We can catch 'em when we like. 'Is Honour's never fretting, is 'e?"

Of course Skeres knew naught of how the Queen would always shy from dealing with her unchancy cousin, unless she saw Mary's treason spelt out. Of how they sought to draw Mary out, before her minions managed regicide. In truth, Tom had a shrewd suspicion his servant wouldn't bat an eyelash — but, the point being best left undiscussed, he just shook his head.

Not that it deterred Skeres in the least. Why, it had him nodding sagely. "D'you know why you're all glum and bedeviled?"

Skeres on the Humour of Melancholy… "You find me glum and bedeviled, Dolius?"

The lad snorted. "You're glum because you're all cooped up in 'ere, with naught to do but fret and 'ear us dunces, and send us out again — that's why!"

That was why indeed! So much so that it startled Tom into a huff of laughter. "Is it? And what do I do with it?"

There was a portentous shrug — the lad being the sort to shrug a good deal to convey all sorts of meaning. "You stay cooped, that's what you do — and order us about, and do your thinking — and blame yerself for it." The booming simmered down to a reproachful mutter. "You 'ad to walk into that nest of papist snakes in France, so now they know your face — and you stay put."

Rheims, and the English College, ay — and the days Tom had spent there a year past. A most reckless thing to do, but there had been three murders to unravel, and a man's name to clear.

"For all the good it did," Tom groused. The good had been little, and the ill was that now John Savage — half soldier and half zealot, and all plotter — knew Tom for a Queen's man.

"Y'know what's good, though?"

"No," Tom ground out. "I do not."

"At least you don't need no fine clothes to go to fine suppers."

Tom gaped, and Skeres shrugged again.

"Now your brother's cut down your pittance again, and the way those fools like to play fops — be 'appy you don't 'ave to go to expenses!"

And trust Nick Skeres to rub salt on a fellow's wounds by way of consolation! And all the worse because the Minotaur himself was lending money to his master — to make up for Sir Edmund Walsingham's unbrotherly stinginess.

Still, what did one say to this, but laugh?

"What would I do without you, Faithful Dolius? And you'd better stay the night, after all: I've had enough of you brawling with the Watch."

Skeres grinned. "Only once, that was — and you worry none, Master. I'll be your eyes and ears, out there."

And for the moment Thomas Walsingham, unpicker of knots for his kinsman Mr. Secretary, had to be content with this — not that he was.

CHAPTER 2

28th of July

After a night of dreaming that he was swimming in the moat back at home in Scadbury, and the water was so warm and murky he couldn't tell up from down, Tom went to the kitchen and found it emptier than it had been in days. The flagstones were still wet with the washing, and the door to the herb garden was thrown open to let in what cooler air there was to be had.

Skeres alone sat at one end of the big table, chewing bread and broiled kidneys, while the cook chided him for eating Master out of house and home.

Of course, Berden was supposed to be watching Father Ballard, and Poley Babington. That Casey had yet to find Gifford was perhaps no great surprise; Finch, though…

"Has Isaac Finch been by?" Tom asked, to a collection of shaking heads from Skeres, the cook, and a scullion.

Ah well. It wasn't as though there were urgent news. Tom sat down to his small ale, kidneys, and buttered manchet. By the time he was done breaking his fast, though, with All Hallows tolling five across the street, there was still no sign of Finch, and all his black humours came thundering back. Had the churl taken offence, and thought to show it by being late?

A quick search revealed that Finch wasn't — nor had been — in the stables, nor in the offices. Young Tobias Chandler said no messenger had come yet, and no one had seen Finch at all.

"Damn the man!" Tom started to count in Latin in his head, and had reached *quattuor*, when it occurred to him that Mylls might have given different orders. "Run off to Tower Hill, Skeres. See whether they know where he is."

Off Skeres ran, and Chandler dithered at Tom's elbow, with the question writ large on his face of why Mylls wouldn't have sent word. Writ large — and unvoiced, though it was an excellent question.

With every minute that passed, Tom found himself hoping more and more that no worse than heedlessness was at play — for otherwise... That would be a fine message for Mr. Secretary: *I've lost one of your couriers, Sir — the one who, only last week, rode from Chartley with the copy of Mary Stuart's letter.* Oh Lord!

When told to run, the Minotaur ran. Very soon he was back, breathless, red-faced, and dripping with sweat.

"Went there last night," he panted. "Left your letter with the porter, and legged it away. And then..." A shrug.

"Where does he live?" Tom asked, because there was still a chance that Finch was snoring in his own bed, oblivious, drunk, or ill. Wasn't it a marvel how slow the mind is to yield to its own misgivings? He asked it of Toby, but it was Skeres who answered, "By St. Helen's church. Do I go?"

"But quietly, mind, and..." Tom paused for emphasis, and glared for good measure. "You don't trounce him. Just bring him here."

Hanging his head like one resigned to never having his way, Skeres departed. Was it worth hoping he wouldn't brawl with Finch, if he found him? Had Rouse Casey been there, Tom would have sent him, but Casey was chasing after Gifford — and, in truth, he hadn't shown much liking for Finch, either.

"What if he's not there, Master?" Toby asked at length, in a round-eyed whisper. Even at nineteen, and only a scrivener, the ills of losing a courier at such a moment were not lost on him. What Sir Francis would think of it bore no thinking.

"Let's hope he is," Tom answered, grim enough that the boy scurried back to his own table without another word.

It seemed to Tom that, in his four-and-twenty years, he had entertained hopes more foolish than that of finding Finch at home. Still, when an urchin arrived with word from Mr. *Skeres* that the bird wasn't in the nest, he wasn't truly surprised. So little so, in fact, that he had a horse already saddled, and was off to Bishopsgate even as Chandler paid the grimy messenger.

In truth he could have walked there, for St. Helen's rose not far from the city walls. It had been a nunnery in the old days, and weathered the change in a way of its own. It looked as though a child giant had torn the old buildings apart to rearrange them, and then, tiring of the game, dropped the pieces at sixes and sevens, so that now two separate naves squatted side by side to make a church, while a burying ground and a stretch of lawn with a dozen trees crowded together inside a walled yard shaped like an arrowhead. A row of houses stood by the church, some looking on the churchyard, some away, towards a tall hall with a huge mullioned window — surely part of the nunnery once.

As he dismounted in the shadow of the trees, Tom caught sight of Skeres on the threshold of the house next to the church.

"Master!" the lad bellowed, with much milling of arms and beckoning. "'E ain't 'ere!"

Ay, well — now the whole of Bishopsgate knew. Tom hastened to join his fool of a servant, but a stern lesson on the virtue of discretion would have to wait, since just inside the open door stood a woman in a grey kirtle.

"This 'ere's the Widow Lovell, Master," Skeres said. "Finch's sister."

Could it be hoped the lad had not given away too many names? In case he hadn't, Tom didn't introduce himself.

"Goodwife Lovell," he said instead, "your brother works for me."

Which wasn't quite true, but near enough, and good enough.

The woman dropped a curtsey, watching Tom with uneasy scrutiny. A few years above thirty, she didn't look much like her brother — narrow of cheek, chin and shoulder, where he was built broad and squat. She had the same graceless voice, though she spoke more respectfully.

"Your man says Isaac didn't show up this morning." She shook her head and lowered her eyes on work-reddened hands. "He came home late last night, when we were all a-bed. We always shut up early when Dr. Lewis is from home. Dr. Lewis is the rector, and I keep house for him, and he's away — he has been these past two days. But that's neither here nor there, is it? Isaac never likes to find the door barred, and he grumbled a good deal — for the door, and because he had to be off early again this morning…"

The snort from Skeres, Tom quelled with a scowl.

Goodwife Lovell didn't take it ill. "Begging pardon, but Your Honour knows my brother. He told his daughter he'd go early, and this morning he was gone, so I thought nothing of it."

She fell silent as the bells began to chime seven. St. Helen's boasted a wooden turret, and a couple of bells with a shrill, scolding ring. Widow Lovell squinted up in the morning light. When the bells fell silent, she looked at Tom again. "I thought he'd gone on Your Honour's errands," she said — and it struck Tom that there was something peculiar in the way she spoke of her brother.

"And can you think where he might have gone instead?" he asked.

She shook her head.

"Does he often go away like this?"

"Ay — coming and going at all hours, never saying when or where…" A sigh. "Sometimes my sister-in-law — rest her soul — would ask, and he always said it was his master's business, and none of hers."

"And he grumbled to you last night."

"To me? Oh no, Your Honour — not to me. I was a-bed. 'Twas his daughter that went to unbar the door for him." She turned to the gloomy interior of the house, calling. "Grace, child — there's a gentleman here as would talk to you."

Grace must not have been far away — nor alone: in a trice, two girls appeared in the light from the doorway. One was a child of eleven or so, with the clever face of a wood mouse, and a likeness to the housekeeper. The other… Tom didn't know what he had expected Finch's daughter to be like — but not this very lovely maiden. Tall and slender, and not a day above eighteen, she had a heart-shaped face, and large grey eyes, half fearful and half angry, and dark auburn curls escaping the confines of a loose knot. Her eager stride halted on the threshold.

"'Tis your father's master," Goodwife Lovell whispered, and young Grace looked down and curtsied.

What had Finch told them of his employers, that his family showed so little curiosity? Only the child, peeking from behind Mrs Lovell's shoulder, was staring, frank and earnest.

"You let in your father last night —" Tom began.

Grace pointed at Skeres, and blurted out, "That man says Father's missing!"

"Grace!" Goodwife Lovell's elbow may have quieted her niece, but it did little to quell her, and the young woman never lowered her unfriendly stare.

Under that stare, it was worth noting, Skeres stood blushing and abashed.

"Does he? Oh no — I'm sure what he did was ask *you* whether he is," Tom corrected — rather untruthfully, he suspected. "Is he?" He gave the three of them a cold look. "Because he had orders to report at cockcrow this morning, and never did."

The the widow and Grace exchanged glances. Wary, and afraid that Finch's master would fire him in absentia — for they couldn't know what Finch had carried from Chartley, could they? Why, the man himself didn't know.

Oh, baggage! Tom reined in an urgency to shake them. "In his years with me, Isaac Finch has never failed to obey his orders. That he has this morning, has me worried, and I want to find out what has happened. I dismissed him late last night — and he came home, didn't he?"

Another glance — and then Grace nodded.

"Ay, he came home late," she said. "He'd been away three days, and we weren't expecting him. We never know when he comes and goes, and still he groused that he must always find his own door barred…"

"And did he say something?"

"Oh, did he!" Grace pouted. "I gave him his supper, and all the time he grumbled that I was taking so long, and did I want my own father to go away before dawn on an empty belly and no sleep, and he pitied —" She stopped short, setting her pretty mouth in a flat line.

"And he pitied…?" Tom prodded.

It was the child who piped up, "The man who takes her for a wife!"

See how Grace turned on her little cousin. "A penance, that's what you are, Peg Lovell!"

And Goodwife Lovell, who possibly agreed with her niece on that score, cuffed the child's shoulder, and poor Peg was sent running away in disgrace.

"She's not a bad child." Goodwife Lovell had the air of having repeated this often. "'Tis that she'll give vent to all that passes through her head…"

"And was she there last night, to hear Finch say what he said?" Tom asked.

"No." Grace pouted some more. "She's just heard it often enough. It was but Father and me, and when he'd groused to his liking, he sent me back to bed — and what he did after, I don't know."

"Could he have gone out again?"

Grace tilted her head in purse-lipped uncertainty.

"Did you bolt the door again before going back to bed?"

There was a shake of the head this time.

"So your father must have done it."

"'Twas latched this morning, so we thought he'd gone."

Tom saw it, the moment when Grace's eyes filled with sudden fear.

"You think Father…"

What he thought, he wasn't going to tell Finch's daughter — not yet, at least — although his next questions must betray his unpleasant doubts.

"Did Finch sleep in his bed last night?" he asked, and it was clear from the blank stares that it hadn't crossed either woman's mind to wonder. "Did he take anything with him? Is anything of his missing?"

Goodwife Lovell was quicker to catch Tom's drift, and paled a little, clutching at the hem of her apron. "'Tis that, until Your Honour's man came, we never thought…"

And of course they hadn't: why should they?

"Would you please make sure now?" Tom turned to find Skeres at his elbow, transfixed in calf-like contemplation of the fair Grace. The Minotaur amorous — yet again! "Go with them, Skeres — unless it's too much bother."

The lad blinked out of whatever idyll he'd been weaving in his mind, and, when Tom repeated his order, trotted after Grace. Could he never see a comely woman without becoming lovestruck?

The housekeeper was dithering, watching over her shoulder as her niece and Skeres, having acquired little Peg again, disappeared into the house.

What people won't tell before others is often worth hearing.

Whether this was a maxim of Sir Francis, or some observation Tom himself had formed in his years of unravelling murders, there was no time to question, as Goodwife Lovell tiptoed close enough to whisper.

"I wouldn't ask before Grace, poor child — but…" She scrunched her face in distress. "Has Isaac stolen from Your Honour?"

"Stolen?" Oh Lord! Had they hired in the Service a man who stole from his masters? "Why do you ask?"

The housekeeper's eyes filled with tears. "I'm a bad sister, Your Honour!" she moaned. "You come here saying he disappeared, you ask questions… 'Tis just that … once, as a youth, Isaac stole a pair of velvet sleeves — or so his master said, and then he ran away…"

Well, of all things! Filching a pair of sleeves didn't sound akin to selling secrets of the State.

"And was it true?"

The housekeeper shrugged unhappily. "Isaac's master was put in debtor's gaol soon after, and died there, so nothing came of it." But what Isaac's sister thought of it was plain.

Still, it seemed a shame that her qualms should only amount to this: Finch wasn't as honest as he liked to claim — or hadn't always been. Couldn't she have seen or heard something helpful?

Unfair as it was, Tom couldn't keep some testiness out of his answer. "Goodwife Lovell — I only know your brother as a faithful servant, and I want to know what's become of him."

Not that she looked convinced. "But couldn't he be at your house? Gone there after you left?"

If he were, then a messenger would have been sent at once, but that was nothing to discuss with this anxious sister — not yet, at least.

"Perhaps," Tom said, and Fates send Finch wasn't galloping away to France instead, after committing a felony. Speaking of which… "Does your brother keep a horse?"

Goodwife Lovell blinked. "He says he has the use of Your Honour's beasts."

"So he has. And … who has windows on the churchyard?"

There was no mistaking the housekeeper's sudden sourness. "Arthur Pratte — he's the parish clerk," she said, pointing her chin at the neighbouring house, which had honeysuckle climbing by its door and fresh new wattle. "He'll be at his shop, now — and his wife's confined. You think they saw…?"

Tom counted on it — but never got to discuss the matter, because Skeres emerged from the house right then, loud with news that *Mistress Grace* missed nothing from her father's garret upstairs, and the cot was all made and tidy.

It was plain as day that Goodwife Lovell would have liked some reassurance — but Tom had none to give. So he dismissed the woman, asking her to send word the moment Finch returned, and waited until she retreated inside the rector's house.

Nick Skeres was still lost in contemplation of the empty windows, so Tom nudged him none too gently.

"Dolius, her own father pities the man fool enough to wed her."

Skeres stuck out his lower lip. "The wits of a cock-pheasant, 'as Finch," he grumbled. "Pity the man who gets 'im for a father-in-law, I say!" And he trudged after Tom, who rather wished he could knock at the door with the honeysuckle, and hunt for that common variety of fowl, the sharp-eyed neighbour. Ah, well — it would have to wait.

"Go back to your quarries," he ordered Skeres, as he mounted his horse. "See whether they seem too cheerful."

"They're always too cheerful for my liking," the lad said. "And why they ain't being cheerful in the Clink, that's for you and 'Is Honour to know."

On this they parted ways — Skeres to find Tichborne, and Tom to Tower Hill.

Mylls, Jove rain on him, sniffed at Tom's news like a cat with a bit of questionable fish. Thin mouth a-working, he squinted at the bundles, reams, and mounds of papers that cluttered up his writing room, as though an answer — or perhaps Finch himself — might appear out of them.

"I say we seek him," he said at length, folding into the one chair. "We can't just assume that he turned coat and ran."

Tom leant on the table, both palms flat on the top, and made himself take a slow, slow breath. There were dust motes dancing in the sunbeams that slanted through the half-shuttered windows, and a child's voice rang outside, singing a rhyme. "But if he did, then it's too late for anything but the arrests, so we'll need the warrants. If he was taken, though…"

"You never think they'd have the wits to do it? To know Finch for our courier?"

"Not Babington — but Ballard? And Savage was a soldier, once." Blunt Savage, so quick to mistrust back in Rheims…

"Or perhaps he fell foul of someone else." Mylls held up a hand when Tom made to protest. "You know Finch; he's the sort to make enemies rather than friends — and we can't hazard to scare them into action just…" *Just because of your fancies.*

"And can we ignore the chance that they've nabbed him?" Tom pushed away from the table. "I'm riding to Greenwich. Right away."

Mylls's brow unclouded in relief that he wouldn't be the one to tell Sir Francis. Why, freed from that prospect, of a sudden he was all zeal.

"I'll have the men warned," he promised, straightening in his chair. "If our traitors are in agitation, we'll know — and I'll send word. And I'll have someone keep an eye on things at St. Helen's."

And wouldn't one think, to hear him now, that the notion had been his?

CHAPTER 3

On the eve of the Royal move to Richmond, the Palace of Placentia was a confusion of harried servants, sweating in their scarlet liveries as they lugged bundles, trunks, and baskets down stairs and along corridors.

Amidst it all, Mr. Secretary's chambers had the heavy silence of still water.

Sir Francis looked up from his desk with a frown as his guard, the huge Welshman Davies, let Tom into the writing room. Two windows were thrown open to let in what breeze breathed from the Middle Court, and their light showed Mr. Secretary withered with care — hunched in his chair, hollow of cheek and eye.

At his side stood narrow, colourless Phelippes, the head-cypherer, not two hours back from Lichfield, wearing a worried grimace of his own. But then Phelippes always looked worried — whether he was or not.

"Thomas! Is anything the matter?" was Sir Francis's salutation.

Tom bowed to his cousin, squared his shoulders, and, there being nothing for it, said what he had to say. "Isaac Finch, the courier, has been missing since late last night."

There was a questioning tilt of the head from Sir Francis, and a click of the tongue from Phelippes.

"The man I sent to Your Honour from Lichfield, with the deciphered copy," the little cypherer said.

Sir Francis's hand went to a paper on the table: Mary Stuart's own letter, surely — the cyphered original, brought from Chartley by Phelippes himself.

"Missing?" Mr. Secretary prodded, and Tom told what he knew — and what he did not.

Phelippes listened, head lowered, picking at the skin around his nails, and flinched when Sir Francis turned to him.

"Did he know what he was carrying?"

Phelippes had never unlearnt to nod and shake his head in answer. "I didn't tell him."

"Not even that it was of special import or urgency?"

Another shake. "Everything's urgent these days, Your Honour — and Finch has always been discreet and prompt."

Discreet and prompt — as Tom had told Goodwife Lovell, and Mylls's opinion as well. Had they all formed the same notion of the man, or passed it from one to another without thought?

Outside, the blackbirds carolled, and a peacock squawked as Sir Francis considered, tapping a noiseless fingertip on the letter.

"Discreet and prompt," he repeated, "…and loyal?"

Was he? Blunt, grouchy, unpleasant, ever-complaining Isaac Finch, onetime sleeve-thief. Was he loyal to his masters, to the good of England?

It was no great surprise, the uneasiness in the ever-wary Phelippes's pale eyes.

"We can't be sure —"

Sir Francis waved this away with an impatience that wasn't often seen in him. "We never can," he said, and turned to his young kinsman.

"In truth, he never gave cause for doubt," Tom began, "but if Ballard's men caught him, if he only let slip the name of Chartley, even just that of Lichfield — willingly or unwillingly…"

Tom let it trail when Sir Francis gave one slow, weary nod, and turned to Phelippes. "So perhaps it's all in vain by now — and at the same time it's all the more urgent that we go ahead with this."

There was a stool by the table, across from Sir Francis's chair, and several ink-pots, and a tray of quills. When Phelippes went to sit there without a word, Sir Francis turned Mary Stuart's letter and pushed it towards him — and something in the cypherer's fierce stare made Tom uneasy. Hadn't he unriddled and transcribed Mary Stuart's message to Babington already, days ago?

"Thomas." Sir Francis rose with the stiff blankness of one masking pain. Bracing himself on the edge of a long table covered in sheafs and bundles of papers, he made his limping way to one of the windows, and Tom followed. "I've been devising steps to precipitate things in London, Thomas, and your news has made up my mind for me. I pray that, within a week, Ballard's complot may be brought to its end, and you and Mylls can have the arrests made. But we need written proof that the Queen of Scots is party to the treason."

And didn't they have just that? Tom glanced at the table, at Phelippes's curved shoulder concealing Mary Stuart's missive. When he looked back, it was to meet Sir Francis's sharp, knowing gaze. It made him seventeen again, feeling his way at the edge of great, deep secrets — trusted, and yet tested.

"Phelippes?" said Sir Francis.

The cypherer twisted on the stool, holding a scrap of paper whose written lines were riddled with crosses. He cleared his throat, and read in little more than a whisper: "*I would be glad to know the names and qualities of the six gentlemen which are to accomplish the design, for that it may be I shall be able upon knowledge of the parties to give you some further advice necessary to be followed therein; and even so do I wish to be made acquainted with the names of all such principal persons —"*

"No." Sir Francis held up a forefinger. "She already asks for the names. Cross out this last sentence."

A shiver crawled up Tom's spine, a burning coldness — because this... Sir Francis had been praying for this from the beginning, and was now playing his last card.

"You will go back to London before night, Thomas." There was something deep in the dark grey eyes, something that was both very hard and very sad. "You will find out what happened to this courier. You will also make certain that, over the next few days, we know at all times where Babington is, and Father Ballard, and all their cronies. Especially... What is he called, your acquaintance from Rheims? The one who swore to murder Her Highness."

"John Savage." Tom did nothing to disguise his uncertainty, and Sir Francis caught it at once.

"You know his whereabouts, don't you?"

"We know his lodgings, and we know whenever he meets with Babington."

Mr. Secretary's gaze narrowed. "Isn't Deacon Gifford watching him?"

Oh, was he — curse the deacon! "We haven't heard from Gifford these past three days. Young Casey is seeking him."

Did Sir Francis also count in Latin when he wanted to rein in his temper? It had never occurred to Tom to wonder — but now he did, as Mr. Secretary stood still, contemplating the rush mats that covered the floor. Even the scratch of Phelippes's pen had stopped across the room, and the cypherer sat in silence, pretending he wasn't listening.

Tom shifted his weight. "It's happened before, Sir. He always turns up."

"But where does he keep disappearing to, I'd like to know?" There was more drumming of the long, thin fingers on the windowsill. "Such a wandering spirit!"

Tom had no answer — but...

But the man knows about Chartley, hung unsaid. He knew more than most, having devised, together with Phelippes, the means of deluding Mary Stuart into a belief that she was smuggling correspondence hidden inside the castle's beer casks.

This time there was no sharp scrutiny in Sir Francis's manner. "You know him best, Thomas, from Rheims. He was there too, I believe?"

"And not much liked or trusted, even there." Such an irony that, of all the men he'd met in Rheims, Tom should most dislike the one who now was on their side. "Gifford had been thrown out of the Seminary in Rome, and taken in at the Collège Anglais — but most of the Catholic exiles there had little love for him. They weren't wrong, considering how he jumped to take the Queen's coin!"

For the first time, Sir Francis's face unknotted in the faintest semblance of amusement. "He was imprisoned, headed for the rack first and then Tyburn. A fellow can jump away quite eagerly from that prospect. Still... He hasn't met you in London yet, has he, Thomas?"

"He refuses to come to Seething Lane, for fear Savage will follow him there." *And I'm as good as caged there.*

There was a small snort from Phelippes, where he bent over his work — the cypherer liking Gifford no better than Tom did.

Sir Francis hummed. "Perhaps it's time our deacon should be brought to Seething Lane, to meet you face to face, Thomas. It will be good for the fellow's conscience to know how long he has been under scrutiny."

And then the danger, the urgency, the uncertainty caught up with Sir Francis again. Grimly, he motioned Tom to another table.

"Will you write down Mylls's instructions for me? I'd rather keep all that we discussed as quiet as can be, and I don't want to distract Phelippes from his work."

His work of cyphering and forging a handful of new, deathly words for Mary Stuart's letter. Sir Francis's own work of ensnaring not one queen, but two.

For a long time Sir Francis dictated the instructions and letters Tom was to carry back to London. No mention of the forged postscript was made to Mylls — and whether this should be surprising or not, Tom couldn't make up his mind.

All the while, as the light slanted more and more golden, Elizabeth's court amused itself, and chattered, and laughed, and wove petty intrigues down in the fine gardens. Did all those greedy, hopeful satellites who orbited the throne in their finery ever wonder what went on behind Sir Francis's windows? And even if one in two dozen did, their wildest imaginings would fall well short of the truth — which was most likely for the best.

Even as he worked, Tom couldn't help, between one letter and the next, peeking at Phelippes. And always, he turned back to find Sir Francis studying him.

The light had yellowed and inched across the rush-matted floor when Davies came to bring the Queen's summons for her Secretary of State.

Sir Francis gingerly straightened his back. "That will do for now, Thomas — and I fear I've had you miss your dinner. Seal the packet, will you, and ride as soon as you've had something to eat. Phelippes will join you in London tomorrow, or the day after."

Phelippes, carrying the letter, the false lines that spelt ruin and deceit and the starkest necessity...

Mr. Secretary stepped close to clasp his young cousin's shoulder, and looked him straight in the eye. "You understand, don't you, child?" he murmured. "She *has* espoused treason, and made it plain. We only make it unassailable — in God's own cause."

There was a long gaze between the two kinsmen, until a burst of laughter from the garden broke the silence. With a quiet sigh, Sir Francis patted Tom's shoulder and walked away with Davies, his silent Welsh shadow.

Fiddling with the wax and seal, Tom was careful not to turn to the mouse-quiet Phelippes across the room. He was left with an uneasy conscience, a dusty ride and a long night before him, and a bleak, blind sense of having been put to the proof — and found wanting.

It was nearing the hour when decent folk headed home for supper, by the time Tom reached London. The warm air was thick with woodsmoke and the river, with cooking and the middens, and people lingered in the streets with lazy summer cheer. They bought a last codling from a peddler, gossiped at corners, took their time walking out of a rider's way, scolded with little heat a bunch of shrilling children. They walked back from the conduit with the day's last bucket of water, leant out of windows with a lamp to beckon the lighter. Just like the glittering courtiers at Greenwich, these people knew naught of complots and threats and unyielding necessity — and Fates send they never did.

Tom knew, though — and was it very foolish of him to feel, together with the weight of that knowledge, something like swarms of sparks in his belly? Foolish, ay — and childish. Let

Sir Francis never know. Or did he feel the sparks too, sometimes?

Fanciful notions, these were, and of no earthly use. Tom shook his head and turned his horse — not towards Seething Lane, nor to Tower Hill. He would have to see Mylls, of course — but first, he made for St. Helen's.

He found Mylls's man Paynter there, loitering under the trees — a lad of eighteen, fresh from the country and bored to tears. Finch, Paynter said, had not returned.

And it must be the sign of an addled mind, that swelling of relief, and the voice inside Tom's head, asking what if he'd arrived to find the courier back at home, with a good reason for disappearing all day? Or what if Finch had been found dead of a calenture, or anything that had nothing to do with Babington's crows? That Finch wasn't there, alive or dead, that Tom wasn't going to end his Service days as the unspeakable idiot rushing England into turmoil over nothing much … ah, well, it was a day for discoveries — one being that relief could taste so bitter.

Paynter had more to recount: Finch's women, he said, were fit to have the vapours. No, he hadn't spoken to them — wouldn't go near a woman with the vapours for all the gold in Spain — but he knew from the sexton. The sexton was an old fellow who'd been mowing grass in the churchyard.

"City folks!" the country lad sneered. "'Tis a miracle he didn't mow his own feet."

Having little interest in the sexton's workmanship, Tom asked about any other tidbits the man might have provided (none, unless you counted whining about the heat, the women's ill humours, and the hard work), about anyone that might have called or carried a message (only the midwife to see

Goodwife Pratte next door), about the rector (still away), and about the clerk (not returned home yet).

It all made for a very empty game-bag, in truth — and Tom would have gladly avoided discussing its emptiness with Mylls — but for the packet from Greenwich.

The packet, and the packet alone made Tom head for Tower Hill — but it was a good thing in the end — for he found Mylls in the greatest agitation.

"Babington and his friends are having supper at the Castle Tavern tonight," the secretary announced, waving an unsealed note. "Berden has a man watching the place, and wants me there at eight — in disguise. The fellow has seen a play too many ... but he thinks Father Ballard may be there."

Tom's heart lifted after all the days of not knowing. "He's in London, then!"

"So Berden says — and he asks for warrants."

Well, those he couldn't have. Sir Francis's packet sat untouched on Mylls's table, and Tom tapped a finger on it. "Not until Babington receives Mary Stuart's letter — and answers it."

And perhaps Mylls struggled with doubt, too. He looked down, frowning as he fingered Berden's note. "It will take days," he murmured.

Days, ay. From where he stood, Tom could see Berden's hasty scrawl, the dark spots where the unsanded ink had soaked through the paper. What if Ballard disappeared again? What if, having Finch, the others knew enough to question the letter when it came? Then again, Mylls wasn't privy to Sir Francis's whole design — and Berden even less so.

"Let's hope it won't. Meanwhile, to be safe, Berden must latch onto Ballard, welcome him back like a lost brother at the Castle, and —"

Mylls gave a lugubrious chuckle. "Ah, but Berden won't be at the Castle."

"Has he gone mad? Why not?"

"He doesn't know that Ballard will be there."

Tom stared in disbelief. "You said —"

The note was held up — this oracle's response! "An acquaintance, one of Babington's lesser men, invited himself to sup with Berden at his lodgings. Himself and a guest — one he wouldn't name."

"And Ballard shares his supper with Berden rather than Babington?"

"Who knows what they have in mind? But, you see…" Mylls raised a forefinger. "'Tis a blessing that you're here — so I can go to the Castle Tavern, and … do you know Berden's lodgings, near the Bedlam?"

Where, Tom noted in passing, it was in fact less likely that Ballard would go. Still, the sparks crackled alive again inside him: oh, to be playing a part at last in this affair — some part beyond fretting in Seething Lane! "But what if I'm seen?"

"Savage is the one who knows you, and he's at the Castle with Babington. That much we know for certain."

"And what if the guest isn't Ballard? What if he turns out to have been in Rheims last year? There were many in the Collège Anglais, I don't remember them all — but any of them might remember me."

Aliudque cupido, mens aliud suadet: desire persuades me one way, reason the other. Never had Tom agreed more with ancient Ovid! Half of him wanted nothing better than to gallop to Bishopsgate Without; the other half, though, reasoned against the scheme, lest his eagerness undo Sir Francis's patient net.

"Besides," the wary half insisted aloud, "what can I do there — or, for that matter, what can you do at the Castle?"

"At least we can make sure. That Poley of yours is with Babington — and Berden." Mylls breathed through his nose as he laid the half-crumpled note on the table with the greatest precision. He was a quiet, serious man, Frank Mylls, level-headed to a fault in the years Tom had known him — but this... This was turmoiling them all, and Mylls's own sort of turmoil took the shape of misdoubting each and all: each step, each move, each notion, each man. Poley was no surprise; Berden, on the other hand... The secretary fidgeted with the papers, squaring them again and again.

"They'll catch no sight of you, Mr. Thomas. There's a garret above Berden's parlour: you'll lie there, and hear all there is to hear."

And this was how Tom found himself in the dust of a garret in Bishopsgate Without, lying still on a sack of mouldy straw in the thickening gloom while three men shared a supper of capon and rabbit in the room downstairs. Capon, rabbit, and treason. The scent of roasted meat wafted through the cracks of the ceiling, together with the bilious light of rushes, and the quiet voices discussing things that, by right, should send them all to the gallows.

That Tom should hear all there was to hear had been, it turned out, Mylls's fond imagining: firstly, the men were never loud, no matter how Berden plied them with wine. Secondly, there were the bells of St. Botolph, whenever they chimed as good as next door. And thirdly, there was the Bedlam. How could one live by this hospital? The howls, the screams, the screeching laughter, the piteous calls of the poor crazed souls locked in there were by far the worst distraction, and the thought of falling asleep each night to this hellish music sent shiver after shiver down Tom's spine, and made it hard to keep still.

For all that, it was not long before one thing became clear: neither of Berden's guests downstairs was Father Ballard. The priest's alias of Captain Fortescue was spoken more than once, always as that of an absent comrade. Which made the whole exercise pointless, and Tom all the more restless.

And restlessness sent his mind a-wander down unpleasant paths: the fate of Isaac Finch, the supper at the Castle Tavern — where perhaps Ballard was sitting — and Mylls's misgivings. What if Berden, downstairs, had whispered to his companions, one forefinger across his lips, the other pointing to the ceiling? What if the nameless guest *was* Ballard, and his discussed absence a ploy? What if Berden had sent Mylls on a false scent to the Castle Tavern, and at the same time fabricated an excuse for himself, not taking into account —

Something wet and quivering touched the back of Tom's hand, making him lash out. He smacked hard against something furry, causing a squeak and a scratch of scurrying feet. Tom hunkered on knees and elbows, heart pounding and ears straining. All plaguey rats be damned — there was quiet downstairs.

Had he moved too sharply, made too much noise? Was Sir Francis Walsingham's design defeated because a rat — a rat! — had startled one of his men?

A heartbeat, two — and was that Berden, grousing? Laughter swelled downstairs, and someone exclaimed of tomcats, and then the bells of St. Botolph called curfew, and made Tom deaf.

Let them deafen the men downstairs too. Breathless — and angry at himself for it — Tom moved, reaching for the sheathed rapier he had unhooked from his belt for stealth's sake, and crouched on the sack, ready to leap, facing the trapdoor anyone must come through who tried to rush him. By the time St. Botolph fell silent, no one had moved, and the men downstairs had gone back to their quiet conversation.

Tom resumed his wait, wishing he'd arranged himself less uncomfortably, and cursing to himself when a cramp seized his calf. In English and French he cursed, and Latin, and Italian. He didn't dare to move, and at long last, when he couldn't feel his legs anymore, the small company disbanded, and the guests departed, leaving behind them the unquiet night, the pained calls, the mindless cackling across the courtyard. Did the Bedlam ever sleep?

Hissing through his teeth, Tom stumbled upright, waiting until the trapdoor lifted and Berden's head appeared, black in the greenish halo of a rushlight.

"Mr. Thomas — what was that ruckus?" was the man's salutation.

After the long, dark hours, Tom squinted against the sudden light. "You do need a cat," he said — and let Berden wonder just what he'd heard. "No Ballard?"

Berden sighed, making his small flame dance. "It can't be that I've lost their trust, though. They spoke so openly that he's out of London, and coming back tomorrow or the day after…"

"Supposing they didn't lie to you…" *Or you're not lying to me.* Tom made his stiff way to the trapdoor, and followed a silent Berden down the ladder.

Downstairs, the remnants of the dinner lay on the table — a carnage of bare ribs and gnawed wings in the light of a candle stump. A single moth danced around the flame, courting death with the horrible heedlessness of its sort.

"There's one thing…" Berden fingered a bit of cheese rind on a trencher.

Oh, God give patience — for Tom had none left. "If this is again about the money, Berden —"

The fellow looked up, soulful eyes full of reproach. "'Tis the warrants. I won't ask what if it *had* been Ballard tonight: mayhap you'll have the warrant in your sleeve, and that's for you to know. But what about tomorrow or the day after? What if they haven't lied, and Ballard comes back, and I've no warrant to arrest him?"

Ah well, Berden was no fool — he was bound to ask, sooner rather than later. When it came to getting answers, though… "Who ever said you are to arrest him?"

"But —"

"They still reckon you a friend, you say?"

"Ay, most surely."

"Then think: their good friend whips out Mr. Secretary's warrant and arrests their leader. They know themselves discovered and observed for a long time, they run to ground, and the next thing we know, one of them turns up at Placentia, hiding among the trees with a pistol."

Berden hung his head. That he was unhappy with the whole game was plain to see — wondering as Mylls had in the morning, as likely as not: *what if they act while we wait?* He squinted at the moth — still alive, still dancing. "Then…"

"Then you do as you're told. Send word when Ballard arrives. See that you know where he is and what he does. The moment will come, don't fear."

And it sounded presumptuous to Tom's own ears — but, if he shared the impression, Berden never showed it.

Tom was on the threshold when he heard a small thud behind him. He turned to see that Berden had hit his palm on the table, and there was nothing hovering around the flame. This was one moth that hadn't burnt itself, for all the good it did it.

CHAPTER 4

29th of July

In the absence of Lady Ursula Walsingham, who spent less and less time in London these days, the house in Seething Lane became a curious sort of place, half office and half quarters, where men of all sorts and stations came and went at all hours — grim, sharp-mannered men, covered in dust or mud and bearing intelligence, or keen-eyed, ink-fingered fellows, stooping over endless pages. Sir Francis's servants, who day and night attended to the needs of sallow clerks and rough messengers alike, asked no questions and made no comments.

The rosy-cheeked housekeeper, on the other hand, was full of questions when, come dawn, she shook Tom awake where he'd fallen asleep at his writing table — not that he'd had much rest.

"Is this the way to live, Mr. Thomas?" the woman tutted, throwing open the window to the damp morning air from the kitchen garden. "Can't a gentleman like yourself find his own bed at night? What would your poor lady mother say to see you like this?"

"Nothing good, Mrs Jeffreys," Tom muttered through a yawn, propping both elbows on the desk to rub sleep out of his eyes. "What time is it?"

"Just past six," the housekeeper said, setting before him a trencher of herrings and manchet bread, and a pot of ale.

Tom reached for the pot, before his still befogged mind caught up with Mrs Jeffreys's words. Six — oh Jove!

"Six!" he cried, and leapt to his feet, half overturning the trencher in his haste.

Mrs Jeffreys jumped to steady it. "Bless you, Master — but do have a bite! You'll make yourself ill!"

This was the way of things when working where the servants had known one from a lad. Throwing down half the ale in one gulp, Tom grabbed a manchet and stepped around Mrs Jeffreys's stocky form.

"Has Mr. Mylls arrived?" he asked.

"Ay, but…"

Tom didn't linger to hear more.

Past the scriveners' rooms, by the closed door of Mylls's room, he was surprised to find Berden, listening as shamelessly as you please.

"Hear what I found you!" the spy mouthed, grinning from ear to ear.

For a wild moment Tom wondered … Ballard? Then an unlikely voice rose beyond the door.

"Have you no eavesdroppers for that? I'm no common watcher!"

It was a young, sullen voice that quivered when it rose — a voice Tom had heard before.

The answering rumble belonged to Mylls — and, whatever he said did nothing to placate his guest.

"The sort of churl that dragged me here, for one! How long have you had him on my back?"

At Tom's elbow, Berden snorted a little. Oh, but this could be the first scrap of good news in days.

"Gifford?" Tom asked.

Berden nodded. "Lugging him here, though — *that* was —"

"I must work as I see fit!" Gifford cried beyond the door. "His Honour himself said so!"

"Did he?" Berden inquired, with an air of being fascinated.

All Tom did was raise an eyebrow. As *he* saw fit, really!

"I have Savage under my thumb, I tell you. I can make him compromise himself and all the others! Didn't I make him take an oath?

There was a bark of "Peace!" from Mylls, and some softer rumbling: the words couldn't be discerned, but there was no mistaking the sharp tone. Another would have gone quiet — but never Gifford. Gifford was all peevish arrogance.

"I won't be treated like this! Mr. Secretary wouldn't want me compromised because of that oaf."

Sir Francis was right: it was time to pare the fellow's nails. With a single knock, Tom entered, closing the door on Berden's face.

"Give you good day, Mr. Mylls," he greeted. "Do you mind if I join you?"

Gifford stopped his ill-tempered pacing at the noise of the door and turned to face the newcomer, slow and straight-backed like a displeased earl.

Was there a gleam of grim amusement in the secretary's smile? "Mind, Mr. Walsingham? But not at all — not at all," he said, and sat back to observe.

Oh, the marvellous power of the Walsingham name! Gilbert Gifford stiffened, as frozen as if Medusa had walked in.

He wore his straight hair a little longer now, and had exchanged the black worsted of the Collège Anglais for worn brown mockado — but otherwise he'd changed little in a year: a slight fellow of five-and-twenty, with a sallow triangular face, a sullen manner, and shifty eyes.

The eyes went rounder and rounder, and the pursed mouth fell open as Gilbert Gifford made his mind match a name to Tom's features — features he'd seen before, at the Collège

Anglais in Rheims… It was a dozen heartbeats before he exclaimed, "Roper!"

Tom had kept steady under Gifford's scrutiny. Now, he tilted his head. "You remember me, then, Deacon Gifford?" he asked. "The name is wrong, of course, but you couldn't have known."

And see how the man gawped, turning from Tom to Mylls. "This man…" he squawked.

"This man is Mr. Thomas Walsingham," Mylls said. "Mr. Secretary's own cousin, and as keen as I am to know where you disappeared to this time."

Tom went to lean against the window's embrasure. He wasn't going to wait while Gifford gathered his wits. "You claim you have a Savage under your thumb, I hear?" he asked, putting all the doubt he knew in the question. "Never the same John Savage we both knew in Rheims?"

In fairness, Gifford was quick to recover his step, drawing himself as tall as such a smallish fellow could. "Ay, John Savage. I made him take an oath to kill the Queen — and won't let him back out of it."

There was a smugness to the words, like that of a child with a trapped lizard. Little as he'd liked Savage back in Rheims — a brusque, blunt fellow, far too distrustful for comfort — Tom found he liked even less the notion of this boastful snake rushing the man to his ruin.

"And would he?" inquired Mylls. "Do you have reason to think Savage would change his mind?"

To see Gifford blush in fury, one would think his honour had been challenged. "I have Savage under my eye, and under my thumb!" he cried.

Oh, Lord smite blustering braggarts! "And what good is that?" Tom snapped. "What good is it to us, if we don't hear from you for days on end, and you're nowhere to be found? Mr. Secretary is very displeased with you."

That Mr. Secretary was also very distrusting, he bit off in time. Upset men did wild things, and Gifford seemed too upset as it was. What could be disquieting this twice traitor?

If Mylls had noticed, he didn't show it. "You'll keep company with Savage, from now on."

Gifford looked up like one stung. "I never did, before. What if he grows suspicious?"

Not an unreasonable objection, in truth — but the deacon had run out of objections — reasonable or otherwise.

"You'll see that he doesn't." Mylls leant across to tap a forefinger on the table in front of Gifford. "And you'll find a way to always know where he's to be found."

"And most of all," Tom said, "we must always know where to find *you*."

For a moment, he thought the fellow was bristling at being ordered about with such briskness not just by the secretary, but also by the one he'd known as Roper, the mercer's son. But there was something else in the hunching of his shoulders, in the rubbing of both palms up and down his faded breeches. It was not mere disquiet: Gilbert Gifford was afraid. Afraid of what, though? Surely, he couldn't fear Babington's fools more than he feared Sir Francis? Unless it was something else entirely?

"Oh — and Gifford…" Tom tried. "What of Finch?"

It had been a long shot, and the shake of the head, the blank stare, came as no surprise.

"Finch…?"

"Isaac Finch, the courier."

"I don't know him," Gifford said, a little too hastily for honest bafflement.

Tom hummed. "And yet you were at Lichfield, weren't you?"

This restored Gifford to petulance. "You know I was." He stuck out his chin, waxing bolder with each word. "At Lichfield and at Chartley, tricking the Queen of Scots for Mr. Secretary. And if you think I had time to waste on the couriers back then..." His voice rose to a squawk. "This Finch — he's never watching me?"

And trust the arrant coxcomb to think all turned around. Still, he sounded startled and indignant, unaware that Finch was missing. Well, let him fret and wonder, then. Perhaps it would keep him on the line, for a change.

Tom smiled at the fellow. "Don't concern yourself, Gifford," he said — and, having accomplished what he'd come to do, he took his leave with a nod at Mylls.

When he opened the door, Berden all but stumbled across the threshold.

"Anything you missed, Berden?"

Never bothering to deny or make excuses, the man followed Tom to the scriveners' room, and there he stood, sucking his teeth in a show of great reluctance. "'Tis just..."

Tom had long learnt it was best to take bait at once. "What?"

"I'm no tattler, Mr. Thomas, you know me. Never the sort to tell tales on a fellow man —"

"*What is it?*"

The spy darted a peek behind him, before leaning in close. "Your Deacon Gifford, he's lying through his teeth," he muttered. "He knows Finch well enough."

From Lichfield? Tom didn't ask — for all that Berden couldn't have missed Gifford's bellows. "From where?"

"They crossed ways at Barn Elms once, and I tell you: there's no love lost between those two."

Which meant little enough, in truth, because Tom had trouble imagining either man being friendly to anyone. Still… "What was it all about?"

"God knows." Berden shrugged, all his fustian reluctance gone. "They glowered at each other, like they'd come nose to nose before. Finch called the deacon a slippery rogue, and the brat made as if he hadn't heard, but…" And here came a knowing tilt of the head.

Tom tried to imagine Gifford doing murder. He was a sour fellow if ever there was one — but was ill-blood enough to kill? Or, more easily, was it enough to betray a man to a foe? And then, if ill-blood was the matter, that must be true of Poley too, and of Rouse Casey, and Skeres — and, come to think of it…

"What about you, Berden?" Tom asked. "Have you ever come nose to nose with Finch?"

Berden snorted. "Show me the man in the Service who never has, Mr. Thomas! The other night, I was right glad you sent him to Mr. Mylls, so I wouldn't have to walk with him Bishopsgate way! The fellow's an ill-tempered pest — and I make no secret about it."

Unlike certain others, hung unsaid — although few would deny that Isaac Finch rubbed them the wrong side.

On the other hand, what of Gifford's fear? Was it the fear of ill-conscience, or the fear that would make a man do ill? Or was it just plain terror at being caught between treason and betrayal?

"Mr. Thomas?"

Tom blinked out of his philosophising to find young Toby Chandler hovering at the door.

"There's Mr. Phelippes, Master," the boy announced, in that portentous whisper he had. "He asks, will you see him?"

He asks…! Tom swallowed a flare of annoyance. Ever since returning from France to take his place as Sir Francis's trusted cypherer, Phelippes had shifted from the close friendship of their shared Paris days to a formality prim enough to sour milk. *Would he see him … * as though Tom were in the habit of refusing audience — to Phelippes or anyone else!

As he made to follow the boy, Tom remembered what he'd meant to ask of Berden. "Ballard?"

Berden shook his head. "You heard what I heard last night: he's expected back, and that's that…"

And that was that. How many times had that been that as Cicero waited for Catiline to act?

Phelippes rose from the chair when Tom entered his writing room.

"Oh, do sit!" Tom wished at once he hadn't made it sound like an order — and, just to make it worse, the little cypherer remained standing.

"I arrived half an hour ago, Mr. Thomas. His Honour is on his way to Richmond by river with the Court, and…" He patted the satchel he wore hanging from his shoulder.

And there was the letter. Mary Stuart's letter, with a few lines added, like a drop of poison in a glass of wine.

All kinds of fool, that was what Tom was: uneasy with the thought of underhand ways, after seven years under Sir Francis's own tutelage! *We only make it unassailable…*

On receiving no answer, Phelippes cleared his throat. "Do you know where my man Casey is?"

"Rouse? Why, I thought — isn't he…?" It dawned on Tom that he hadn't seen Rouse Casey since the other night, when he'd ordered him off to find Gifford.

Tom went to the door to call to the waiting Chandler. "Have you seen Rouse Casey since the other night, Chandler?"

Chandler had not — nor had he heard from him.

Phelippes took this with a deep frown. "I meant to send him to deliver the letter." He fidgeted with the satchel's strings. "What of Berden?"

Tom shook his head. "He's been passing himself off as one of them."

"And so has Skeres, hasn't he?"

"And Poley. And Chandler never did anything of the sort."

Phelippes pursed his lips. "I don't think we can trust a servant with this," he murmured.

And here was the dilemma of secrecy making itself plain: they'd kept the workings of this conspiracy as close as possible, trusting as few men as was practical, and planting more and more of them with the traitors. It was one of Sir Francis's maxims that trust needed to be a narrow ring — so narrow that now they lacked one trusted man to deliver one most important letter.

It was not hard, Tom found, to convince himself it was nothing but the strictest necessity — and to ignore the sudden thrill, the sparks coursing through his blood.

"If I were to go..." He held up a hand to forestall the protestations written in Phelippes's raised eyebrows. "I know, I know — but 'tis Savage alone who knows me by sight. If we make sure he's not with Babington, then I can go disguised as a servant."

"I don't know, Mr. Thomas..." Phelippes's whole face wrinkled in a grimace. "If we could get Gifford to draw Savage away..."

Tom grinned. "Ay, well — it happens that we can."

Once Mylls was talked into acquiescence, if not agreement, and Gifford sent off with Berden to watch him, there was the matter of the disguise.

A plain blue coat was easy to borrow from the returned Skeres, together with a soft cap, and Tom owned more well-scuffed shoes than he liked. After unearthing a plain shirt and riding Venetians, he thought himself so inconspicuously attired that nobody would look at him twice.

"Well?" he asked, turning around to offer his new self to the scrutiny of Phelippes and Skeres — and, devil pinch them, must they both shake their heads?

"A gentleman disguised," Phelippes pronounced. "Look at your hands!"

Tom did. They were the hands of one who spent far too much time within walls. "So? I'm a house servant, not a peasant toiling in the fields! And I've been riding in the sun, these weeks past. I've browned —"

"Browned, 'e says!" Skeres snorted. "There's a bottle of walnut juice, down in the pantry…" And he was gone, even as Tom protested.

"I've fooled a college full of priests into believing me a mercer, haven't I? If I lived through a week of it in Rheims, I can well play the servant for an hour, I daresay — never mind my smooth hands!"

Phelippes slumped his shoulders, more mournful than ever. "His Honour won't like it."

On this he wasn't wrong. Sir Francis had not liked Tom's jaunt in France — although he'd never quite said so — and wouldn't like this other any better, but then…

"His Honour's on the river, halfway to Richmond, and he'll like it even less if we dither," Tom said.

Skeres barged through the door without a by-your-leave. He had no walnut juice, but carried a folded scrap of paper instead.

S. at the Castle with the D., Berden wrote. *Staying awhile.*

Tom handed the scrawled note to Phelippes, who, instead of looking cheered by it, asked Skeres if Rouse Casey had come in, by any chance.

"Did you say to ask?" the Minotaur grumbled, even as he went to inquire.

Tom shook his head, and looked sideways at the fidgeting Phelippes. "Do you think I'd take a needless risk...?" he asked through gritted teeth.

Whatever Phelippes heard in the question, it seemed to decide him. With a slow sigh, he drew two letters from his satchel.

"One from your supposed master," he explained. "He promises to name himself next time and warns Babington to ask no questions — so they won't bother you. And this..."

Oh, the cold, bleak weight of a square of paper, when it carried treason, and fear, and deceit, and death in its folds. Tom turned it between his fingers. On the back was a mark of some sort, like a square lacking the bottom side.

"Gallows." Phelippes was fidgeting — blushing, even. "When I first read it, my first thought..."

Gallows.

For an hour Tom had almost forgotten as he argued with Phelippes, and Mylls, and Skeres. All of a sudden, the cold truth rushed back. There was no adventurous thrill to this — only a complot of men who were no less dangerous for being a pack of fools, and the necessity of cozening them, and their mistress, to their ruin. But this was Service work, wasn't it? The Queen's own work, and God's...

Phelippes cleared his throat. The blush had ebbed away from his pitted cheeks.

"Do you remember, back in Paris?" he asked under his breath. "When you needed to ride back to London, and had no passport?"

Five years gone, Tom had been nineteen and meddling with murder for the first time, at the risk of wrecking what career he had. And Phelippes had been right there, with quills and inkhorns in his satchel.

"Do you remember what we added to Skeres's passport?"

Oh, Tom did remember. "*And one servant*, ay," he murmured. "Hardly the same, was it?"

"Hardly," Phelippes agreed. "We had the vaguest suspicion, then — but now there's the Queen's life at stake, and all England. We had the vaguest suspicion, and we did it, didn't we?"

But nobody goes to the gallows over a passport that's been tampered with. We were not pushing a queen to her ruin, then, and another to deeds beyond repair. It was a different, much darker stare that Tom felt on himself as he swallowed his qualms and slipped the letters inside the blue coat.

Perhaps it was sympathy in Phelippes's grimace, or perhaps it was relief — and it struck Tom that it was this that made the cypherer reluctant: not a lack of trust in Tom's abilities, but an awareness of his uneasy conscience.

Phelippes twitched, and for a moment Tom thought the man would pat his arm — but then he turned away to open the door to the gallery.

Down in the hall stood Skeres, glowering thunderously. He looked up as he caught sight of Tom on the stairs, and bellowed, "Rouse ain't 'ere!"

"Quiet, Dolius," ordered Tom, exchanging a glance with Phelippes.

And to Phelippes perhaps it was just the last confirmation that Tom had to play messenger. To Tom it was a fresh disquiet. Where was Rouse Casey? Had he gone Finch's way — whatever way that was? It was a most unpleasant question to carry in one's head, on the way to the plotters' lair — even if it was only to knock on the door, drop a letter, and walk away.

CHAPTER 5

Anthony Babington lodged in Holborn, in fine gentlemanly fashion — and why wouldn't he? It was only in the tales of old that villains burrowed in the darkest ruins. Wasn't Catiline a nobleman? Never the sort to dwell in hovels, surely.

So it was no surprise that Hern's Rent was a well-sized house, two storeys high, the second jutting over the street in painted arrogance. The door-knocker had the shape of a fox's head — and Tom had enough time to consider the irony of it, before his knock was answered.

The man who opened the door was no servant. Around Tom's age, he was tall and finely clothed, although his damask doublet hung open at the front. Did the handsome, narrow face and the pearl earring belong to Babington himself?

Face schooled into blandness, Tom let Kent colour his voice. "Beg Your Honour's pardon, I've a letter for a Mr. Babington."

The hand that held the door went white-knuckled, and when Tom made to unbutton the top of his coat, he found himself grabbed by the wrist.

"Not in the street, confound you," the man hissed, and he pushed the door just wide enough to let Tom in.

And there went any chance of dropping the letter and being gone.

Tom blinked in the gloom as the door slammed shut behind him. Had Finch done the same before they'd dragged him downstairs to a cellar and a makeshift rack? Or had he walked in here to peddle what he knew? Either way, the courier had seen a largish hall, with dark tapestries hanging from the walls, several doors, and a carved staircase at the far end. Tom fought the urge to hide his tell-tale hands, until the man turned to call over his shoulder, "Tich!"

By which, when someone else emerged through one of the doors, Tom guessed him to be Chidiock Tichborne — the one Skeres was following.

Tichborne had less finery about him, and was stockier, with round cheeks and the beginning of a gingery beard: on hearing Tom's errand, he took a hitching breath.

"I'll fetch him," he said — and bounded up the stairs.

The man who wasn't Babington remained, tapping a foot and looking over his shoulder now and then. Tilney, perhaps? But servants didn't stare at gentlemen, so Tom kept his head low, until three men crowded atop the stairs and hastened down.

One was Tichborne, the other Poley, and between them, glowing in straw-coloured satin…

"I'm Anthony Babington," he announced far too loudly, even before he reached the foot of the stairs. "You bring something for me, boy? Where have you come from?"

Tom blinked as stolidly as he knew. "'Tis all in the letter, please you, Master."

Poley murmured something — some caution, surely. All was thrown to the wind. Babington strode along the hall to receive the letters.

Under cover of fumbling with his buttons, Tom observed the man who fancied himself an arch-conspirator. Anthony Babington was young and slender, with the sort of long-jawed face one saw on painted saints in France. Here was the would-be regicide, courting Spanish fire for the sake of the old religion. With his domed brow and fervent manner, he might have looked the part — but for the deep-set eyes that roamed restlessly.

He snatched up the letters, and picked the one from the Scots Queen, nostrils a-quiver, shoulders tensed, long fingers fussing with the wax seal which, in the scant light from the one oriel above the stairs, glowed scarlet.

Like spilt blood, half of Tom's mind offered — the other half scoffing at the garish simile.

"Perhaps…" Poley threw a cold glance Tom's way, and leant to whisper in Babington's ear.

At first it seemed this second warning, too, would be ignored — and so much for Poley's vaunted influence. But as soon as the seal broke, Babington smiled — a boyish smile that changed his face entirely.

"My prudent Robin!" he said, patting Poley's hand. "Let me just…" He unfolded the letter, grimaced, and passed it to Tichborne.

"I'll need help, Tich," he said.

Help with the cypher, ay. Tom looked down to hide a flash of scorn as Babington opened the second letter, and the others hovered with bated breath. Had this fop expected Mary Stuart to entrust her treason to plain writing? Skeres was right: if these were the Queen's enemies…

"Well, boy…" Babington beckoned Tom closer. "Your master begs that I should ask no questions — and I won't. Tell him I'm grateful, and pray that the Lord may bless him. As for you…" He held out a silver coin — a groat.

Four pence for carrying a letter! Well, if there was something Master Babington lacked — besides his wits — it was a tight fist.

Still, it rankled to take the traitor's silver and give humble thanks for it.

"I'll have the answer done in a day or two," Babington said — and then his friend with the earring, who had been watching in cross-armed, quivering stillness, stepped forward.

"You know the Castle Tavern, near the Exchange? Ask the ostler there whether they're stabling Mr. Tilney's bay horse. If he says they are, then come and pick up the answer."

Yes: Charles Tilney. The well-heeled courtier, the Gentleman Pensioner who had hitched his fate to this wretched venture.

Tom bowed. "Mr. Tilney's bay horse," he repeated. "At the Castle."

This seemed to satisfy them, and Tichborne was shepherding Tom to the door, when there was a knock. They all froze, and Tichborne shoved Tom aside to spy out of the peep-hole.

"The Captain," he threw over his shoulder, beaming, and his companions lit up as one — Poley with them.

Tichborne hastened to open the door — far wider this time — and a man strode in, tall, broad-shouldered, swarthy of face and black of hair and clothes. He wore tall riding boots and, in spite of the hot day, a black cape thrown over his shoulder like an ancient Roman's mantle. There was gold trim on the cape, and silver button flashed on the high-crowned hat...

All this Tom caught in sideways glimpses, and it was hard work not to gape. For this dark man they called Captain was Captain Fortescue, or Black Foskew to some who thought they knew him. But to Sir Francis's men this was Father John Ballard, Rheims man, priest, and traitor.

And see the adoring awe of these young fools! Babington's crows, Berden called them — but he was wrong: Ballard's gudgeons, they were, one and all.

Behind the priest came a big-boned man with a hard, flat face. This henchman — Bernard Maude, surely — had hardly crossed the threshold when Tilney came to hurry Tom through the door.

"Off you go now, fellow," he whispered, but not so low that Ballard didn't hear.

This was how Thomas Walsingham, kinsman to Mr. Secretary himself, first came to lock gazes with Father John Ballard — and found himself dry-mouthed of a sudden.

He had the warmest grin, this traitor, as he turned away from his friends to observe the man in the blue coat. And he had large black eyes that burned through to a man's soul.

Or perhaps not so deep — for when, after a long moment, Tichborne explained, "He brought the letter," Ballard lost interest, and Tilney resumed his pushing.

"See how the Lord brought me —" Tom half heard, before the door was shut behind him — and he had no doubt the rich, warm tones belonged to the priest.

He walked down the street with a manner of unhurried purpose, in case it occurred to someone in the house to make sure of him. Not that it was likely, now they had both the letter and their leader to occupy them — but this last encounter had left Tom feeling scoured and exposed.

Temple Bar was in sight before it occurred him to unfist his hands, and he found the mark in his palm where he'd been gripping Babington's groat.

There was a beggar crouching at a corner, bemoaning his palsied legs. Tom dropped the coin into his grimy palm and ran for the river, the man's loud blessings following him like a pack of stray dogs.

From Phelippes and Mylls's fretful welcome in Seething Lane, one would have thought Tom the greenest schoolboy in the Service.

Even as he resumed his own plumage, Phelippes plied him with myriad questions, down to the minutest detail. Tom answered, and answered, and answered, quashing his annoyance with the thought that Sir Francis would want to know.

"And I can't swear to it, for I only saw him once before, but the one who arrived with Ballard was Bernard Maude," he offered, when the cypherer ran dry at last.

Phelippes clicked his tongue, and Mylls, who had been scowling all along, snorted, "Maude! Much good it does to have that one!"

Bernard Maude had been long foisted on Ballard to be his inseparable companion, only he'd done precious little reporting. They had little luck with their men, lately.

The thought made Tom look up from the buttons of his doublet.

"Has Rouse turned up?" he asked.

Phelippes shook his head most mournfully, and Mylls' scowl darkened.

"No, Rouse hasn't," the secretary said. "But it may be that someone else has."

"*It may be?*" As half of Tom's mind sifted Mylls's words, the other half noticed that this must be news to the frowning Phelippes, too.

"A body was fished out the Houndsditch," Mylls said. "They think it may be Finch."

A body! *And were you keeping this for sweetmeats? Still making little of it?* Tom made himself swallow the angry retorts.

"Who are *they*?" he asked instead — which he thought showed great restraint. "How did we come to know?"

"A constable went to tell the clerk at St. Helen's, it seems."

"And when was this?"

If Mylls observed Tom's irritation, he discounted it. "Early this morning. I was advised about an hour ago — but what with you being gone, and all…"

And see how Phelippes pursed his lips. Was it in displeasure at Mylls's silence, or in recognition that, much as Sir Francis trusted him on the matter of the letter, Finch's disappearance wasn't his to sort? Ah well, he was welcome to argue it with Mylls, if he liked.

In a trice Tom was hastening downstairs.

"Are you for St. Helen's?" Mylls asked from above.

"I don't know about you, Mr. Mylls — but I'd rather know if it's Finch."

"I sent your man Skeres there," Mylls said.

Tom swallowed more sour words as he clattered downstairs. Skeres — and so much for discretion!

There was a man knocking at Sir Francis's door. A man wearing the soberest black, followed by a boy carrying a box.

A normal and innocuous occurrence, at any other time — but now?

Already on horseback, and ready to head for Bishopsgate, Tom dismounted quickly and reached the steps just as Fisher the head-servant, opened the door.

The visitor turned, showing that his black garb was of the professional sort, and he was no stranger. "Mr. Walsingham, is it?" he asked.

Tom had already met this young man with the long, glum face, but…"I'm afraid I don't…"

"Lopes," the young man offered, dipping his dark head in a nicely judged bow. "Ambrose Lopes, at your service."

"Of course!" Tom smiled. "Doctor Lopes's son, aren't you? We met once, when your father attended on Mr. Secretary."

Dr. Roderigo Lopes was the Queen's Portuguese physician, who had risen to the post on Sir Francis's own recommendation. The son, who could not have been much older than twenty years, nodded with great solemnity. He was, he said, on an errand for his father, bringing a few cordials and powders he himself had made for His Honour's comfort. He nudged forward the boy, and Tom had Fisher receive the box, with a promise that it would be delivered at Barn Elms before night. He exchanged solemn greetings with this most solemn young man, and had his foot in the stirrup when a thought occurred to him.

How many times had he pored over a corpse, and wished for a medical man to tell him what meant what? And here he was presented with one — just at the right moment.

"Master Lopes, I believe I've never been more in need of a physician."

Lopes gave another small bow. "I'm not that, yet. I'm reading for my doctorate, and training with my father."

But he was still the apprentice to a Royal physician — and he risked killing no one for what Tom had in mind.

"I'm on my way to see a body … a corpse, and I would have a more learned opinion than my own. I wonder if you would assist me?"

Though Ambrose Lopes wore the sober ways of a man twice his age, he was still an eager youth underneath. See how he lit up at the prospect, even as he hummed and rubbed his long chin.

"'Tis more a surgeon that you'd need, perhaps — but … where do we go?"

So Tom walked his horse to St. Helen's, with young Lopes in tow, telling him as little of the matter as he could without appearing discourteous. All of a sudden, he wasn't all that sure of his whim. Beside Sir Francis and the Queen, the elder Lopes also physicked Lord Leicester. Did the son do the same? And, even if he didn't...? As they made their way through the streets of Bishopsgate, Tom found himself tying his tongue in knots around what few facts he had — until he caught a glint of amusement in Lopes's dark eyes.

"Mr. Walsingham, my father has long caned out of me all indiscretion," the young medicus said. "I'll observe this corpse, and what I can learn I'll tell you — and you alone. No one else will hear of it. Not even my father."

Tom smiled ruefully, and asked Lopes's pardon. Of course a man didn't gain the trust of such exalted patients — Sir Francis first and foremost — without being as prudent as he was skilled. Oh Jove — but Mylls's fretfulness must be catching!

Or was it the stifling heat, befogging Tom's wits? The morning air was thick with the damp odours of a London summer — but there was something else, a festive cheer about the chattering groups, the knots around the ballad sellers. And in the noise, the name of Drake sounded again and again.

Unexpectedly, Ambrose Lopes knew the cause of it. "Captain Drake is returned from the Americas. Laden with Spanish treasure, our scullion swears."

Which would, no doubt, darken the humours of Philip of Spain — and meanwhile it made Londoners wild.

By the time they reached St. Helen's, it was a comfort to enter the quiet shade of the plane trees. Mylls's man was nowhere to be seen, but there was no mistaking Skeres, who lounged against the curved wall, pretending to pare his nails as he kept the most lowering watch, in plain sight of both houses — and to Tartarus with prudence.

"This Pratte fellow, the clerk, 'e lives there," he announced, as soon as Tom was within hearing distance. Skeres pointed his knife towards the house with the honeysuckle.

"Have you talked to him?"

The Minotaur's sullen shrug wasn't reassuring. "'Tis 'im as talked to me," he said. "Came out like a charging bull, said they're honest folks 'ere, and want no truck with Finch and us all."

"Oh, they don't?" Tom rather disliked the clerk on principle. Now it was time to dislike him in person. "Where is he?"

Skeres jerked his chin towards the church, and there Tom went.

Inside, St. Helen's was as its peculiar frame promised: a nave and a quire just as large, separated by a row of pillars. It was also unusual in that its large windows and lack of side chapels made it lighter than most old churches, and the floor lay on different levels, with sets of shallow steps leading up and down at odd places. It was squat, white, chilly after the July heat outside, and smelt like damp chalk.

Tom's steps echoed as he moved along the nave, seeking the clerk. It wasn't long before other, fussier steps answered from the other end, and a red-faced man emerged from the transept with the air of wanting to give the intruder a piece of his mind.

Tom didn't give him the time. "Are you Arthur Pratte, the parish clerk?" he asked, letting his voice carry.

"Oy!" Pratte — for who else could it be? — hastened close. He was a stocky fellow of five-and-thirty or so, ruddy and curly-headed. "Who would you be, to barge in like this?"

From his three-step vantage, Tom looked down on him with all his severity. "Isaac Finch works for me."

The clerk stopped short, taking in the gentlemanly clothes and manner. The reckoning was plain to see in his face;

servants prying in the churchyard had been one thing, but this...

Once again, Tom cut his calculations short. "Or should I say that he did? Why did you tell my man out there that Finch is dead?"

"I didn't..." Pratte protested. "I never said that, Master. 'Tis just that Finch comes and goes as he pleases, never saying a word — not even to Dr. Lewis — and nobody bats an eyelash. Now he's gone a day, and his women fret, and you and your men come asking questions, and then the constable says there's this body they found in the Houndsditch. I ask you, in good conscience: what am I to think?" And Pratte could have stopped there, having made his point, and a fair one in truth — but no. He had to do more hawing, and purse his lips. "And we all know about Isaac Finch, don't we?"

We all know... Tom's stomach clenched, and he made himself observe the man coldly. "Do we truly? And what is it that we all know?"

"Why, I..." Pratte's chin fell as he gawped, for all the world like a curly-headed tortoise. "Now, I don't blame Goodwife Lovell for her brother's ways — but... Unneighbourly, that's what I call him. And ... and ... Your Honour will know..."

Having gone from "Oy!" to being His Honour in the course of a short minute, Tom did nothing more than raise one brow. He'd learnt the trick from Sir Francis, and it seldom failed to work.

Pratte was all but undone. "'Tis Dr. Lewis!" he blurted. "He says we must put up with Finch's uncouth ways, for he does the work he does — and we must ask no questions, he says, and never gossip..."

He does the work he does... And surely Dr. Lewis thought himself subtle! To how many of his parishioners had he played

75

the oracle about Isaac Finch — leaving them to conjecture the wildest hugger-mugger?

Tom swallowed a sigh. "Why did the constable come to you with news of the body?" he asked.

This seemed to settle Pratte somewhat. "He didn't come to *me*," he said, all clerkly again. "That is… When a dead body is found, they go to all the parishes, ask about missing people."

And they'd go to the clerk. "Did you tell Goodwife Lovell and her niece?"

"Ay, well…" The clerk shifted his weight. "'Twas not my place to tell the constable about Finch. When Dr. Lewis returns —"

Could this be a small mercy? "But you told the women?"

Tortoises had no crest, and nor had parish clerks — but Pratte's had fallen. "What was I to do, Your Honour?" he moaned. "If I told them, they'd rush to see the body, and name names, and make a noise, and Dr. Lewis isn't here…"

A small mercy, ay — bound to be short-lived, but a mercy all the same. Sorry as Tom was for Goodwife Lovell and pretty Grace…

"You did well. Where do they keep the body?"

"At St. Botolph Without," Pratte said. "Down in the crypt, the constable says." He was eager all of a sudden, pointing northwards, as though Tom might not know where the gate lay.

Dr. Lewis's doing — with his Delphian pronouncements.

It seemed fated that Tom must spend more time than he liked around the Bedlam. The cries of the poor souls in the hospital seemed less loud in the bustle of daytime, but angrier — and he, Skeres and Lopes had a good earful of them while they waited for a distrustful old beadle to open the crypt for them.

"Not that there's much to see," the man kept grumbling, as he fumbled with the biggest of the bolts.

"I'd 'ave drawn that thing twice," Skeres said in what he perhaps thought a whisper, "and tied it around the gaffer's neck! Do I trounce 'im, Master?"

"No, you don't," Tom said — lest the Minotaur took silence for assent. Apart from the unseemliness of trouncing elderly church servants, Tom had a shrewd suspicion that the beadle wasn't half as slow as he made out.

As if to prove him right, it wasn't long before they heard a cry of "Stop, Uncle!"

A very large young man pushed through the church's side door, panting and waving as he called out again. "Stop!"

The beadle obeyed, beaming as the newcomer advanced — a fellow possessed of a bovine face and the arms of a blacksmith.

"What d'ee think 'ee's doing, eh?" he bellowed. "Coroner's inquest's tomorrow. Then 'ee can see all 'ee like."

Tom stepped in front of the simmering Minotaur. "And who are you, to give orders like this?" he demanded, although he had a fair notion.

There was some chest-puffing, and a trumpet-like announcement: "Constable Hallet, of Bishopsgate Ward!"

It took a newly minted constable to parade himself like Hannibal at Cannae — but then, the older ones were no better in their own way. Young Hallet seemed far too full of his own dignity to cede to browbeating. Would he listen to reason?

Tom doubted it but still… "Well, Constable, you do your duty, I'm sure. And part of it is to find out who the poor deceased was, I believe?"

Hallet scrunched up his face. "Ay, but —"

"Very good. Now, this man you see…" Tom hauled Skeres to the front. "His cousin went missing two days ago."

"Ay, but —"

"You know the coroner's work would be a good deal easier, if you had a name to give him."

It was plain as day that Hallet knew nothing of the sort, and had to chew on it.

"Sometimes I forget just *how* the peace is kept," Lopes murmured at Tom's shoulder. He'd been observing all, as quiet and dark as an owl, and now he was studying young Hallet with philosophical fascination.

"Am I taking too much of your time?" Tom whispered back.

"Not at all, not at all. This is all so…" Lopes gestured with both hands. "I'm a student of human nature, as well as the human body."

And Hallet was undoubtedly a prime sample. See how he sucked his teeth, weighing the matter in what mind he had — until, alas, he shook his head. "Coroner said naught of folks seeing it."

Oh, now! Were there justice in this world, slow-witted churls should have been easy to lead — but no! Did Hallet need to hear the Walsingham name?

This once, Tom was spared the need of naming his great cousin, for right then another fellow trundled inside, calling, "Hallet, you big lout!"

It was an older man, just as sturdy and far more jaded. Hallet's better in the ranks of local Law, perhaps? That this might be for the good was a short-lived hope, as Hallet and his uncle no sooner saw the man than they fell on him, and the three started squabbling.

Apparently, Portsoken Ward had come to poke its nose where it had no business.

Ambrose Lopes looked much amused. "Is it always like this?" he asked.

"Oh, this is nothing. You should see France," Tom snorted — and then caught the glint in his servant's eye. "And before you even say it, Skeres: no, you trounce no one."

Meanwhile, Hallet, his uncle and their foe were still at it, trading insults and jeers in a most useless manner, until Tom shouted, "Enough!" and the three men fell silent.

When bid to explain, the Portsoken man proved more limber-tongued than Hallet, and said the body was found in his ward, giving him authority over the matter.

That Hallet knew how to counter this was dubious, but the beadle jumped in the fray.

"In the Houndsditch, it was!" the old man cried. "And that's not inside that thing you call a ward!"

Hence the ruckus. The Houndsditch hugged, moat-like, a length of the city walls, and was nicknamed for all the carcases that floated in its foul waters. Who had jurisdiction over it was debatable — as it was being debated at the moment, with young Hallet wanting to know why then the coroner had had the body brought to Bishopsgate.

"So what of it? 'Twas Portsoken men as found it!"

"Right under the Gate…"

"This side of it, you lurdane!"

Once again, Tom made himself heard: he cared naught one way or the other, he said, as long as they let his man see the body and be done. And, when Bishopsgate still fretted, he asked, "Just to make matters clear: which ward is rounding up the jurors for the inquest?"

Hallet had to concede it was the Portsoken fools.

Just as Tom had surmised — and hoped: see how smug this particular Portsoken fool was in announcing that he had no objection to the gentleman seeing the body if he liked.

As the beadle, grousing all the time, at long last drew the bolt and lit a candle to light the way, Lopes leant close to Tom to ask, "Is that entirely legal?"

Ah well, now… "City Law is more tangled than most." Tom shrugged. "I never met a wardsman who knew his way around it. Are you worried that we're breaking the law?"

"Not in the least!" There was another of those amused flashes in the dark eyes. "So the trick's to pretend you know better?"

It was a miracle the young man didn't tumble down the spiral stairs when Skeres elbowed him in the ribs, with a wink and an approving chortle. "'E learns fast, this one, eh, Mr. Tom?"

Swallowing a laugh, Tom caught young Ambrose by the arm to steady him. Like the Minotaur, he was beginning to like Dr. Lopes's son very much.

CHAPTER 6

The stench met them atop the stairs. Not just the nasty Houndsditch muck, but a strong odour of rotting meat. Once down in the crypt, the gloom was so thick with it that Tom had to swallow back the rising of his gorge — and was Skeres gagging behind him? The two constables lingered, a good deal less zealous of a sudden. Ambrose Lopes alone was unaffected — which was fitting in one of his calling. The beadle scurried in to put his candle on a trestle that stood between two huge pillars. What lay shrouded on it was easy to guess.

"We'll need more light, Beadle," Tom said in his coldest, steadiest manner.

The man shuffled away in the darkness and reappeared with a handful of dusty wax candles, some half burnt, some little more than stumps. He made quick work of lighting one after the other, dripping a few drops from each to stick it to the trestle. As soon as he was done, Tom walked close, with young Lopes at his side. *Would these matters be easier in the dead of winter?* he wondered — and was thankful when Lopes reached to lift the shroud.

Or not so thankful, perhaps.

Stifling a cry of revulsion, he turned away from the miasma, and had to shield his nose in the crook of his elbow before he made himself look again.

The sight was no better than the fetor: the flesh was swollen, the skin macerated to a sodden, pale greyness. The lips and eyes were gnawed away, and a hole gaped where the belly had been.

"The soft parts are eaten first," Lopes explained.

As ugly a memento of mortality as could be.

As he leant over this rotting horror, the medicus threw a meaningful glance Skeres's way. "Shouldn't he…" he murmured — and right he was.

It took some throat-clearing before Tom's voice allowed him to summon his suddenly timid servant.

Very green around the gills, the Minotaur came to stand at Tom's shoulder and peered over it for a heartbeat, before shaking his head with great vehemence.

"He didn't even look!" Hallet called from the foot of the stairs.

"Make sure, Nick," Tom ordered. "Is this your cousin?"

Although, how anyone could be expected to find a kinsman's likeness in such a ruin? Tom swallowed hard. God send Goodwife Lovell and Grace never needed to see this as their last memory of a brother or father.

There was no blaming Skeres when the lad shook his head again, and ran for the stairs — but, hypothetical cousins apart, the trouble remained unsolved. Could this have been Isaac Finch? Steeling himself, Tom looked again, taking in the body's shape and what little remained of the filth-soaked clothes. And if the clothes were too ruined to tell, the height could perhaps be right. But bony men of middle height — how many of those were to be found in London?

This was hopeless … or was it? Ambrose Lopes was still busy with his observations.

"When did you say Nick's cousin went missing?" he asked, never turning from the body.

Tom had to rake his mind for the answer. It seemed he'd been searching for Finch for a long time, but in truth… "His daughter saw him last the other night."

"Hm." The young man straightened to question the wardsmen, huddled at the crypt's door. "He was found this morning, you say? And you brought him here at once?"

The Portsoken man stepped forward. "They were opening the gate a bit early, right before dawn."

"So the body wasn't left out in the sun." Lopes pitched his words to an almost court-like formality. "All is possible according to God's will, but I don't believe this can be Nick's cousin."

He bent over the body again and, with thumbs and forefingers, almost daintily, pried open the dead jaws. Tom was almost proud of the fact that he didn't look away.

"How old was he, your fellow?" the medicus asked, as he peered inside the black maw.

How old now, indeed? "Not yet forty," Tom croaked, not at all sure that it was true — but he knew what Lopes was aiming for, and a memory flashed in his mind, of Finch biting into a chunk of bread. "He had most of his teeth."

Lopes straightened. "I don't know what lives in the Houndsditch, but no fish will eat teeth. And no dead body will undergo so much decay in a day and a night. Your Nick can keep worrying." And then he asked the beadle for a place to wash his hands.

Tom was very glad to stumble up the narrow stone steps, and never had a church's air felt sweeter to him than that of St. Botolph that day. Also, he was very glad to have brought Ambrose Lopes with him.

How glad he was of the young man's findings, he was still turning over in his mind as they made their way back into the city with the recovered Skeres.

Lopes waited until they were back inside the Bishopsgate before he spoke. "I'm afraid I wasn't much help to you," he said. "And of course I'm no surgeon, nor a physician yet — but…"

Tom waved it away. "I'm not questioning your judgment in the least," he said — and he truly didn't, for it had been spoken with such quiet and considered steadiness. "If you say it couldn't be my man, I believe it. And I'm glad this will spare the fellow's daughter such a sight."

But if Finch didn't lie dead and rotting in the crypt at St. Botolph, where in Tartarus was he? Fleeing to France with Babington's gold — or someone else's filched possessions? Spilling secrets in the wrong ears? Tom shook his head. In all the ado, it hadn't crossed his mind to say a prayer for that poor dead soul from the Houndsditch — killed or drowned.

"Could you tell how that man died?" he asked the medicus.

Lopes hummed. "I'd have to examine him a little more. Feel his skull, his bones… Do you want me to go back?"

There was a grunt from Skeres — half distaste, half alarm.

"No," Tom said in haste. "But if a more likely body should turn up, could you observe things like…" *Like signs of torture*, he bit back. "Like bruises, or a stab wound, or froth at the mouth…"

"Froth at the mouth?"

The swarthy, sneering face of a French archer flashed in Tom's memory from long ago. "For drowning," he said. "Although I reckon it would wash away after some time…"

"Oh — but not all who are drowned froth at the mouth, you know. That is, if you find froth, it's likely a drowning, but the lack of it doesn't mean it isn't."

There! Tom swallowed a bitter chuckle. There went the froth at the mouth — one of a few tidbits, amassed with such care over the years — and it wasn't even true.

Never presume you know, Thomas, was one Sir Francis's oft repeated maxims — and a very true one.

"Ah, well…" Tom smiled ruefully. "Serves me right for taking French archers at their word! One should trust the ones with learning and experience."

Young Lopes stopped at the corner of St. Martin Outwich, where Threadneedle Street branched off Bishopsgate Street. "I wish I'd more of both, Mr. Walsingham," he said, tilting his head in not quite modesty. "And I can't promise to find bruising and stabbings for you. It depends on the body's state, you see. But if you have another, please have me fetched: I'm most definitely at your service. Thank you for a most enlightening afternoon." And, with a little bow, this singular young fellow was gone, wending his way through the crowd.

Skeres exploded in a stentorian huff. "Lord love the lad — not squeamish, is 'e?" A jutting of the lip, a shake of the head. "I'm not finical meself, but I tell you, Mr. Tom — I'll be 'appy if I never see the likes of *that* again!"

And so would Tom, but needs must. "You may have to, Dolius — each time a body is found hereabouts, until either Finch turns up or Babington's crows are caught."

"Cuds-me!" Skeres kicked a scrap of fly-ridden rubbish into the runnel. "Tell you the truth, Master — 'tis a shame it wasn't Finch, down there. At least we'd know 'e's dead and done, and not 'elping the traitors!"

It was because he'd been thinking much the same, and was ashamed of it, that Tom scolded, "A most unchristian thought, Nick! And besides, there's no earthly reason why one cannot turn traitor first and then be killed."

Beside knowing Tom too well to be abashed by his rare flares of piety, Skeres was always quick to see when a reproof was not truly aimed at him. But the logical portion of the outburst left him scratching his curly head. "Ay, well…" he muttered, brow knotted in effort.

But, Tom decided, the Minotaur could philosophise another time. "Go back to St. Helen's," he ordered. "Tell the clerk — and him alone, mind — what we found at St. Botolph. Tell him that, for the time being, there is no need to tell either Goodwife Lovell of the body, nor the constables of Finch. I'm sure he'll see the wisdom of it."

Skeres trotted away, looking pleased at the prospect of ordering about the clerk. Tom, with a sense that nothing was resolved and all hung by the thinnest thread, directed his steps back towards Seething Lane.

A most enlightening afternoon, young Lopes had called it. Tom tried to arrange the enlightenment of it in his mind as he rode — to arrange it in the form of a letter for Sir Francis. Surely Phelippes had already sent word of the letter being delivered, and therefore all that remained was: *We still know nothing of Finch.* How momentous, after venturing into action for the first time in months!

It was in a sullen frame of mind that he arrived home, and he wasn't pleased to hear a din of raised voices in the stables. Two voices. Of one Tom wasn't sure — but the other… Oh, Jupiter!

Throwing the bridles to Fisher's son, Tib, Tom strode inside with the bad humour of relief — and there, covered in sweat and dust, hatless, wide-legged and fist-handed, stood Rouse Casey, facing another, very angry fellow.

"Where have you been?" Tom barked.

Young Casey startled — and his opponent half turned, showing himself for none other than Tobias Chandler, the scrawny little scrivener, doubled in size and stance as he upbraided the miscreant. Sir Francis's two stable grooms watched with great glee.

"He's back, Mr. Thomas," Chandler proclaimed — quiet, soft-spoken Toby! — and pointed a stern forefinger at Seething Lane's particular version of the Prodigal Returned.

"So he is." Tom turned a hard stare on the grooms — and on Tib Fisher, peering from the nearest stall.

"My horse needs seeing to," he said. "And then you can tell Cook I said to give you supper early."

The three stablemen vanished in hunch-shouldered haste — for idle curiosity and gossip were very black sins in Sir Francis Walsingham's household.

Once they were gone, Tom turned all his severity on young Casey, demanding again to know where he'd been.

Casey shuffled and blushed in that glowing way of the red-haired. "Just where you sent me, Mr. Thomas," he said, with a most unconvincing effort at bluster. "Hounding Gilbert Gifford."

"Hounding him for two days — and all for naught. Berden ran into Gifford early this morning."

The lad blew out his cheeks. "But how was I to know? I tried everywhere I could think of, and then I thought perhaps he'd run. I thought I'd try the road to Staffordshire, but I didn't go past Dunstable —"

"Dunstable!" Lord give patience and give mercy! "And you never found it in your empty head to send word? To let us know where you were going? Isn't it enough that Finch is missing? What were we to..." Tom stopped short when Casey's jaw dropped. "You didn't know?"

Casey gawped and shook his head.

No, of course not. Gone two days: for all Casey knew, Isaac Finch was still galloping up and down the Greenwich road.

Tom clicked his tongue. "Go fetch Mr. Phelippes, Toby," he said.

"I sent for him —"

"Now go fetch him yourself. Tell him we'll be in my writing room."

Chandler stalked away like an avenging angel, carrying his chin so high that Tom had to ask Casey what he had done to him.

"I called him an inkhorn rat, fiddling with his quills all day and hiding while others —" Casey blanched as it occurred to him, most surely, that his own master was a scrivener, if a more important one. "Please you, Mr. Thomas, I didn't mean…"

Oh, the young dolt! "You'll do well to remember that in this business, an inkhorn rat outranks servants and couriers. Now, come."

Tom waited until they were in his room before explaining about Finch — not that he had much to explain yet.

"Did you see him again after leaving here?" he asked, when he was done.

Young Casey looked shaken. "We parted ways right out of the door. I was gone out of London the next day."

Yes, very shaken — and yet he must have had little cause to love Finch, who'd had such scathing words for him.

Out of the corner of his eye, Tom caught movement behind young Casey as Phelippes, come to retrieve his errant man, stopped in silence on the threshold.

Tom made no sign that he had seen the newcomer. "Have you known Finch long?" he asked.

"Why, all my life…" And from the lad's sourness, one wouldn't think it a great joy. "He's friends with my father —

regular gossips, they are. And then I entered Mr. Phelippes's service, and here Finch was — just for my sins."

"You don't much like him."

"Nobody *likes* Isaac Finch — but 'tis more that he doesn't much like *me*." Casey grimaced. "'Tis hard, at times, with folks that have known you from an urchin."

Was it not! Tom wanted to laugh at that — a little bitterly. "It won't be easy even with those who haven't, if you do these stupid things."

There was a hum of agreement from the door — and see how Casey winced, and spun around, and blurted, "Master!"

Never had it occurred to Tom that Phelippes must be a student of Sir Francis's manner too, but there was no mistaking the way he stared at his servant in blank severity.

"We'll discuss your conduct, Casey," he pronounced. "Go and fetch a scrap of supper, and wait for me. And no gossiping."

Had Casey ever spoken face to face with Sir Francis, to know where the forbidding air came from? He bowed and scurried away with no more than a meek, "Ay, Master."

When he was gone, Phelippes closed the door and wilted back into his own stooping, grimacing stance. "He's no dimwit, or I wouldn't keep him — but he has no discretion. No discretion…" He shook his head. "Did he say where he's been?"

"Chasing Gifford all the way to Dunstable." Tom went to sit, and motioned Phelippes to the other chair. "And he knows Finch better than most of us."

The cypherer sat in turn. "Something he never mentioned before," he mused. "He knows Finch, and doesn't like him."

"Does anyone, truly? In all honesty, do you?"

Phelippes's grimace twisted deeper. "At times I think the fellow doesn't want to be liked. Or *didn't...*?" He raised both pale brows in question, only to flatten them when Tom shook his head.

"They have a body indeed, with Bishopsgate and the Portsoken squabbling over the coroner's inquest — and they are welcome to it." For the moment, he decided, he could appropriate Lopes's findings. "Far too rotten for two days, and too many teeth missing."

"Good to know in itself, but..." There was an inkwell of carved silver on Tom's desk, a gift from his cousin Frances. Phelippes fiddled with it, squaring it with utmost care to the table's edge. "But it doesn't help us much, does it?"

It helped not at all, if truth be told.

"Skeres was most disappointed that it wasn't Finch." Tom rose and began to pace. "And we can rush to see each and every corpse that turns up in London, but we may well never know. Not that it will matter, once Ballard's game is undone."

Except for Grace Finch and her aunt, of course. Tom stopped at the window, pushing open the casement. The garden herbs had wilted all day under the sun; now the cook's boy was busy with a pail, watering the little bushes one after the other. Rosemary, marjoram, sage, and the scent of damp soil wafted in, along with the kitchen smoke, the river, and the swallows keening overhead.

"Do you reckon he's dead?" asked Phelippes.

Soft as the question was, Tom startled a little. Did he? What if he was, then? And what if he wasn't? It was hard to imagine an innocent reason why a living Finch could have gone astray — but this didn't make a dead Finch innocent. Tom brought his mind back to Babington's place and made himself see the men there again. Babington first, glowing with zeal; Tichborne, brisk and earnest; the unquiet Tilney — and most of all Ballard. Ballard was capable of all sorts of deceit, no doubt — but the others?

Tom turned back and perched on the sill. The room was glum in contrast with the light outside.

"The way the letter was received… There's no saying with Ballard — but the others had no wariness towards it, or towards me."

Phelippes fiddled some more with the inkwell. "I'll send a man to the Castle Tavern, tomorrow," he said. "But they're not much good at their cyphers. The day after tomorrow, perhaps."

Two days to wait — praying the plotters didn't have Isaac Finch in their cellar, tortured into spilling how the letters from Chartley shouldn't be trusted. And, Finch or no Finch, they had to pray that Babington's men swallowed Phelippes's forgery.

CHAPTER 7

30th of July

Night had brought a dream of the ado in the stables — only, the errant fool returning was Finch.

Morning, of course, brought nothing of the sort — neither the man nor tidings of him. It brought, however, reassurance that none of their crows had taken flight yet — and that was something. Or rather, it was all there was, until the imaginary bay horse appeared at the Castle Tavern, and the warrants arrived.

It was proof at least that the traitors didn't have Finch, Mylls observed — and, much as one who had disposed of a child's petty preoccupations, he went back to gnawing at the matter of the arrests, which instead worried him. How were they to be done — by day or night?

Not that Tom was convinced. They had not fled — so what of it? If Mylls was right, then all the better. But what if he was wrong? They could well know, and bide their time while Babington sent his answer to Mary Stuart in some other manner. As for how they could know...

Perhaps it was persistence, or perhaps it was a petty wish to prove Mylls wrong that, well before mid-morning, brought Tom knocking on the rectory's door with a list of questions ready in his head.

Young Grace answered the summons, throwing the door open and then losing all her breathless vehemence on recognising the visitor. Waiting for her father, poor child — and there was no denying that Skeres wasn't wrong in his moonish admiration: Grace Finch was lovely, even with worry marking a line on her brow.

"Good day, Grace. Do you remember me?" asked Tom.

Grace never lowered her gaze, even as she curtsied. "Father's master," she said. "Is there...?"

"No — no news. I came to see whether I can have a word with Dr. Lewis?"

Grace steadied her voice and crossed her hands on her apron — a little maid playing housekeeper. "Master isn't back yet. We expect him this evening or tomorrow."

"Then perhaps I can speak with you?"

"Me...?" She glanced over her shoulder, into the gloomy little hall.

"Perhaps you can help me."

She looked away, and then back to the hall again — but not before Tom caught a flash of something in her eyes. Doubt, perhaps? Or was it fear?

"But what would I know to help?" she cried. "I thought Your Honour'd sent him somewhere..."

"Sometimes we know more than we think," Tom said — and never mind how sibylline he sounded, for something in her distraction made him want to question her. "You'll help me find your father, surely?"

She could have pled ignorance, or she could have called for her aunt, or she could have run away in a storm of tears. Instead she stood there, her head lowered and her bottom lip caught between her teeth. Then, with sudden decision, she went back inside and reappeared carrying an empty bucket. Drawing the door behind her, she led the way around the church's corner, and across the walled churchyard.

"The Prattes, they're such babblers! The wife would be kind enough, if he let her — but..." A twist of the lips. "Who

93

knows what the tales would be, if they saw me speak to Your Honour on the door!"

And would the tales be any better, if they saw her walk away with His Honour? But this didn't seem to worry Grace, who, once out of the yard's gate, dove without hesitation into a small crooked passage between two houses — heading for the well, and waiting for questions.

This deserted alley was as good a place to start as any.

"Grace, do you know how your father earns his living?"

"He works for Your Honour."

"And what does he do for me?"

"He carries things." Grace hesitated, slowing her step and fiddling with the bucket's handle. "Messages. Things of importance."

"Things of importance." Now, this was a surprise. "Did he tell you this?"

Grace gave a small snort. "Tell me! He tells naught — and to me least of all. Am I a son, that he should tell me?"

Tossing her head, she stomped out of the alley, into the thick press of what turned out to be Bishopsgate Street.

Leading to one of the city gates, it was always more crowded than most, with carts, barrows and horses making their way in and out of London at all hours, even well after the last sellers bound for Leadenhall and Stocks Market had come in from the country, dragging their poultry and pigs. It was a good thing that it was a short way to the pump. Grace joined the line, mopping at her red cheeks and damp forehead with the back of her hand and, because it would draw attention if he stood in line with her — a gentleman waiting on a servant — Tom retreated a few steps and curbed his impatience, keeping an eye out for pickpockets, and considering. Grace Finch was angry at her father — there was no mistaking it. For disappearing, perhaps — for that was the shape worry took in some — but there was more.

Am I a son, that he should tell me?

Here was a new thought: had Tom's sisters chewed such bitter gall, before their father's death? Old Sir Thomas, before his declining health had forced him to rely on Ned as his heir, had never been one to talk much to his children, except to upbraid them — and even his alleged partiality to Tom had come with a good deal of harsh words. His daughters he'd ignored, except for calling Barbara a termagant, and Mary a shameless malapert. Had they resented it? Sir Francis was kinder to his daughter — but then Frances was all a man could want in a child: keen-witted, thoughtful, gentle and sweet-mannered, elegant of speech and thought... And yet, how many times had Tom heard Frances wish that she were a boy — for her father's sake?

It wasn't long before Grace returned. She walked awkwardly as she carried her bucket two-handed, sloshing water with every step, on her skirts and on Tom — until he lost all charity and snatched the bucket from her.

"I've carried worse and heavier," he cut through her protestations. Never in the streets of London, if truth be told — but still. "Now, tell me again of how your father arrived home, the other night. What was it that you argued about?"

Even if he hadn't been watching her, it would have been hard to miss: the catching of her breath, the rising of her shoulders.

And Jove fulminate the fat fellow with the handcart, who all but ran over them in his heedless haste. Tom jumped out of the way, cursing after the man and dropping the confounded bucket.

It was a heartbeat before he found Grace again, and her face had changed.

"We argued, ay," she hissed, eyes filling. "He made me cross, and if this was the last I saw of my father…" She snatched up the bucket, half-empty by now, and ran away. Tom followed and found her where the alley bent in a sharp elbow, sobbing quietly.

"Grace Finch, heed me." He lifted her chin with a finger. "I'll do my best to find your father — but you must tell me the truth."

She sniffled, seeming very young of a sudden. "But what can I know?"

"You say your father carries things of importance. How would you know, if he didn't tell you?"

Grace swallowed, dabbing at her eyes. "Dr. Lewis says so," she said. "And, on account of it, we must not vex him when he's mistempered."

Hadn't Clerk Pratte said much the same? It was beginning to seem that Dr. Lewis had done a good deal of this — whether in the way of peaceable advice or officiousness.

"And was…" Tom caught himself. "And *is* he often distempered, your father?"

If Grace noticed the slip, she didn't show it. She gave a wet, bitter chuckle instead.

"And has he been different, of late?" Tom pressed.

"He's been the way he always is. Never a smile, never a kind word — and it made me so cross! But when he comes back —" Face crumpling, she ran away again.

Tom followed at a slower pace. *When he comes back…* Young Grace expected Finch to return.

A sudden burst of shouts, a growl, and the girl's screech rang from the direction of the church. What the devil now…? Tom broke into a run and spilled into the yard to see a clutch of ragged children armed with sticks, busy harassing an old mastiff. They hooted as Grace shouted names at them, but knew to jump out of the way when she began to swing the bucket in angry arcs — and there went the rest of the water.

"Runagates!" she yelled. "Whelps!"

Be it her fierceness, be it that the dog stood by her, bristling, be it the arrival of a man, the brats dispersed, still cackling like magpies.

Grace glared after them for a heartbeat, panting and quivering, and then hurried around the corner of the church, the dog on her heels and the handle of the empty bucket clanging as she ran.

When Tom took the same route, at a slower pace, he was just in time to see her under the churchyard trees as she wrenched away from her aunt to disappear into the house.

And, catching sight of Tom, Widow Lovell must have had bad thoughts, mustn't she? See how she glared at him from afar — half timorous and half warlike, twisting the hem of her apron, ready to defend her niece against this ravisher.

"She had a tussle with some ragamuffins," Tom explained, as soon as he was within talking distance. "Over the dog."

Goodwife Lovell's brow cleared in guilty relief before it creased again. "Rascals! They're from a tenement past old St. Mary, and the good Lord can count them — for their slatternly mothers can't!" Her unfriendly glare travelled past the rectory. "There, past the Leathersellers' Hall. Dr. Lewis says it all used to belong to St. Helen's, back in the old nuns' days. All I say is, if it still did, we'd have more peace, without those brats. A tribulation, they are!"

A tribulation, ay — and Finch being such a paragon of amiable meekness... Now, how foolish would they look —

how foolish would *Tom* look — if the man had been clobbered over the head by an angry father from the tenement?

"And how does your brother bear with these ruffians?"

"Bear with them!" the widow exclaimed. "Bless Your Honour, when was he ever here long enough to bear with aught? Oh, he did chase them away now and then — but…" She shrugged her narrow shoulders. "'Tis Grace as can't abide them, poor child. Grace and my Peg, too. If it's not the sexton's Sturdy, 'tis a bird, or a cat, or a suckling pig, or even some poor lackwit. There's no creature that's safe from those rapscallions. And now, with Joan Pratte confined and to give birth at any moment, you'd think they'd keep their noise away — but no. And with Dr. Lewis away from home, and Isaac gone — though how they come to know such things…"

When was he ever here… He did chase them… "Gone, Goodwife? You don't expect Isaac back?"

It was in the nature of the work he did, Tom supposed, that he should have to deal with many crying women, much as he'd rather not.

The widow gave a tremulous sigh. "I've always known Isaac was meant for trouble. From a boy, he was always harsh, and grew worse after the pox. His little boys died then — both of them — and he himself was left so scarred that, as a small mite, Grace was frighted of him."

Not the way to endear a daughter to her father — or him to her. Poor Grace — and poor Finch.

"But that must have been long ago. What of these last days: was he different? Glum? Frightened? Preoccupied?"

Unlike her niece, to give her credit, the housekeeper thought about her answer, tilting her head in that way she shared with her brother. "I wouldn't say that he was, no. We saw little enough of him, but when he was at home…" She shook her head. "For all that he was my brother, he was always harsh-tempered and unkind."

All of it true enough — but still… "Still, if all harsh men should be murdered…"

Goodwife Lovell looked up sharply, blanching at the ugly word.

Tom bent close, watching her face. "If you believe your brother dead on account of his bad temper, what on earth do you imagine happened to him?"

And, bless her with hot water, there was not just surprise in her glare, but, of all things, reproach. Her brother's sister, after all.

"Your Honour doesn't need me to say it," she hissed. "Those who do the Queen's work must ever be in mortal peril!"

But of course — of course! Tom swallowed a huff of unamused laughter. "The Queen's work!" he groused. "I'll take a guess: your brother never talked of it, and you know because Dr. Lewis says so."

It was little wonder when the housekeeper opened her mouth and closed it again. She didn't stay disconcerted for long, though. "My brother kept his thoughts to himself, Your Honour, and Dr. Lewis knows best. You'd better talk to him when he's back." And, with a curtsey and a quick wish of "Good day," she retreated to safety behind her door.

Tom was left with an ever-growing itch to meet the oh-so-knowing Dr. Lewis. Also, right as the rectory door slammed over the hem of the widow's grey kirtle, there it was! A movement behind a window in the house with the honeysuckle.

Someone under Clerk Pratte's roof was keeping watch.

Tom's first urge was to march up to the door, pound on it until they opened up, and corner the watcher — whoever he — or she — was.

Learn to mistrust your anger, Thomas, and any course of action it dictates, was one piece of wisdom Tom had learnt in his early days with Sir Francis — and he was considering it when Rob Poley came around the church's corner at a brisk pace.

"They told me you'd come to St. Helen's," the fellow said. "'Tis lucky I didn't miss you."

And there was something about his manner... Oh, the smile was in place, but when Poley suggested they talk over a bit of dinner, Tom much misdoubted it would be good tidings. With a last glance at the door with the honeysuckle, he ordered Poley to lead the way.

The Pewter Pot in Leadenhall Street had prospered for many years as a coaching inn. These days, it looked to be on the decline — narrow and dingy, little more than a stable-yard with a cramped, sooty taproom.

Poley caught Tom's dubious scrutiny. "Safest place in London, Master: can you see our fine crows in here?"

Ah well, he wasn't wrong. Tom followed him into a gloomy little parlour whose one window overlooked the yard, and was placed so that no one could walk near it without coming in sight.

Trust Poley to know such things! Tom took a seat and let the man order ale, and two well-laden trenchers of cheat bread and cheese.

Once the pot-boy had retreated, Poley sat across from Tom at the narrow table.

"The fact is..." he began, then stopped and started anew. "Young Babington's grown loose-tongued."

"Has he now?" Tom narrowed his eyes. This could be very good — but for Poley's twitching hesitation. "And…"

"And he's told me of the plot." Poley sat forward, both elbows on the table. "Not that they want to kill Her Highness, mind. Just that they want to overthrow her and her ministers."

Tom exhaled slowly. *To overthrow her…* This wasn't enough. This wasn't half of what they knew already. Were they putting Poley to the test? Were they baiting the Queen's men? Had the letter — Finch or no Finch — made them wary enough that they tried to feel the air? And that was supposing Poley told the truth.

"What did he say? What were the words?" Tom asked.

The words, it seemed, had been that Babington and some of his friends had the means to keep the State as it was, or to snatch the crown from Elizabeth's head, and to restore the true religion.

"So he grasped my hand and asked for my promise, and my good faith." Poley shook his head. "Trusting fool!"

"Not quite so trusting, is he?" Tom took a thoughtful sip of ale. "He did keep to himself the small matter of regicide."

Poley hummed. "I don't know about that." He tapped fingertip after fingertip on the table's edge, like one trying out the virginals. When he reached the thumb, he looked up. "Oh, Ballard thinks of nothing else. And Savage, too, and the other lads — they're all afire with it. Master Anthony, though…"

Tom gave a huff. "Master Anthony's too good and loving a subject for murder?"

Poley's smile was back, the bland, amiable one he wore the way another would wear a feather in his hat. "Master Anthony's a misled young gudgeon, and very much afraid. He's like a boy who let his friends dare him to climb up a tree. He liked it well enough at first, with everybody cheering — but now he's too far up for his liking."

"Very poetical, Rob —" Tom broke off at the burst of shouting from outside. Oh, Jove… He rose and went to the window.

"They've made a strip of the yard into a bowling alley," Poley explained. "I don't think they have a licence for it."

A game of bowls! A mindless game, and for a heartbeat Tom had feared Ballard's men had started their crowd-seizing! Jumping at shadows — like Mylls, like Sir Francis himself. Tom turned and leant his back against the blackened wainscoting. "There's a fine for that, isn't there? Nothing to what befalls boys who climb up the wrong tree."

"Ah, but, you see…" Poley sat up straighter. "This one boy only wants to climb down — if he knew how."

"So he throws ha'penny secrets at you?"

"Well, what with me being Her Ladyship's servant…"

"He hopes it'll get to the ear of Her Ladyship's father." And little wonder. It was, after all, why they'd foisted Poley on Babington. "I'll have your tidings sent to Mr. Secretary at once." And again, there was a twisting of Poley's mouth. "What now?"

"D'you reckon, Mr. Thomas…" A grimace. "Maybe I could ride out myself, and tell His Honour? Now, don't think ill…"

But Tom did. "So here's why you came to me with this — and not to Mr. Mylls."

Not that Poley denied it. "There's this to say for you, Master: trust me or not, you'll listen, and think on it." *Whereas Mylls won't.*

But while it was true that Mylls's ears would be closed to Rob Poley's notions, it didn't mean Tom would do well to pay heed. "And what is it that I should listen to?"

"I think…" Poley pushed aside his untouched trencher. "If we let the boy stew a little longer, he'll be ripe to give us all the others, trussed hand and foot."

Or are you playing us false — rather than the boy? Gaining him time while he and his cronies prepare disaster? It was a game two could play: lead them and let them think they're leading you … and never be too eager. "Just how far does he trust you, Poley?"

"A good deal. More than his friends like."

"Enough to tell you, if they'd nabbed one of our men?"

Poley pursed his lips in thought. "Ay," he said slowly. "He'd swear me to great secrecy and tell me. And if he didn't, it'd still show in his manner."

"You say Babington has taken fright."

Poley shook his head. "He and the others… They'd all be a lot more jittery, if they had Finch."

Of course, the man was no fool. Just how clever he thought himself, though, was another matter. Let him have some more rope. "Off you go, then: ride to Richmond, see how Mr. Secretary likes your notion."

Not very much, most likely, but Sir Francis would want to sift Poley's intentions for himself. Of course, Tom would send word separately, warning his cousin — and Poley knew it well, even as he rose, smiling back with every show of gratitude.

No doubt the man would smile as amiably if he were aiding Babington, or playing both sides. And if he was, and Finch had somehow smelt his game…

"Oh — and Rob, speaking of Finch…"

Poley stopped, hand on the doorjamb. "What of him?"

"Have you seen him since the other night in Seething Lane?"

More cries and laughter came from the bowlers in the yard — and Poley turned to the window. After a heartbeat, he shook his head grimly. "I've been thinking," he said. "And I mislike the thoughts I have. Poor bugger…"

Truly! Tom raised a brow. "The poor bugger called you a knave to your face in front of half the household."

"And he called Rouse Casey names, and Berden, and Skeres — but that's Isaac Finch for you: all are knaves in this world, but for himself."

"And is he so unknavish?" Barring the theft of velvet sleeves — if that was true.

There was no chance Poley could miss the implication. He considered, pacing back to the table. "Finch is a pain — but a turncoat…? I'd peg him for the sort to stay where he's content, and he seems content enough to take His Honour's coin."

And Tom would have thought much the same — until two days ago. Now, of course, there was no saying. "Off with you, then. The sooner you're back with Babington, the better."

He would have liked to ask if Master Anthony was writing letters — but didn't.

Outside, the bowlers sounded ready for a tussle.

Poley quaffed the rest of his ale, crammed a chunk of bread into his pocket, and left.

Ay, let the man have some more rope — and see whether he'd hang himself or Babington with it.

Asking for ink and paper, Tom jotted down a letter for his cousin, sealed it, and enclosed it inside another for Mylls, with a request to have it sent to Barn Elms as soon as it could be arranged. *Not by means or to the knowledge of Poley, if you please — who is riding out*, he wrote. Mylls would like that.

CHAPTER 8

Having made quick work of his dinner, Tom emerged from the sooty gloom of the Pewter Pot into the summer haze.

He arrived back at St. Helen's to find one of Mylls's watchers loitering just outside the churchyard's gate, and sent him off to his master with the packet. The yard was empty and quiet in the early afternoon, but for an old fellow shuffling along the churchyard wall, nose in the air, muttering at the wilting rambling roses that covered the wall. The sexton, then — the one who, to hear Paynter, was no good at mowing lawns.

Whatever his skill with a scythe, the fellow wasn't keen of hearing. He didn't hear Tom until he emerged from the trees, and he squinted at him, shielding his eyes from the sun with a brown, gnarled hand.

"Were ye wanting Dr. Lewis, Master?" he called, in a deep rumble. "He ain't at home yet."

Tom stepped closer. "In truth —"

"Ah!" the old man smiled, showing a few missing teeth. "Isaac Finch's master, eh? That's who Yer Honour'd be!"

A fleeting vision of the whole of St. Helen's discussing him flashed through Tom's mind. "And you're the sexton here."

"Ay, Yer Honour. The sexton, ay." He made as if to doff his hat, but finding himself bare-headed, he bowed instead. "Lambsfoot, they call me."

"Good day then, Lambsfoot. Finch hasn't returned, I take it?"

There was more shaking of the half-bald head, and also a knowing squint at the gate behind Tom's back. *If you don't know yourself*, the sexton didn't say.

So much for watching with discretion — Jupiter rain on Mylls's men! Tom only half feigned the flare of annoyance. "Never a hint of trouble in six years, and now... What possessed him to wander away like this, I'd like to know."

And he watched as the sexton pursed his lips.

"Never one to chase after whims, was Isaac..." he rumbled.

Was. Did Lambsfoot know more than he said? Or was Tom just hoping to find that Finch's disappearance had nothing to do with Mary Stuart's letter? It was a constant risk, to allow oneself to see what one wished to see.

"When did you see him last?" Tom asked.

"When did I see him last?" the sexton repeated, rubbing at his chin. "*Talk to him* ... ah, that was around St. Swithin's day." A twist of the mouth. "He's been away more than not, of late — but Yer Honour will know — and when he's here I've little to say to him."

But St. Swithin had been a sennight ago, and Finch had come and gone several times since, surely? "You've seen him without talking, though?"

Lambsfoot snorted. "Heard him, more like, Yer Honour. When he's about, ye hear him. Always knows better than other folks, does Isaac."

Well, Finch hadn't endeared himself to his kin and neighbours, had he?

"And did you hear him on Wednesday last?"

"Wednesday, now, that was..."

"He came home late, I think."

"Oh, ay!" The sexton raised a gnarled forefinger. "Right late, it was, and did I hear him! Knocking on the door, hollering for his daughter like a Dutchman — a din to wake the dead!" He jerked his head towards the church. "Dr. Lewis lets me keep a room over the vestry, Yer Honour — see? Didn't I hear him — for all that I sleep on my good ear!"

"And then?"

The old man had been warming to his tale — yet to this one simple question he had no answer. "Then…?" he repeated.

"You heard Finch make a fuss to be let in — and then?"

"Then I don't know," was the answer — as bland as you please. "I went back to sleep, Yer Honour, for the hour was late, and I was right forspent."

"You didn't hear the door barred again?"

A purse-lipped shake of the head.

"You didn't hear Finch leave in the morning?"

More of the same.

"You never heard him again?"

And more still. "But then, I sleep on my good ear…"

So here was another who had little love for Finch, and naught to say of his disappearance — which seemed to be the common condition of all who knew the fellow.

"If that's all, Yer Honour…" Old Lambsfoot shifted his weight, eyeing the wall of rambling roses. Just what he'd been doing that was useful, muttering to the faded flowers, Tom wasn't certain — but, having no more questions to ask, he released him and watched him hobble back to his inspection.

Ah well.

There was another person Tom wanted to question, so he turned towards the door with the honeysuckle — its scent almost too sweet in the high summer warmth, and the buzz of bees so drowsy.

He was still half a dozen steps away when the door opened, and a thin-lipped woman of middle age walked out. Behind her came the clerk, in his shirtsleeves, fretful and flushed.

"What I can do, I've done for now," the woman said, with an air of great patience. "'Twill be another day, or even two. And mind, there's no need — but I'll come and see her tonight."

"I'll send for you, if..." Pratte began, and went no further, for the woman shook her head.

"Only if Goody Lovell says so," she said — and then hurried away.

Pratte gaped after her for a heartbeat, before he noticed Tom. "You heard that, Master?" he asked, pointing an indignant finger at the woman. "Ask Goody Lovell! Because she thinks I'd have my wife give birth on her own, before asking..." He hiccupped to a halt, in the way of one remembering himself. "Beg pardon, Master. My wife's young, it's her first child, her time is nearing, and the midwife... You heard her. But please you, Master..."

Glancing towards the rectory door, Pratte stepped aside to let Tom in.

"In the absence of Dr. Lewis," he said, restored to self-importance, "I understand that it falls to me..."

The hall was narrow and cool, with a scent of mint and lavender in the air. Even as he apologised for intruding at such a moment, Tom found himself as good as pushed into a high-backed chair, old-fashioned and polished to a gleam. Whatever the condition of Goodwife Pratte, her house was well cared for.

The clerk hovered close, though Tom had a suspicion that the obsequent manner wasn't going to last.

"I've come for news of Finch, and found none. But since I'm here, there are a few question I'd ask of you, Master Clerk."

It was amusing to see Pratte bristle at the demand, and then mellow at the formal title — which in truth didn't befit a mere parish clerk. Amusing and promising, for importance loosened tongues.

And, indeed, the fellow preened. "About Finch, Your Honour? I fear I've little to say. We pray for his safe return, but…"

What the clerk thought of such a return was plain in the grimace of doleful piety.

Ah, but this one and Finch must have been a torment to each other! "Very Christian of you, I'm sure," Tom said, trying to keep the wryness to himself. "And towards such an irksome neighbour…"

"Irksome! Why, Your Honour, I never said —"

Tom waved away the protestation. "Unneighbourly, you called him — and your midwife jests that you won't ask counsel of Finch's sister. She stretches it a good deal, I'm sure, but…"

All dolefulness gone of a sudden, Pratte's piety soured. "I bear much for Dr. Lewis's sake," he cried. "But truly, as blustering a churl as Isaac Finch is hard to find. Very quarrelsome — very."

A sin in Pratte's book, judging by the way his red cheeks quivered with the thought.

"So you quarrel with Finch often?"

Such a stare of pious horror! "No — oh no, Your Honour!" Such a shake of the curly head! "Not I. Dr. Lewis says the meek are blessed, and forbearance is a virtue loved by the Lord. A most Godly notion — and so I try to use charity."

Which Tom guessed to mean that Dr. Lewis often singed both men's ears.

"It must take much patience. Such rough ways, and coming and going at all hours…"

"As I said, Your Honour, we bear."

In all fairness, it wasn't hard to see why Finch would be quarrelsome with this fellow.

"Did you have to bear last Wednesday, too?"

Pratte took a reproachful air. "You'd think," he sniffed, "with my wife in her state... But no: loud as a trained band! And his women took their time to let him in, too."

"And did they bar the door again?"

"I wouldn't know, Your Honour. I've never been one to eavesdrop on my neighbours."

"You must have heard him go away in the morning, though?"

"No, I..." Pratte stopped short, forefinger to his lips as he recalled. "I didn't," he said slowly.

"You didn't." And Lambsfoot hadn't either. Tom sat up straighter, with a feeling of glass pieces shifting inside his mind. "And is this unusual? What with him being so loud?"

"Well, I must have been fast asleep."

Which was as good an answer as the plainest *Ay* — and perhaps the first finding of any note in these past two days.

Tom rose to his feet. "I've imposed on you enough, Master Clerk," he said. "I may be back soon — but for now, I say good evening."

Pratte bustled to show him out, with the air of one uncertain that he'd spoken unwisely. Ah, well — let him fret.

Out of the clerk's house, Tom all but walked on young Peg Lovell when she emerged from a bush right in front of him, with dirt on her skirts and her hair full of leaves.

"You mustn't believe Goodman Pratte," she announced, adding in a rush, "Beg Your Honour's pardon."

"Have you been eavesdropping, Peg Lovell?" Tom demanded.

If he had thought that sternness would discompose the child, he'd been wrong. Instead, she jutted out her chin.

"I don't need to," she said. "He's always saying wicked things of us to make himself look good to Dr. Lewis. He says I'm a hoyden, and will always be. He's no call to say that."

"No," Tom agreed. "He has no call — though I think he's more irked at your Uncle Isaac than yourself."

Peg sniffed. "It doesn't signify," she said with great dignity. "He tells lies about us, and Dr. Lewis says that lying, no matter why, is always a sin."

An impossibly simple tenet, in the face of the world's maze-like depths — but, quite likely, a wise thing to teach a sharp-witted girl of eleven. She had time to learn how tangled truth and lies could be.

"Dr. Lewis is a wise man," Tom said. Perhaps it was wicked of him to take advantage of a child's truthfulness, but ... "So, if I ask when you last saw your Uncle Isaac, you'll tell me the truth."

Peg liked being taken seriously. It made her earnest. "Oh, it's been days..." She wrinkled her nose in thought. "He came home the other night, but we were all asleep. Grace ran to let him in, and she was angry when she came back to bed. She woke me again."

We argued, Grace had said. *He made me cross.* "Were you still awake when he drew the bolts again?"

Again Peg thought, closing her eyes as she went back to the night before her uncle disappeared. When she shook her head, it came as no surprise.

The surprise was that, with her mouselike face intent, and sounding uncannily like her mother, she asked, "You think my Uncle Isaac's dead, Your Honour?"

"Ah…" Tom floundered. What did you tell such a young child — a child who thought all lies a sin? "I don't know," he said. "I hope I can find him."

Of course, if he found her uncle alive, Tom would have to arrest him and put him to the question, but Peg didn't need to know that.

Before she asked more thorny questions, he sent her running to her mother.

At Mylls's house, Tom found two rather boorish men lounging in the kitchen garden. The younger one squinted up from their game and, observing Tom's lack of urgency, went back to the dominoes.

The pursuivants, no doubt — and a more unprepossessing pair was hard to imagine. But then, one didn't end up chasing Jesuits in the streets out of grace and wit.

Mylls, it turned out, was just back from Seething Lane.

"You've seen my hounds?" was his glum salutation. "Heaven send I can unleash them soon, and be rid of them!"

He begged Tom's company for supper, and — Mrs Mylls being off to spend the summer in the sweeter airs of Kent — the two of them shared trout and pike in a stuffy parlour that had all the evidence of dust-sheets removed in haste.

That the fish was finely cooked, and the Rhenish that went with it quite good, did little to relieve the secretary's bleak humour. There were no warrants yet, he said — not that Tom had expected otherwise — and no bay horses at the Castle Tavern.

"Phelippes brought your letter himself, for His Honour summoned him to Barn Elms." Mylls hesitated, eyes fastened on the goblet of green glass he turned between his fingers, catching the sunlight from the window. "Poley went on your orders, did he?"

A most pertinent question — and it struck Tom that perhaps he shouldn't have waited for Mylls to ask it. He watched the secretary as he told his tale — or rather Rob Poley's — and the man's mien grew grimmer and grimmer with each word.

"That Poley…" Mylls leant both elbows on the table. "I've long thought he's playing both sides, and…"

Tom had known Frank Mylls for a long time, long enough to know the searching peer for what it was. "And you feared I was taken in by the fellow's smiles."

The thinning of the secretary's lips was answer enough. "I'm glad you prove me wrong."

And still he made it a question — neither persuaded nor very glad of it.

Tom made himself set down his knife with utmost care. *Unus … duo … tres…* "So little taken in, in fact, that I'm half-minded to suspect Poley killed Finch."

And there it went again — the grimace, the slow exhalation.

"Mr. Thomas…" The secretary didn't quite speak with that slow patience one uses with a fanciful child — but it was close. "First you thought Finch was in Babington's hands; now Poley killed him?"

Oh, pinch the fool! "You never believe the man vanished by accident?" Tom snapped. "Oh, perhaps he did — and perhaps not. Perhaps they have him — willing or not. Or perhaps he caught someone playing us false and was silenced. And now Babington bides his time, and meanwhile warns the Queen of Scots behind our backs."

Mylls thunked down his goblet. "How? They've no way, other than what we've arranged."

"They'd seek no other while they thought the ale-casks safe — but what if they had cause to think they aren't?"

The secretary didn't answer for the longest moment — and, when he did, there was a colour of uncertainty to his words. "Poley doesn't even know of Chartley…"

Or did he? "I wouldn't swear by it," Tom said, in slow consideration. "The other night, Finch let slip that he'd ridden from Lichfield, and Poley was there."

"If Poley knows Lichfield is near Chartley…" Mylls's bushy brows drew together. "But how would Finch catch Poley at it?"

Oh Jove, what did it matter? "Just suppose he stumbled on it. Whatever that could bring for the plotters, it would be disaster for Poley. The rack, the gallows… Well worth killing for."

The silence stretched. Chin on his chest and lips pursed, Mylls fiddled with the green goblet, turning it around and around. The very likeness of one eating gall. Then he looked up, sour at this man of half his years, who had the cheek to tell him off.

Well, Tom wasn't shying away. He held the unfriendly gaze until it fell.

"What do you want done then, Mr. Thomas?" Mylls asked.

And it sounded so much like a request for orders, that Tom's unease bit even harder. But fools alone recoiled from an advantage won, surely? Those who were not fools put their advantage to good use.

"We send warning to our people at Chartley, and…" Tom considered carefully. "Nick Skeres hasn't put himself much forward. He can wind deeper into the group, sound out what our crows are about."

"Poley knows him for your man."

"So he'll know he's being watched. And if Skeres finds himself distrusted of a sudden, we'll know why."

"Very well, Mr. Walsingham. I'll have it done." There was something half sad and half amused in the way Mylls sat back in his chair — as though he had, after all, been expecting such a day.

And, having won his battle, Tom was eager to grant the honours of war. "Thank you, Mr. Mylls," he said, as he rose. "And be good enough to have Mr. Secretary informed of what we have decided."

Stiff and formal as it sounded, it loosened Mylls's glower a little. And if they both knew that Sir Francis would question Tom on the matter, the thought of having won graciously enough lightened Tom's mind a good deal.

That Skeres didn't protest against his new orders could have been deemed a minor miracle, but for two mitigating facts: one being that, while he said nothing, the lad sulked mightily; and two, that he was much absorbed in mending a tear in his doublet by candlelight.

Perhaps, though, "mending" didn't describe it: he sat cross-legged on his truckle-bed, butchering both the cloth and his own fingers.

"Why don't you do these things by daylight, Dolius?" Tom asked from his own bed.

"'Cause by daylight I'm off watching unchancy asses who'd murther the queen —" was the muttered reply, broken by a yelp and a string of curses when Skeres pricked his finger yet again.

"Why don't you have the kitchen-girl do it for you, then?" Tom insisted.

The lad sucked at his gouged thumb. "She's mad at me."

"Have you been singing Grace Finch's praises to her?"

Tom's half-hearted attempt at condoling fell short. The Minotaur snatched the candle from the trunk at the bed's foot to plunk it on the corner of the truckle, showering molten wax on himself and the hapless doublet.

"Well, I ain't seeing 'er again, Mistress Grace," he grumbled. "Should be 'elping you ferret out Finch — and you'll need me, mind — but no: instead I must stick to Master Tichborne like a leech!"

So there it was: the Minotaur resentful. "'Tis more than Tichborne now. I need a man watching them all — a man I can trust."

Skeres was not mollified. "Ay, ay." He wiped his finger — blood, spittle, wax and all — on the doublet's hem. "And if the asses won't 'ave me?"

"Why wouldn't they? Tomorrow you go to Tichborne, moan that your master sacked you —"

"For being a papist?" The lad bounced on the truckle, hard enough to topple the candle if Tom hadn't leapt to catch it.

"Don't set us all afire, you disgrace! See?" He held up the candlestick before putting it back on the trunk. "That's why you were sacked. A half mishap with a candle, a bit of swearing, and your protestant master threw you out, the cursed Pharisee!"

The Minotaur's face knotted, all knobs and shadows in the flicker of the disturbed flame. "Not for being a papist?"

"Right now they might be shy of one who comes with such a noise. An angry fellow, however, they're bound to like. Would Tichborne pity you enough to take you into his service?"

Skeres tutted. "'Im or else Mr. Tilney. But it don't mean they'll open their 'earts to me. Mr. Babington's all familiar with Rob Poley — and they don't like it a jot."

And let no one call the Minotaur thick-witted! "Never mind their hearts. You just hang upon them and sniff the air. See whether they bestir themselves — and let Poley see you do it."

"Poley, ay! 'Ow will 'e like it? If 'e's made lard of Finch…"

"If he raises a hand to you, then you have my blessing to trounce him. But I'll wager you he won't."

"You'll wager, eh?" the lad snorted. "If 'e ain't no murtherer, then 'e's a traitor —"

"Which is why he'll watch you like a hawk: if anything happens to you, we'll know why."

"Much comfort it'll be, in me grave! And if 'e's neither?"

"Then he'll watch your back out of good fellowship."

"Ay, and pigs fly with their tails forward!" Skeres went back to his mending, wielding the needle like a pike. "I'll go, if you want, and cry misery, and make them 'ire me…"

"Never let them see you mending clothes, and they might."

How minotaurishly the lad scowled up from the poor doublet! "Laugh all you like, Master," he groused. "But I mislike it: you go alone after Finch's murtherer, and when you need Nick Skeres and 'e ain't there, what will you do then?"

And, in spite of the lure of fair Grace, in spite of the implication that Tom couldn't look after himself, one could almost feel touched.

"I'll try to manage, Dolius," Tom said, not bothering to hide his grin. "And if you want to help, do listen to what I've learnt since Finch disappeared." Receiving a grunt in the way of assent, Tom lay back against the pillows, crossed his hands over his stomach, and, staring into an imaginary distance, began his recitation.

"Item: Finch left here with Rouse and Berden — but they parted ways at the door. Item: Finch went to Mr. Mylls's house, left my note with the porter, and went away. Item:

Finch arrived at St. Helen's, found the door barred, and roused the whole place until his daughter let him in."

A small sigh saluted the mention of Grace. Tom ignored it.

"Item: if anyone saw him after that, nobody will say. Item: Grace Finch, the Widow Lovell and her daughter, the sexton and the clerk — all deny hearing the bolts drawn again later in the night, or Finch leaving in the morning. All, when asked, admit it's unusual, though not impossible. Item: it seems Finch didn't sleep in his bed, and nothing of his is missing. Item: he never arrived here in the morning — nor at Tower Hill. Item: his daughter is distraught, but speaks as though she expects him back. Item: his sister thinks he must be dead — because of his bad temper and (on the rector's authority) of his mysterious work. Item: the sexton, the parish clerk and the people in the tenement all have reason to dislike Finch. None of them are murdering matters in themselves, but then rage heeds no reason. Ergo: the possibility can't be discounted that Finch's disappearance is no Service matter. Still…"

"Master?" Skeres had been quiet for so long that Tom had half-forgotten him.

"Yes?"

"If I end up in the 'Oundsditch, you won't think I've sold you out, will you?"

"In the Houndsditch!" Tom raised himself on an elbow to glare at his servant, who had set aside the doublet and was undressing. "You won't end up there at all — and if you do, I'll think nothing of the sort."

Another grunt, and the lad flung his slops on a stool halfway across the room. The chances of the Minotaur being taken into service seemed thin indeed.

To the music of the truckle-bed groaning under Skeres's weight as the lad squirmed and settled, Tom lay back and resumed.

"Item: for all we know, Finch could be in Scotland or France by now, counting his ill-gained money, or hanging chained in a Holborn cellar, spilling all he knows under torture … or he could be dead. *Quartum non datur…* No fourth possibility," he translated for Skeres. There was no answer from the truckle bed but a soft snore.

Tom knelt up, leaning to blow out the candle. The smell of smoke and burnt wax wafted in the warm darkness.

Item: Robert Poley could have killed Finch to protect himself.

Item: Robert Poley could have betrayed Finch to the plotters — for the same reason or out of zeal.

Item: Robert Poley knew of Lichfield — if not of Chartley.

Item: logic dictated that the three items above were also true of Berden, young Casey, and even Skeres…

And it must have been the heat, the long day, Tom's tiredness, or too much thinking in circles — but all these stubborn facts refused to combine into a semblance of meaning.

Had Cicero sat up late like this in some Roman night, cursing Catiline to himself, sifting through his thoughts, and finding precious little that was of use?

CHAPTER 9

31st of July

There was no knowing about the nightly musings of Cicero of old — but a morning letter showed those of Sir Francis to have been rather like Tom's own. Mr. Secretary approved, he wrote, of Tom's actions regarding Poley — whom he had charged to cultivate this new frankness in Babington — but he wished that more could be known of Finch's fate. Would please Tom apply himself to the unravelling of this particular tangle?

And just what his cousin thought he'd been doing, Tom wondered a little sourly — although the sourness was more for himself: three days — and what had he found? And, worse, he saw little in the way of paths he hadn't trodden yet in his inquiries.

Well, there was Dr. Lewis, the great authority of St. Helen's. Even if all his caveats about Finch's all-important work were to prove empty air, the man was bound to know about his household, wasn't he?

To that end, it being Sunday, Tom considered his clothes-press for church attire. He settled on the suit of grey velvet, with a small ruff and a flat cap that had belonged to poor Guildford, his dead brother. He spared a sigh for the fine court things he'd never worn since Paris. No matter how much lavender he coaxed from Mrs Jeffreys, the moths were going to eat his burgundy silk — and it wouldn't matter, because the suit had gone out of fashion. Even with Skeres's loans, he'd never have the money to squander on a new one.

A most childish discontentment to carry — and yet it lingered at the back of Tom's mind as he rode to St. Helen's and took his place in the nave for Dr. Lewis's service.

The rector proved to be a tall, rosy man of middle years, warm-voiced and noble-headed, and perhaps a touch conscious of both virtues. He spoke like Benignity itself, which put Tom in mind of the exiled Dr. Worthington saying Mass back in Rheims. It was not an endearing reminder — but...

Never let preconceit form your judgment for you, Thomas — not of men, not of circumstance.

And, having admonished himself with Sir Francis's words, Tom left the rector for later, closer consideration, and joined in with the singing. Only his tongue was busy with the hymn, though, and it must have been its own kind of sin that he had chosen his place so to keep an eye both on Finch's women and on Arthur Pratte.

The clerk fretted, glancing towards the door now and then. If the midwife had returned to see his wife, she must not have taken pity on his flustering. The women, on the other hand... They stood close together, tight-mouthed and stiff-shouldered, ready to brave ... what? Ill tidings? Rumour? Was Isaac Finch's disappearance already the talk of the whole parish? Far from unlikely, human nature being what it was — and yet, if it was, the congregation seemed quite placid about it. Through the years Tom had found himself in the midst of crowds of all sorts: small and huge, joyous, and angry, and maddened with zeal, and alight with curiosity. They were like wild beasts, crowds, ready to pounce on all they might enjoy or dislike. But this small crowd of St. Helen's felt more like a drowsy cat at her summer rest, not even alive to the scent of the three women's unease.

It was young Peg, even more mousy in her Sunday kirtle, who caught sight of Tom and nudged her cousin. Grace peeked over her shoulder, and leant to whisper in her aunt's ear — and, while Goodwife Lovell didn't turn, there was no mistaking the tautening of her narrow shoulders.

After a bland sermon, the Eucharist, and several hymns, the service trundled to its end, and the congregation dispersed. Goodwife Lovell and her girls were among the first to go, and from the church door Tom watched them hasten across the yard like a small troop in enemy land, until a man approached them, doffing his cap and greeting the housekeeper and her niece in turn. He stood so that Tom couldn't see much of him beyond a lean frame, a wilted ruff, and sandy hair. Also watching the little group, as he held the door for the departing faithful, was Lambsfoot.

"Good day, Sexton," Tom greeted — and see how the fellow startled!

"Good day, Yer Honour!" Lambsfoot smiled askew and bowed. "Beg pardon, I hadn't seen... Ah, but Dr. Lewis, he's back! Ye were wanting to see him, eh? He's back..."

And what on earth had the rector told his people to make them so nervous of Finch's master? A question that wouldn't stay unanswered, for here came Dr. Lewis himself, sailing along the nave in his priestly robes, and steering his course towards Tom.

"Good day, Master," he saluted, all smiles and rosy cheeks. "I'm Dr. Lewis, the rector here." He stepped a little closer and lowered his voice. "Are you the gentleman asking questions about Isaac Finch?"

And what had Dr. Lewis's people told him in turn? Ah, well... Tom moved away from the sexton and bowed back. "I'm most pleased to meet you at last, Doctor. You'll be thinking that I played at mysteries with your household. I'm sure you'll understand when I tell you I work for Mr. Secretary Walsingham."

"Ah!" The rector's eyes, which were a faded blue, lit up in earnest pleasure on hearing this — a boy guessing a riddle.

"But..." Tom held up a warning hand. "I must ask you to promise me utmost secrecy on this."

"Of course, of course." The rector nodded most zealously. "You needn't fear. I understand the importance of a matter of the State, and always... I won't speak of guesses, and much less of suspicions, no — but I always conjectured that Isaac Finch must have to do with the Queen's service."

"And these conjectures, Doctor, were based on something Finch said?"

"Something...? Oh, no! Not once in all these years did Isaac let slip a word about his masters. But this very silence, and the way he came and went, you understand..."

Tom understood. "And you made hints to Finch's sister and daughter about this, and to your clerk, and your sexton."

It came as no surprise when Dr. Lewis coloured a little. "Hints? No — what I did was teach them forbearance, in view of the burden Isaac must bear. Forbearance of his blunt manner, as you must know, Mr..."

"Walsingham."

The rector gaped for a heartbeat, and there was a spell of silence as he did his reckonings, no doubt. Most of the parishioners had gone their way — but a few still lingered, chattering in small knots under the trees, or visiting the graves. Across the yard, Goodwife Lovell and Grace were still talking to the man in the drooping ruff. Grace, it was worth noting, was leaning away from him.

"Doctor, would you know who that man is, speaking to Goodwife Lovell?"

Dr. Lewis blinked shortsightedly. "Oh, that's Alderman Casey, of Aldgate Ward."

Casey! This could never be…? "Casey?"

"Deputy Alderman, in truth. Our Grace's betrothed."

It was Tom's turn to stare. *My father thinks aldermen only heed the Queen and God himself.* How many Aldermen Caseys could there be in London?

The rector mistook Tom's frown. "A great difference in years, yes," he said, shaking his head. "John Casey is a widower, and an old friend of Isaac's. I fear Grace is bitter about it."

"Is she?" Oh, it showed plain as day in the thin line of her mouth as Deputy Alderman Casey took his leave from her. And yet, both she and her aunt had not seen fit to mention this when questioned.

"Well," Dr. Lewis tapped his chin with a thin forefinger, as though Tom's question had been in earnest. "I suppose young women dream of young grooms. John Casey is a good man, no question about it — but his children are older than Grace."

His children… "Are they?" Tom asked — and, sure enough, it set the rector prattling again.

"Oh, but she won't have them under her roof: the daughter is married, and the son is in service, I believe. In time, Grace will come to see that her father has secured for her a good husband and a life of comfort."

Meanwhile, though, she was bitter and angry, and wishing herself rid of a groom twice her age. *We argued. He made me cross,* she'd said — never thinking to mention why.

Dr. Lewis was still canvassing paternal wisdom and youthful fancies, when Tom cut through his argument.

"With your licence, Doctor, I'll have a word with Goodwife Lovell," he announced.

The rector blinked at the sudden interruption. "Of course, of course," he murmured, half eager and half wary as he led the way to his door, where Grace and her aunt had disappeared.

With much of his amiability turned to worry, Dr. Lewis did not seem at his ease in the severe room he called his study.

Did all rectories in England boast a study with black wainscoting, and black, gaunt-backed chairs, and blackened portraits on the walls? Tom wondered vaguely, as the rector groped for words.

"This betrothal…" he began, only to stop and begin again. "But perhaps I should ask you this first, Mr. Walsingham: do you believe it possible that Isaac Finch still lives?"

Well, this was bluntness! All the more so because it was grimly plain that Dr. Lewis believed nothing of the sort.

"If I knew, Doctor…" Tom started, to have it waved away.

"No, no — I understand you don't. What I wonder is…" He shook his head. "Grace is not yet nineteen, and betrothed to a man of her father's choosing. She has no mother, no family besides her aunt, and I feel a burden of care towards her. If she's an orphan now, I believe she should be married as soon as she's out of mourning."

"But that would be for Goodwife Lovell to decide, I'm sure — with your counsel."

Dr. Lewis lowered his voice to a fretful murmur. "But Mr. Walsingham, what if he's alive and…"

What if he's alive and a traitor? What would become of a traitor's child? Tom didn't believe there was much in the way of goods the Crown could seize, and besides, Isaac Finch was a lowly courier: his felony, if he'd committed it, would make little noise amongst those of gentlemen and priests. At worst, Grace's matrimonial prospects might suffer a little.

"You are letting your misgivings lead you too far, Doctor," Tom said, a little more brusquely than he'd meant.

Not that the rector took the hint. "I wish it were so," he said, in a soberer version of his sermon manner. "I pray that it is… And yet, will you deny that, for Grace's sake, we must all hope her father dead?"

Well, now! Tom swallowed a bitter laugh, and with it whatever itch he had to scoff at Dr. Lewis's gall. How could he, when he himself hoped to find that Finch lay dead somewhere of any cause that had naught to do with the cursed plot? Poor Isaac Finch, without a soul to pray that he was safe and hale!

A knock on the door spared Tom the need to answer. Dr. Lewis called to come in, and the housekeeper entered, still in her Sunday best, with a way of great wariness about her.

Oh, yes — the housekeeper, summoned by Dr. Lewis at Tom's request. It seemed a little pointless now, beyond Tom's irritation that the women had kept the matter of the betrothal from him. Still, people hid things for a reason — and those reasons often proved more important than what was hidden.

When asked about her niece's betrothal, Goodwife Lovell peered at her master aslant. "I never liked it," she said, "but Isaac would hear no reason. The Caseys used to live nearby, and John and my brother grew up together. A terror, they were — a terror and a penance. Old Mr. Weste, as was rector then, had a white hair for every trick they played. My father belted them both, when he could find them — for they had all sorts of hiding holes around the church…" She shook her head. "Such friends, they were — but I ask Your Honour: is that a reason to give John Casey a girl in marriage, young enough to be his daughter?"

A good husband, and a life of comfort, according to the rector. "Finch's reasons are his own, Goodwife. I'd rather hear what yours were for not telling me of this."

"But why would I?" the widow scoffed. "'Tis a common thing, naught to do with…" Her eyes filled. "And now…" She turned to Dr. Lewis. "Now that she's fatherless, Your Worship, will she have to…?"

"All the more now — if he'll have her —"

The door burst open then, and why they all must be surprised to see Grace half-stumble in, Tom didn't know.

"Father's dead?" she cried.

When Goodwife Lovell made to go to her, Grace flinched away.

"Father's dead!" she said again — and this time it was no question.

"Grace, child…"

Dr. Lewis floundered, and the housekeeper had no words, so it fell to Tom to answer.

"In all truth, we don't know," he said.

Grace held his gaze. "But you think he's dead," she said.

"We won't know until there is a body found."

"Then wait!" Grace turned to her aunt first, and then the rector. "You don't know that I'm fatherless, to make me wed John Casey! And even if I were… Father has changed his mind. Pray he comes back, and he'll tell you!"

She had a knack for leaving all speechless, this one. In the stunned silence, Tom observed for the first time young Peg. How long had she been there, peering around the doorjamb? Jove — but the daughters in this house were running wild!

"What do you mean, Finch changed his mind?" Tom asked, when it became clear nobody else would.

Grace wiped at her tears, and when she spoke her voice was small and shaking. "What we argued about," she said. "It was John Casey. I'd been crying, and Father wanted to know why — as if he didn't know! I said I didn't care a whit to be an alderman's wife — I'd rather drown in the Ditch..." She stopped at the twin gasps from her aunt and the rector, but never looked at either. "And then he laughed, all angry and bitter. *You can quit fussing*, he said. *I don't reckon you'll wed John Casey!*"

"But this..." Dr. Lewis stammered. "Are you certain, child?"

Grace stuck out her chin. "He cursed when I asked why. He said it was his business, and none of mine..." Her face crumpled at last, and she let her aunt embrace her.

How very convenient — now Finch couldn't give her the lie. Tom didn't bother to hide his doubts. "And you told no one? Not even your aunt?"

"I wanted it to come from Father!" Grace wailed, face hidden against the housekeeper's shoulder. "*Him* you'd all believe..."

She started sobbing hard, and over her pretty head Goodwife Lovell glared at Tom. Even Dr. Lewis frowned in disapproval — and, had he been there, Skeres would have trounced his master when Tom asked one more question.

"Had your father told Alderman Casey, Grace?"

The girl redoubled her sobs for all answer, and Dr. Lewis went to stand between the women and the overbearing guest.

"Please, Mr. Walsingham — you'll question her later." He raised a pleading hand — half to beg Tom's indulgence, half to pacify the housekeeper. "Take her away, Mrs Lovell. Put her to bed, give her a posset ... there, there."

With one last glower for Tom, Goodwife Lovell led her weeping niece away, murmuring to her. Peg scurried after them.

"Mercy on us!" Dr. Lewis rubbed at his brow. "This is unexpected. *Most* unexpected."

Most unexpected indeed — to the rector, who had been away for days — but also, by the look of it, to Goodwife Lovell. Did Finch's sister believe her niece? Did Tom, for that matter? Whether he did or not, though, this betrothal added a few new pieces to the collection in his mind.

"You wouldn't know where Deputy Alderman Casey is to be found, Doctor?" he asked.

"Why, I believe he..." The rector fell silent as he gleaned Tom's meaning. "Oh. Oh, you think...?"

And the man a Doctor of Divinities! Weren't they taught the ills of hasty conclusions? "I don't know what I think, yet," Tom said with all his sternness. "But I want to question Isaac Finch's friend."

But of course, it was too late. "Yes, yes — 'tis wise of you, I'm sure." Dr. Lewis tapped a long finger on his chin. "John Casey, now... He keeps shop in Fenchurch Street. A mercer's shop..." And the more he rambled, the more his brow smoothed. "Yes, yes — men have been known to take ill a breach of promise, haven't they? And arguing can lead to fighting, and..."

Oh, let the rector be relieved, Tom decided. It was a good thing that Dr. Lewis was missing the point — the question being, if Casey had killed Finch for reneging on their understanding, why had Finch reneged on it at all?

And they called London such a huge place!

Not even a blind cat could have failed to see that John Casey was kin to Phelippes's servant — not that Tom had truly expected otherwise: the two men shared not just the same thin face and sparely-fleshed body, but also the same whitish voice.

Only, John Casey dressed rather better than his son and, where Rouse owed his nickname to his gingery mane, his father was sandy-haired, and beginning to grey. He even moved as loose-limbed as his son, as he approached across the yard at the back of the mercer's shop.

"I'm John Casey, ay," he announced — and then, with a mercer's quick appraisal of clothes and bearing, he changed his manner to a more respectful one. "May I serve you, Master?"

Tom wished he'd taken the time to question Phelippes. Just how much did this fellow know about the business of his son's master? The roundabout way often being the safest…

"I've heard of you from Isaac Finch, Alderman," he said. "He used to call you his good friend."

Casey stared. "*Used to*? But Hannah Lovell says there are no tidings. I've come from St. Helen's — Your Honour was there too… Isaac's master, Hannah said."

So it hadn't been appraisal, but plain recognition — and who knew what else the housekeeper had said?

"I saw you talking with Goodwife Lovell and her niece."

Casey nodded, rubbing at the bark of the yard's one spindly pear tree. "Old friends they are, the Finches."

Tom raised a brow. "Well, Goodwife Lovell, perhaps. But Grace is rather more than that?"

Whether this was an innocent question depended much on Casey's circumstance, of course. There was no guilty start, no shifty glance — but there was *something*. The man chewed on it with an air of not liking what he tasted.

"My daughter lives Smithfield-way," he announced. "I walk to have dinner with her, on a Sunday, and take the air. Would you keep me company, Master?"

The yard was surrounded by houses, so that a good few windows overlooked it — and yet this play at hugger-mugger disagreed so much with Finch's tale of the Exchange… But Tom liked discrepancies. He liked them very much — and was well armed, in case the mercer should prove to be the murderer after all. "If you will lead the way…"

They left the city through the old, squat pile of Aldgate, Tom leading his horse by the bridle — and Casey pointed to the wide street that ran south, between the gardens at the foot of the Walls and what remained of the old Minories abbey. It was a pleasant walk, well-sunned and lined with a few trees, and quite tranquil of a Sunday. There had been no talking in the press at the gate, but once they were out of it Tom lost no time in mentioning Grace Finch again.

"She's my betrothed, ay." Casey stuck out his chin. "There's no question of a wedding right now, of course — but…"

"But if she's left fatherless, she'll be all the more in need of a husband, won't she?"

Here was another thing John Casey shared with his son: a way of colouring like a rosy tide.

"'Tis not that I'm heartless, Master. I pray to the Lord that Isaac Finch may come back safe and sound — but if it turns out he's dead… Grace is too much of a handful for her aunt, and Isaac always meant that she should be my wife."

The words of an innocent man — or of a culprit sounding the ground. "Ah — but not quite always. It seems Finch changed his mind."

Deputy Alderman Casey stopped in the middle of the road, so suddenly that Tom's horse all but walked into them both. "Changed his mind...!"

"He meant to renege on the betrothal. You didn't know, I take it?"

Once Tom had seen a player instructing his apprentice. He would command a passion, and the boy would reshape his face and his stance, like molten wax — ire, melancholy, supplication, the wildest cheer, all in the blink of an eye. He was put in mind of it now, seeing confusion and anger chase each other across the mercer's face.

Anger won.

"Changed his mind!" he cried. "Did Hannah tell you this?"

"I much doubt Goodwife Lovell knew before this morning."

"Ha, never believe it, Master! Did it come from Grace? Then Hannah put her up to it. She's never liked that I should take Grace as my wife."

Had the housekeeper feigned her astonishment, then? From the beginning she'd shown little hope of her brother's return. Had she made up this charade together with Grace? Could she have thought the girl would be given credence on such a matter? Unless, of course, John Casey was lying through his teeth.

No certain way to know — but there was no harm in throwing a little bait. "Or perhaps Finch himself told me," Tom ventured.

Again the melting-wax play of confusion and anger. "Your Honour jests! Why would he go back on his word?"

"Ay, Alderman — that's what I wonder: why would he?"

When Tom tugged his horse into motion, John Casey didn't follow at once. He stood gaping, rooted in the middle of the street, as pale as he'd been ruddy. Then he broke into a jog and caught up with Tom, grabbing him by the sleeve.

"Isaac wouldn't…" He paused, flustered. "The gain's all on his daughter's side, and he knows it well!"

"Young Grace sings a different tune. She claims Finch wouldn't tell her why, that it was his business — and yours."

"You can't believe a word the chit says, Master — nor her shrew of an aunt! Hannah never wanted me for a nephew, and Grace is young and foolish. Now Isaac can't gainsay them, what's to keep them from lying?"

"Can't he? You seem very sure that Finch is dead."

"Why, his own sister —"

"But she can't be believed, can she? Unless, of course, you've other reasons to think Isaac Finch won't come back."

"Other reasons!" Casey choked out.

They'd reached a place where the street forked, to the Tower's Postern Gate on one side, and through a large common on the other, where people strolled and played games. At the fork's head stood a tall wayside cross, and Tom stopped there, watching the mercer.

"I'm cursed with a curious mind, Deputy Alderman: did you happen to take the air Wednesday last, too? Late at night, perhaps?"

"Wednesday last? Why, I was at home…" It was plain, the moment when the man saw through the bewildering question, and his eyes went wide. "Because a slip of a girl makes up a Canterbury tale, you…?" John Casey forced a hard laugh through his teeth. "With all respect, Your Honour's horn-mad! Even if Isaac Finch had changed his mind — and I can't think why — would it be a blood matter, I ask you? The courts are full of people suing for breach of promise!"

True enough, but then in all those suits the bride's father hadn't gone missing — nor had he ridden for Sir Francis Walsingham. That, and how it all depended on why the promise was broken, Tom kept to himself for the moment.

"Men have killed for less," he said. "Or they've grown angry enough to kill where they never meant it."

Without waiting for an answer, he leapt into the saddle and heeled the horse into a narrow turn. "Good day, Master Alderman," he threw over his shoulder, and he spurred his horse back towards the gate, leaving a disconsolate John Casey to wonder how deep in trouble he was — and, perhaps, even to make some useful mistake.

CHAPTER 10

Gilbert Gifford, Mylls's servant said, wouldn't come to Seething Lane, nor to Mylls's house. He had, however, weighty information to impart, if anyone were to open for him the little wicket door at the back of Sir Francis's garden, the one in Mark Lane.

Tom went to draw the bolts himself — and, when he peered out, there stood Gifford, hunched and white-faced in the greenish light of the lowering afternoon.

His mouth thinned at the sight of Tom. "I'm not coming in—"

"Yes, you are." Tom pushed the door a little wider. "Or do you think it'll seem more innocent, if you stand chatting at the back door?"

Gifford squinted this way and that along the lane, and then threw himself across the threshold, tearing the door from Tom's hand to slam it shut. A fine show of innocence!

See how he leant against the door, trembling and gaping. When distant thunder rolled overhead, he startled.

"You weren't followed, were —"

Tom was cut off when Gifford began babbling in a wild-eyed torrent.

"They all spent the morning together at Babington's house — Babington himself, and Savage and Ballard. I found out but an hour ago —"

"Soft and fair, now." Tom held up a staying hand. "Are they still there? How do you come to know?"

Gifford stamped his foot. "Savage told me! And Poley was there. *Anthony's Robin*, Savage calls him." A twist of the thin lips, the voice waxing shrill… "Ballard would be in gaol now, if he'd sent word —"

"Soft, devil pinch you!" Tom grabbed his shoulder. "You sent no word, either…"

"I never knew until I met with Savage — and then I couldn't hare away at once! Poley was there this morning, then went away… You could have arrested Ballard! You could have arrested them all…"

Gifford didn't know they couldn't — not yet. Whether Poley did, though…

"You say Poley went away. Why?"

"How would I know…?" Under Tom's unamused glare, Gifford checked himself and looked away, scuffing at the gravel with a worn shoe. "Babington asked him, I think. When Savage and Ballard arrived."

"And Savage dislikes him?"

"Very much."

Which was a little alarming: were the plotters suspecting a snake in their collective bosom? At the same time, though… "This should assuage your suspicions, Gifford. If they mistrust him, Poley can't have played us false — at least not too much."

Oh, how Gifford scoffed at that! "As though Savage couldn't lie about it, to keep us complacent, to cozen us!"

Tom thought back to the soldier he'd met at the Collège Anglais, with his blunt, stubborn manner. "I'm sure you know Savage best — but the man I met in Rheims never struck me as devious-minded. Unless you believe he's been befuddling you all this time."

"He never struck *you*, Mr. Walsingham?" Venom flared in Gifford's dark gaze. "What would *you* know of it? You sit here, day after day, hidden behind His Honour's name, sending others out to risk their necks — if it *is* you sending them, for it seems to me it is Phelippes and Mylls doing the work —"

Hades take the lout! "You scurvy toad!" In sudden fury, Tom shoved hard at Gifford. "Another who believes 'tis just my name —"

"Mr. Walsingham?"

It was like a bucketful of well water down his back. Tom froze, his mind clearing of a sudden. What was he thinking?

"Yes?" He took a breath and turned around — and there stood Phelippes.

"There are letters from Richmond, Mr. Walsingham," he said. "And Mr. Mylls needs to consult you, if you please — and there is this…" He held out a folded paper.

"Thank you, Phelippes." Tom had himself in check again as he took it, half hoping it was from Poley — but no. Berden warned of a gathering at the Rose Tavern: Babington, Ballard, Savage, Tichborne, Tilney… Tom turned back to Gifford. "Do you know where Savage is taking his supper?"

Oh, how the deacon would have liked to have an answer — and how it galled him that he hadn't! "He spoke of an engagement," he muttered.

"Ay, at the Rose Tavern, near Temple Bar. He didn't invite you, I take it?"

The tossed head was answer enough.

"You may go, then. Keep watch on Savage — and keep yourself where we can find you."

As soon as a sullen Gifford had disappeared through the wicket door, Tom closed it and leant against it. Smite all self-regarding, rancorous assheads! *Unus … duo… tres … quattuor…* Tom would have laughed at himself — but Phelippes was still there, squinting in the grey light and shifting his weight from foot to foot. Phelippes, who, after shrouding their friendship in a stranger's distance for the sake of his career, still thought he had to come to the rescue of Tom's dignity and pride. "What is it, Phelippes?" he ground out. *Quinquies ... sex ... septem...*

"You still count in Latin!" the cypherer blurted.

Caught! And must Phelippes grimace so uncertainly?

But yes — he must, the way he always did — whether worried or not. All of the heat drained out of Tom like water from a cracked bowl.

"Oh, Philippus!" he sighed. "Where did you think Tityrus had gone?"

It took a moment, but the old Paris nicknames drew a thin smile out of Phelippes. It was crooked and a little rueful — the way it had been in the old days.

"I think I just caught a glimpse of him," the cypherer ventured. "He was minded to throttle Gifford — and small blame to him."

With a huff of laughter, Tom dropped onto the bench under Lady Ursula's medlar tree. There was more thunder, and the garden smelt like rain to come. "That fellow! He..." *He irks me into foolishness. He pricked an old megrim.*

Tutting, Phelippes came to perch on the bench at Tom's side, a little stiffly. "He's afraid, to my thinking," he said.

"Of them?" But no — or, at least, not just. "And more afraid still of us, isn't he? That we'll throw him to the lions in the end."

"A traitor sees betrayal everywhere."

"Ay — but I think..." Tom sat up, elbows on his knees. "I think he's trying to give us Poley as a Judas, instead of him."

"Mr. Mylls rather agrees."

Oh, yes — Mylls, too. "And he'll agree more still, when he hears of what Poley didn't do this morning." Tom recounted Gifford's tale. "It may be true or not, and if it is, there may be all sorts of reasons — but in the end I can't find it in myself to trust either of them. Can you?"

Phelippes was leaning forward, running a twig through the small dusty mound of an anthill, watching the ants' frenzy. "There's still no bay horse at the Castle," he said — not half the *non sequitur* it seemed.

Two full days and a half now… It seemed easier to imagine Poley whispering in a traitor's ear — and perhaps killing Finch — until one remembered Gifford's subtleness with the beer casks at Chartley. But would he be cold-minded enough to keep reporting and feign fear?

The skies opened of a sudden — the breeze picking up, carrying the first fat drops of rain — and Tom, still in his grey velvet, sprinted for the house, with the cypherer on his heels.

By the time they stumbled through the door the rain had gained in fury, whipping the monkshood and the roses. Lady Ursula would be displeased, and Frances vexed, for she loved the monkshood. But Lady Ursula almost never came to Seething Lane these days, and Frances must be halfway to Flushing, where her husband had been made governor.

For the first time in a long while, Tom clapped Phelippes's shoulder. "Come, Philippus," he said. "We can't all have fine suppers at the Rose, but I reckon Mrs Jeffreys will feed us poor Queen's men."

And, for a wonder, instead of bowing, the cypherer nodded awkwardly, and even curled his lips in the hint of a smile.

Mrs Jeffreys was only too happy to spread a half feast in the kitchen, with roast ham and, much to Tom's liking, a well-sugared pie of early plums. After fussing a little about the bread that was only cheat, she left them with their trenchers, a jug of rosemary ale, and a candlestick whose golden light glanced off the copper pots on the walls.

The evening had cooled, and the whisper of the rain came through the open window, together with a scent of dampened herbs. They ate in silence — or Phelippes did, never being one to start conversations, while Tom picked at his ham and brooded.

He thought of the group drinking Mary Stuart's health at the Rose, and the missing Finch, and the unwritten letter, and Gifford's fear.

"And they won't have him for supper..." he murmured to himself.

Or he'd meant it for himself, but Phelippes looked up from his trencher, where he was cutting his wedge of pie into little squares. He must have been thinking much the same, for he asked, "And Poley? You reckon he'll be there?"

"Babington is more trusting than Savage. Whether he's wrong, now..."

Phelippes clicked his tongue. "'Tis a good thing Poley knows naught of the letter."

Except... "He knows of Lichfield," Tom said. "And what if he and Finch met again that night? Say Poley tried to draw more out of Finch, and Finch grew suspicious?"

"Ah." The little cypherer chewed thoughtfully. "It could be, couldn't it?"

"Although what goes for Poley could be true of Berden and Gifford as well. And then there's the matter of the daughter."

Phelippes frowned in question, and Tom told him his findings of the day. When he reached Grace's betrothed, the cypherer choked on his pie.

"Casey...?"

"Deputy Alderman John Casey, of Aldgate Ward." Tom watched as Phelippes set down his knife, and exhaled through his nose.

It was a known fact in Seething Lane that Phelippes never laughed. Tom suspected it was because, when he did, he tittered.

It wasn't a cheerful titter. "If I heard it in a tale, I'd scoff..." He shook his head, and listened in grim silence to the rest of the tale.

"Do you believe the girl?" he asked at the end.

Throughout the day Tom had wondered more than once. "It's an easier lie than most, if Finch is dead. Hard to gainsay her."

"Still, getting rid of an old suitor is one thing — but sending him to the gallows as a murderer..."

"She never thought that he would fall under suspicion. She made up her father's change of heart, and thought that would be that."

A click of the tongue. "Little fool! But ... Rouse's father, of all men!"

"What do you know of him?"

The cypherer pursed his lips. "His son calls him a pompous, meddling ass — a most unchristian thing to say of one's father. I've never met him: does he make a likely murderer?"

Tom gave a small shrug. John Casey was self-righteous, brusque, and not half as clever as he thought — but... "What I can't help wondering, though, is this: if Grace speaks true, why did Finch change his mind?"

Who knows? said the tilt of Phelippes's head. *And, what's more, what's it to us?*

"Has Rouse told you of the noise his father made at the Exchange? Rouse was there, watching Babington's friends..."

"Was he found out?" Phelippes's glare was sign enough that Rouse had neglected to mention the incident.

"Both he and Berden say he wasn't."

"And Finch was there to see?"

"'Tis from him that I had the story," Tom said. "So, if there was something more to it than meddling ass-headedness — or even if there wasn't…"

Outside the rain hissed like a creature angered, and Tom and Phelippes sat in the yellow candlelight, each thinking much the same, Tom would have wagered: that these days even an ill-founded suspicion of treason was a great danger.

"Fear can move men to —"

The rest of Sir Francis's maxim was lost when the door was thrown open, and Nick Skeres hurled across the threshold like cannon shot, wet to the bone and calling with great cheer, "Oy, Master!"

"Don't —" Tom warned — too late.

Other men, coming in from the rain, might drip; the Minotaur shook himself like a hound, spraying a river's worth of water on all around him.

"Oh, go to!" Tom groused, brushing rain from his sleeve, and wishing he'd changed out of his newish suit.

Skeres laughed as if for a fine joke. "Mrs Jeffreys scolds if I do it in 'er sight," he explained.

And Phelippes, having escaped most, if not all, of the pelting, blinked, and likely thanked Heaven that Skeres was not *his* servant.

Having long learnt the uselessness of challenging the lad's logic, and wanting to hear the tidings, Tom took the easier course of having Skeres out of his sodden doublet and sat at the table.

"Did you have a fine supper?"

"Cuds-me!" The flushed cheeks and the smacking lips told their own tale. "Best quails I ever 'ad, and the blancmange! A fine place, is the Rose, and crammed to the eaves, all toasting Drake like 'e is their own coz. Not where I'd plot treason — for all that Mr. Babington paid to 'ave a parlour all to ourselves. But there were servants in and out all the time, and Lord knows who was eavesdropping." He shook his head and cut himself a slice of the sweet pie, choosing the side that had more plums. "'Ow this band of fools can be a danger to anything or anyone, I'll never know. They babble of naught, all 'ugger-mugger like villains at the play."

Which wasn't all the consolation it could have been, for it took little wit to wield a poniard. "Did Tichborne hire you?"

"Says 'e will. Not that 'e can pay me much: 'e asks if I'll go as a companion — which means less wages, don't it?"

He said it with such affronted bitterness that Tom couldn't help but laugh. "Then I won't worry that you'll leave my service for his. Now, less of the hypothetic, Dolius: who was there?"

"Who was there now..." Skeres sat back, chewing as he frowned at the dark ceiling. "Babington, and Mr. Tichborne, and Mr. Tilney — and you wouldn't credit the pearl 'e 'ad in 'is ear tonight! Then that tall fellow, Savage, who never talks much, and three more that I don't know, and then Foskew."

"Captain Fortescue?"

"'Im — and you should see the others, drinking up every word 'e says... Why, I drank it up meself! I won't say 'e made me afeared — but..." The Minotaur's eyes shone strangely, round and large. "But 'im I'd nab and 'ang if I were you, Mr. Tom — just to be safe."

Wouldn't they all like to be rid of Father Ballard! Tom thought of the burning gaze and the warm, commanding voice.

It said something that even the Minotaur had felt the priest's power. But was one strong-willed man enough, if he was beset with well-covered enemies? Supposing he truly was…

"What of Poley?"

"What of 'im?" Skeres answered through a full mouth. "Stuck to the Babington boy like a louse. Always smiling, always Master Anthony this and Robin that, always fetching and carrying…"

Phelippes had kept quiet; now he had a question of his own. "Would you say they trust him?"

The lad laughed at that, slapping a palm on the table hard enough to make the flames dance. "Trust 'im! Bless you, Master — and save the addlepate who does! Babington, ay — but the others…" A snort. "Mr. Tichborne trusts 'im like 'e would a rat. Savage, too — and even Mr. Tilney, for all 'is pearls, 'as the wits to mislike Rob Poley. But then, none of them likes that Maude of Captain Foskew's either — and the Captain goes nowhere without 'im." A shrug. "Berden's the one they don't mistrust too much. And me… I'm a fool of a servant-lad. I gape at all they say, moan 'ow 'ard it is for a poor man to keep the faith, play wretched…" He demonstrated. "They like that."

And, quite pleased with his doings, Skeres helped himself to another slice of pie, bigger than the first. To think he'd come home from a fine supper of quails and blancmange!

"Didn't they feed you at the Rose?" Tom snatched away the plate with what remained of the pie. "What will Mrs Jeffreys say?"

And see what amazed innocence! "Does she want that I go 'ungry?" Skeres moaned, and had the cheek to cast a longing look at the last wedge of the pie.

And what did one do then, but push back the plate before the lad, earning a huge grin in return?

Phelippes waited until the pie was disposed of, before he asked another question. "But did they seem astir to you, Skeres? Keen to move…?"

There was some purse-lipped humming and a shake of the head. "'Tis all air, if you ask me. Boys playing at secrets — 'till someone tells them what."

"But they do have that someone, don't they?" Tom asked under his breath.

For once, Skeres's countenance darkened. "You take away the Black Foskew, Master, and down they all go like skittles."

After that, Tom dismissed a well-fed Skeres and remained alone again with Phelippes, who raised a pale brow in question.

"And so…" the cypherer said.

"And so, we don't know much more than we did before." Tom rubbed at his eyes. Ah, these long days of chasing thoughts, and facts, and shadows — and always coming up with precious little! "We'll hear what Berden has to say — but…"

"But there's no saying what's afoot," Phelippes moaned. "No saying whether they know."

"Nor whether they found another way to get their letters through."

Phelippes's perpetual worry darkened to bleakness. "Oh, we'll come to know, in time — but by then it will be too late."

The rain had ceased, and outside a solitary owl was hooting in the garden. Tom went to the window and stood leaning against the sill, peering at the wet darkness outside. "Mr. Secretary must be informed," he said — wincing at the thought of how Sir Francis was going to like it.

Phelippes's chair creaked behind Tom's back. "And the warrants. We must know what to do about the warrants, in case Ballard decides to make his move."

Ah, yes — the cursed warrants. It would require a day at best to obtain them, more likely two! But then... Tom turned away from the window, grasping at the one trickle of light in the whole bramble.

"At least, for a mercy, they don't sound ready to disband and run to earth."

"You trust your Minotaur's judgment?"

There was no scepticism, no mockery colouring the cypherer's question — just plain curiosity.

Tom half surprised himself as he answered. "He rather lacks in graces, doesn't he? And he makes a dismal servant — but, as he's fond of saying, his mam raised no fools."

"And you don't think..." Phelippes leant over to fiddle with one of the candles. "You say that if we suspect Poley, then we must also suspect Gifford and Berden. What of Skeres?"

Tom was startled into a laugh — but, in truth, they didn't call the lad a Minotaur for nothing. "I'm not saying he couldn't have killed Finch in a rage — and yet I have a notion that, if he had, he'd up and tell me."

This drew from Phelippes something that was half snort and half sigh. "'Tis good to know at least one of our men is too plain-minded to have done murder in secret!"

Such a droll atomy of fact to possess — when all the rest remained tangled and unfathomable. Outside, the owl hooted again, and Tom slumped his shoulders, wishing for the thousandth time for the smallest scrap of certainty on the fate of Isaac Finch.

CHAPTER 11

Tom was busy penning his letter to Sir Francis — and wondering whether he should rather ride to Barn Elms himself — when a note came from Dr. Lewis at St. Helen's.

He found his fingers stumbling as he tore the still wet seal. Could it be that Finch had come back? And if he had, could the Fates be so generous that the fool had a reason for his absence?

But this was baggage, truly, and Tom knew better than to heed his own rosy hopes.

Mr. Walsingham, the worthy rector wrote, *A constable has come here, seeking a convenient place to preserve a most horrible object that was found in a yard near the grounds of Crosby Hall. Because of the sadder duties of my ministry, I do not conceive of myself as over-sensible in matters of death — yet I still shudder to think of the instant when the cloth was lifted, showing a human hand — or what remains of it. While I pray this most cruel maiming is nothing to do with our Isaac Finch, it seems to me that you should be made aware of it. Trusting in your good council, George Lewis, DDiv.*

A hand… Bless the good doctor and his flowery prose!

In a trice Tom was out of his writing room, shouting for Toby Chandler, who hurried from the scriveners' room.

"Get this to Mr. Phelippes first, and then to Mr. Mylls," Tom ordered, thrusting the note at the youth. "And send word to Wood Street, the house of Dr. Lopes: *Mr. Walsingham asks for Master Ambrose Lopes's kind assistance at the church of St. Helen's in Bishopsgate.*"

"*At his soonest convenience…?*" young Chandler called after Tom, who didn't heed him.

There being always a horse kept saddled in the stables these days, Tom was out in the lane in a blink, and trotting towards Bishopsgate.

A hand! Now, a body would have told its own tale — but a hand? Tom pushed his horse past two fishwives squabbling in the middle of the street. How even Lopes would tell from nothing but a severed hand, Tom didn't know. Nor did he know why he'd decided to ride rather than walk, at this hour of the morning, with the streets aswarm with market goers. But a hand! Those young crows, looming over a shackled Finch, holding a knife over him… Tom swerved his horse around the corner of St. Andrew's. It was hard to imagine Tilney in his silks, cutting a man's hand, or Tichborne, and Babington would faint at the mere thought … but Savage? And Ballard? Catiline's swarthy face and piercing eyes haunted Tom's thoughts as he dismounted in St. Helen's churchyard, tossing the bridle to the nearest urchin among a number of hovering people.

Not the wisest of choices, perhaps, if these were Goodwife Lovell's runagates — but Tom had no leisure to change his mind as, catching sight of him from the rectory's door where they stood holding onto each other, Grace and Peg ran to meet him.

"Is it Uncle Isaac's hand?" Peg asked, clutching at her cousin's arm.

"Is that Father's?" choked Grace.

In his life Tom had faced bullies, brigands, rabid dogs, rogue soldiers, angry French crowds, madmen in their frenzy, and more than his fair share of cornered murderers — and never had one of them dismayed him the way a grieving woman did.

"How would I know?" he snapped. "Where's Dr. Lewis?"

The two cousins pointed as one towards the church, and made to follow when he moved. Now all he lacked were two girls having the vapours... He asked for Goodwife Lovell; Peg and Grace shook their heads. When he bid them see to his horse, Peg gave a silent nod, but never left her cousin's side.

"Now, wait here — both of you!" Tom ordered, as sternly as he knew. "I don't want you in there!"

And, for a wonder, Grace stopped, putting an arm around a mutinous-looking Peg.

Good.

At the church door, Arthur Pratte stood together with a staff-carrying watchman — the clerk waving to catch Tom's eye. Tom hastened to join him, and they entered the empty nave.

"'Tis horrible, Your Honour!" Pratte gasped. "The pig... But come this way, if you please. Today of all days!"

"What's with today?"

Pride and unease vied for possession of the ruddy face. "My wife was delivered of a boy this morning, and all went as it should, but as portents go —"

Oh, Jupiter! "Portents are rank superstition, surely?"

Under Tom's glare, the clerk wilted and led the way up the aisle.

As he followed, Tom caught a glimpse of Grace and Peg on the door, arguing with the watchman. Tartarus seize those two — and the fools who'd raised them! So let them see if they liked.

The vestry, when Tom strode inside in an ill humour, was revealed to be a narrow room, lined with walnut cupboards and smelling of beeswax, dampness, and decay. There was a slender window on each end, and through the one facing east, the morning light slanted in all its summer strength. Four men were gathered around a cupboard, where the source of the sickly odour lay. They turned as one to face Tom.

Dr. Lewis and old Lambsfoot were there; Constable Hallet (save and deliver!) made a huge third. The fourth, with cap in hand and a shrinking manner, was a smallish, grey-haired fellow in faded clothes.

"Oh, Mr. Walsingham, Heaven be thanked!" Dr. Lewis called, brow clearing, and then he halted in his tracks in sudden doubt.

Ah, well — but then, reckoning by how Constable Hallet's thick features reshaped themselves from contrary to questioning to wrong-footed, it was just as well.

"Walsingham…?" the wardsman repeated, blinking in the way of the lost — thinking back, surely, to his first encounter with this grandly named fellow.

Tom assumed his most Sir Francis-like steeliness. "We meet again, Constable … Hallet, is it? I'm sure you understand, by now, that I'm seeking someone. I'm also sure you'll see the need for the greatest discretion. May I see what it is that you've found?"

In all fairness, young Hallet recovered his dignity soon enough — not that he knew quite what to do with it. He began by grumbling of dead cousins, then snatched off his cap, and stepped aside.

"Go ahead, then, Yer Honour," he said. "Not that it was me as found it, mind."

It was the hand — or what remained of it, as Dr. Lewis had written. A right hand, lying palm-up on a grimy cloth in the full glare of the August sun. It bore an unpleasant likeness to a very large dead spider, the colour of old wax. The thumb and three fingers curled inward, the ring finger missing its tip and nail. It seemed as though the little finger and the outer edge of the palm had been gnawed away, and, where the wrist should have been, the grey-white flesh was shredded, showing lumps of bone. An ugly thing — though not half as bad as the drowned body at St. Botolph. Also, it was neither sodden nor swollen.

Wishing Lopes would make haste, Tom straightened from his examination. "If you didn't find it, Constable, then who did?"

There was some shuffling as the old man bowed his way to Tom's elbow.

"That was me pig, Yer Honour," he said bashfully, and shrunk back when Hallet scowled at him.

"No it wasn't, 'ee bootless lackwit!" the wardsman scoffed. "A woman did, down past Crosby Place." He turned to Tom. "This fellow's pig had brought it."

A pig.

Some of Tom's new steadiness roiled away, and he tried hard not to think of last night's ham at supper. "A pig?"

Dr. Lewis beckoned the small man forward. "I think you'd better listen to what Faldo has to say, Mr. Walsingham."

Under so much attention, poor Faldo shrunk like one who'd rather hide in the nearest cupboard. Now that he observed him, Tom noticed how the man's right arm hung stiff at his side, the elbow crooked, and the shrivelled palm facing outward. Some childhood illness, perhaps — for Faldo wasn't built for soldiering.

"I'm listening," Tom said.

Faldo squirmed a little, cleared his throat, and began in a thin, hoarse voice. He lived, he said, close by the walls, where the old Papey friars had had their church. There were tenements, there, and houses — some fine and some not — and a garden or two. Well, there Faldo lived, and kept a few chickens and a pig. This pig had a liking for wandering, and he'd gone astray last night. Faldo hadn't worried, for the pig always came back.

"Not that 'e's wicked at 'eart, Yer Honour, just a little wild, being a young pig —"

Just when Tom was losing charity with the pig and its owner, Hallet butted in.

"Ay, well, the pig ran, and this woman found it mucking in her herb beds right after cockcrow. She shooed it away with a spade, and it left that behind." He jerked his chin at the hand. "Gave her the vapours, it did."

And small blame to her. "Not what one expects to find among the gillyflowers," Tom said. "And this was down by Crosby Place, you say? A good way from the Papey."

"Pigs go a-wander, Yer Honour," Faldo piped up. "Young pigs more so."

"And do you know where your pig likes to wander?" Tom asked, feeling very foolish.

Nobody so much as snickered as Faldo shook his head mournfully.

"Faldo's pig has a reputation," the rector said. "A wandering spirit."

The sexton joined in. "Once it ran all the way to Bishopsgate Without, didn't it, Faldo? And once in Aldgate…"

Of course. *Of course.* Tom wanted to laugh. The Queen's enemies were plotting murder, Sir Francis expected him to gauge the joints and flexures of the matter, and here he was, contemplating a rotten hand that a pig had found. And it *had* to be a pig with a wandering spirit. Tom wanted to laugh all the more: just what Sir Francis had called Gilbert Gifford…

And then Pratte reappeared in the doorway, saying that a gentleman was there, asking for Mr. Walsingham — and, Fates be thanked, over the clerk's shoulder Tom spied the gloomy countenance of Ambrose Lopes.

"This is Master Lopes," he announced. "He'll examine the hand as a physician. Master Lopes, if you will…"

With one of those sideways nods of his, Lopes entered the vestry. Did he fashion his solemn manner after his father, the way Tom did with Sir Francis?

"Thank you, Mr. Walsingham," he said, and, as unmoved as he'd been at St. Botolph, he went to peer at the ugly thing.

There was a spell of silence — but for the throat-clearing from Faldo, and the unamused shuffling from Constable Hallet, who most likely wondered just what he'd got himself into — until Dr. Lewis spoke up.

"I fear the pig mauled it…" He faltered. To hear him, one'd think he was making excuses for a burnt pie.

Lopes blinked. "The pig?"

When the story of Faldo's pig was told again, young Lopes took it in stride. "It explains the way the wrist was severed," he said, pointing to the ragged edges of flesh and bone. "Chewed away."

Oh good Lord. Tom's wrist twitched of its own accord, and he must have looked a little green, because Lopes hastened to explain.

"After the death, most certainly." He pointed again. "You see the way the flesh was torn. Living and dead flesh do not behave the same way."

Not that he saw anything of the sort, but Tom made himself observe more closely. Dead flesh… "How long dead, Master Lopes?"

"'Tis hard to tell, but I'd venture…" Lopes bent lower, touching the greyed skin with a careful fingertip. "Four days, or three perhaps."

"No less than that, though?"

"Not if it was buried — and, in this season, a body could never remain unburied and not be found."

Three or four days. That would match with Finch's disappearance.

"But Yer Honour..." Faldo shuffled forward. "Me pig didn't run for a good week before last night..."

"Shut yer trap, Faldo!" Hallet groused. "Nobody thinks the pig did murther. It *is* murther, eh?" This last was addressed to Tom, together with a prodigious glower. "The murther of yer man?"

Ah, to know that! Finch's hand presented itself in Tom's mind — reaching out, talon-like, to grab a sealed note, candlelight playing on the pox scars.

Swallowing hard, Tom turned the thing with a cautious finger — and sure enough, there were the marks.

"Is this all the pig's work?"

Lopes squinted at the marks. "Some of it — but mostly, it looks like pockmarks."

Pockmarks indeed — and, between thumb and finger, a pit the size of a three-farthing coin.

Tom exhaled slowly. So this was Isaac Finch's hand, not severed in torture, but torn from his dead body.

"Mr. Walsingham..." Lopes caught him by the elbow and drew him a little aside from the gaping group. "You understand: pox scars are very common."

"That large one, though..." Tom touched the back of his own hand. "But let's not upset these good people yet."

He turned to the four waiting men. Dr. Lewis and the sexton looked perplexed, and Faldo anxious to be gone. He scurried away, all bows and thanks, when Tom dismissed him with a penny — which the constable didn't like by half.

"Now see, Yer Honour —" he began, only to be cut short by Tom.

"What are you going to do now, Constable Hallet?"

"Well…" The young man wasn't very good at keeping his truculence. He sucked his teeth, glancing sideways like a schoolboy rehearsing his lessons. "The coroner —"

"The coroner won't hold an inquest for a piece of body," Tom cut in again. "What I'm asking is, how do you propose to find the rest of it?"

And see how the fool gaped, and muttered…

Truly, how London ruled itself without sinking into the Thames was a mystery sometimes. It was time to take charge — and let Bishopsgate Ward go cry to whom it liked.

"You heard Master Lopes, didn't you? The body has been buried these past three or four days. Where could that be?"

Hallet was still raking what brains he possessed for an answer, when Dr. Lewis entered the conversation.

"They're digging up old graves somewhere nearby — but I forget…" he said. "Is it the graveyard at St. Andrew's, Sexton?"

But Ambrose Lopes shook his head. "This is not from an old grave. I'd say the pig must have disturbed a fresh one. They do that, pigs, and dogs."

"Not here, my masters!" Lambsfoot protested in his deep rumble. "Not one of my graves!"

And so outraged he was, that Dr. Lewis felt a need to pacify him, and assure Tom that his sexton never dug shallow graves.

Not that it meant much, Tom's country boyhood whispered, for pigs were persistent beasts — but… "And if you don't, Sexton, then who does? You'll know how graveyards are kept hereabouts?"

Lambsfoot hummed and hawed, but it was not long before he named St. Ethelburga nearby, St. Andrew's, St. Martin Outwich, St. Anthony, where the French did their worship, and, most of all, St. Benet Fink. "Not a week passes without a burial, there," he said. "They can't always be thorough, I reckon."

Which sounded promising, if one were to hide a corpse. "If I were you, Constable Hallet, I'd have a look at St. Benet's graveyard."

"But, Mr. Walsingham," Dr. Lewis protested, "they won't let him disturb the graves — and very rightly. It would be most unchristian."

"Never as unchristian as having buried there a murdered man in secret — but I'm not saying our constable should start digging up graves." Tom turned to Hallet. "Just seek any recent burial that may have been disturbed again last night. If you find any, then we'll see what needs to be done."

And this appeased Dr. Lewis, but not Hallet himself.

"St. Benet Fink, 'tis out of bounds," he complained. "'Tis Broad Street Ward, and besides, the coroner..."

Oh, Tartarus swallow all wards, and wardsmen, and coroners! "I tell you, we've still a good way to go, before this becomes coroner's business —"

"Coroner's waiting, Master."

But was St. Helen's a cursed port of passage, that there was never a moment's quiet? There on the threshold, loud and brisk, stood Nick Skeres.

"What are you doing here?" Tom snapped. "What do you mean the coroner's waiting?"

And of course no amount of snapping ever moved the Minotaur in the least.

"I mean 'e's 'ere," he said. "Someone sent for 'im. And the midwife."

All the retorts burning on his tongue, Tom swallowed back — mindful of being in a church — but the glare he turned on Hallet was enough to make even this stolid fellow squirm. "Is this your doing, Constable?"

He tried — oh, he did try to hold his ground. "Ay, for that's what you do —"

"That's what you do when you have a dead body, you churl — not just a scrap of it!" And Tom stormed out, with Skeres on his heels.

All they lacked now — *all* they lacked… Coroners were no city men. They were appointed by the Crown, and who knew who this particular fellow's friends were at Court? Oh, Sir Francis was going to love this!

But wait! He wasn't thinking straight. Tom caught himself, and stopped short just out of sight of the door.

Skeres bumped into him. "'Orn-mad," groused the lad. "That's what you are, these days."

"Ay — and I'll end up in the Bedlam, if I can't see through this rigmarole. Now, fetch me Hallet."

Grumbling on principle, Skeres hastened away — to return in a trice with the red-faced constable.

Tom glared as coldly as he knew. "Now, Hallet, you tell the coroner how things stand — but say naught of me. You beg the man's pardon, say there's naught but the hand, and you're searching for the rest. You'll have him sent for when it's found."

"What if he wants to…" Hallet half-gestured towards the vestry.

"Why would he? By law, he can't inquest parts of a body. And if he does —" for there was no discounting zeal or plain curiosity — "if he does, then let him. I won't be there, and you never saw me — and much less heard my name."

It was a very good thing that Bishopsgate Ward had no seasoned officers to send around. Young Hallet mumbled and scratched his chin, but in the end he could find no objections. In fact, in the act of squashing his cap on his head, he stopped, struck (oh, portent!) with a thought.

"Jem there — my man, that is, he saw 'ee, and belike yer surgeon, too."

So even thick-headed wardsmen had wits on occasion. And there was Skeres too.

"Have they seen you, too, Dolius? What did you say?" asked Tom.

"Nothing, I said. Came in through there." Skeres jerked his head towards the unwatched large side door across the two naves — and coloured a little. "'Twas Mistress Grace as told me of the crowner, and showed me."

Mistress Grace. Tom hid a grin. "Then that's no trouble. As for myself and Master Lopes … gentlemen come to see Dr. Lewis on other matters, and then gone. Now, off with you, Hallet, and send the midwife on her way, too. What did you think, that she'd wash and dress a hand?"

Of all things, this seemed to irk the constable the most. He puffed and squared himself. "That was the clerk's wife, not me," he announced with great dignity — and was gone.

Oh yes, the clerk's wife. A new little Pratte — and the mother now delivered. Would it be worthwhile to question her about Finch? Well, never in front of the midwife. Tom went back to the vestry to fetch Ambrose Lopes, and to advise Dr. Lewis of what the coroner needed to be told.

"Much as I mislike asking you to lie, Doctor," he said, when the rector's brow darkened, "I hardly need to tell you what's at stake."

And see how the man lit up! "The Lord will forgive a minor trespass for the sake of…" He cleared his throat and stopped demurely. Lambsfoot also gaped, struck with awe.

"One should always look well into what you say — and what you don't, Mr. Walsingham," Lopes said, as they hastened out into the walled yard.

"I didn't want to burden Dr. Lewis's conscience — but he fancies himself such a fine keeper of secrets."

Lopes's chuckle was short-lived: his long face closed into the soberest Aesculapian composure at the sight of Hannah Lovell waiting by the gate.

"Your Honour…" She twisted her apron's hem. "Dr. Lewis won't have me in there — but the watchman told Grace… Is it true that they found a hand?"

"A hand, yes — but we don't know whose."

Never had Tom observed how large the housekeeper's eyes were, gleaming deep in their sockets.

"Dr. Lewis says to wait and pray," she murmured, and hastened away.

Oh Jupiter…

Lopes rubbed at his chin, his head tilted most owl-like. "I've found that oftentimes not knowing is what affects people worst."

True, no doubt — but wasn't it enough to unravel the darkest knots of mankind's doings? Must he also bring ill tidings?

"I'll tell her when I can be sure." Or perhaps, for a mercy, Dr. Lewis would tell her before then. "Well, my thanks, Master

Lopes. You have been of great help." A sudden thought struck Tom. "As for your charges…"

This would go down as Service expenses, surely?

Lopes smiled his thin-lipped smile. "My charges, Mr. Walsingham? This is all learning to me! I've a notion you should charge *me*."

And with that, he took his leave.

"And they say Jews are all silver-sick!" Skeres exclaimed, not half as softly as would have been polite.

"Quiet, you savage!" Tom elbowed him hard. "For one thing, Master Lopes is no Jew, and for another we owe him."

"'Tis not me calling Dr. Lopus a Jew."

"A dunce, as well as a savage, that's what you are. Young Ambrose and his father are Christians just as you and I."

Skeres shrugged, placid and unconvinced. "I ain't saying different, Mr Tom. I like the lad. I wish 'im no ill. So, what now?"

What now, indeed? Tom strained his ears. There was quiet inside the church — or at least nothing that sounded like an overzealous coroner. It seemed that, after all, Hallet had done his part.

"You know, Dolius, Hallet isn't wrong. He can't go charging out of bounds without stirring a riot among the wards."

"So we do it ourselves?" Skeres groaned heartily.

"So we do it ourselves," Tom said. "And — no offence to Lambsfoot — we begin here."

CHAPTER 12

It was quick work to see that no grave, and no portion of ground, had been disturbed at St. Helen's, so, with Skeres in tow, Tom moved nearby to St. Ethelburga, whose small walled yard was a model of fussy neatness, and then to St. Andrew Undershaft — where old graves were being dug up, to make place for a new rank of the dead.

St. Andrew's sexton — a rather younger man than Lambsfoot — was hard at work together with a boy, disinterring bones, skulls, and rotten scraps of shroud from the soil that last night's rain had made heavy. The fellow had no qualms about stopping to chat with a pair of idlebys.

When Tom spun him a tale of an old servant being buried there, the man leant on his spade. "'Tis always a sad day, when we've to dig up the old 'uns," he said. "Not that it happens often, mind you — but..." He nudged something in the mound of earth he'd been making, and bent to retrieve a jawless skull. "Makes you think, eh? What was he called, Your Honour's servant?"

Before Tom could come up with a name, Skeres beat him to it.

"Smith," he said, all mournful. "Old Ben Smith, as was me dad's Godbrother. I was an 'obbledehoy when 'e gave up the ghost."

The sexton held up the skull. "Who knows? Mayhap this here's your Uncle Ben. Oy!" This was for the boy, who had followed his elder's lead and was slacking in his efforts. "You're not paid to count the birds in the sky!"

Which was a little unfair, seeing as the sexton himself went back to his conversation, shaking his head. "Lazy rascal! If he were a bit more awake, we'd have finished before it rained yester-night. Now, 'tis like digging clay."

Tom saw his opening. "Have you been long at it?"

"Why, no…" The sexton pushed back his cap. "Well, yesterday was the Sabbath. Saturday all day, though, dawn to sunset. Weeks without a drop, and not one poor soul to bury — but when must it rain hard? When we're a-digging!"

And indeed, apart from on this side of the yard, none of the graves looked recent.

"Lean days, eh, Sexton?" Tom asked.

The man pulled a face — a dearth of burials clearly being a matter for commiseration to him. "At least 'tis quiet. Even the mongrels have been staying away from my graves."

Tom gave the man a penny for the sake of old Ben Smith, and left him and his boy to their work, half hauling away a fidgety Skeres.

"Do you really have an Uncle Ben buried here, Dolius?" he asked, once they were back in the street.

"Never you mind 'im." Skeres waved aside his Uncle Ben. "Those 'oles, we must go back and dig! I'll wager Finch's stuffed in there!"

"You heard the sexton: no grave was disturbed before Saturday at dawn, and Master Lopes says the hand's owner has been dead these three or four days."

"Maybe they buried it on Saturday night — or last night."

"It rained last night. The sexton would have noticed the footprints in the mud, if nothing else. Besides, where would they have kept the body until then — in this heat?"

Skeres tried hard to find an answer, with much humming — but, in the end, he had to concede defeat.

Next they tried St. Katharine Cree, so old that the church floor was half a dozen steps beneath the yard. Cramped amongst the houses all around, the small churchyard was only accessed through the church: how would a murderer with a body slung over his back make his way to this dank well of a place?

Martin Outwich's burying ground, it turned out, instead of lying by the church, had been long moved all the way to Camomile Street, by the walls: quite convenient for Faldo's pig, and poorly fenced — but not ransacked last night.

Back at Threadneedle Street, St. Anthony seemed more promising. A square-faced young woman showed them the graves behind the church.

"This was the cloister of the old monks," she said, in a French-tinged voice, and pointed to the remaining corner of a covered walk. "There was a hospital, back then, and the cemetery was over there."

It was a largish square of ground, fenced all around.

"A big place to keep in order…"

This earned a sigh from the young woman. "You have no idea, *Monsieur*!" she exclaimed, and moaned at some length about how hard it was to keep pigs away. "*Mon frère*, he is the pastor here. He says it is because the monks used to fatten up pigs here, and the nasty unclean creatures never forgot."

Which struck Tom as not just unlikely, but also a fanciful notion for a Huguenot pastor — a literal-minded sort, in his experience. But then perhaps the ills of papistry were the one subject on which Huguenots unbridled what fancy they possessed. It all seemed rather promising, until the pastor's sister explained that the council had had the fence remade last month. "'Tis sturdier now, and taller, so we have no more pigs, and now the graves are safe."

So, if St. Anthony had ever been a haunt of Faldo's pig, the creature had lost it well before Finch's disappearance.

At St. Benet Fink, where things weren't half as dire as Lambsfoot had described, they drew another blank, and Tom was contemplating St. Bartholomew across the street when a sweaty Skeres thought to dig in his heels.

"Look, if you were a pig, would you come all the way from the Papey to nibble an 'and from a grave 'ere, and then bring it back by way of Crosby Place?"

Tom had seen pigs back in Scadbury — enough to doubt that they'd go rooting several large streets away when they could do it close to home.

"And besides, would a murderer go all this way carrying a body?" He wondered aloud — and, as he did, a new notion sprang to mind. "St. Helen's used to be a nunnery, didn't it, Dolius?"

Skeres had no idea, but the mention of St. Helen's perked him up. "We go back there?"

"Indeed, we do." Tom picked up his pace, winding his way through the press of Bishopsgate Street. "We've been thinking of graveyards — or at least I have, because pigs wreak havoc on the graves all the time — but truly... Wouldn't it be easier to bury a body in some half-abandoned place? And if this place were close by, all the better! Don't you see?"

"Not a whit," Skeres grumbled, puffing as he strove to keep up. "Me sight goes dim when I'm a-famished."

Leave it to the lad to hunger more for dinner than for a glimpse of the lovely Grace. Tom laughed and clapped his sturdy shoulder. "I won't let you go blind, I promise. But before we eat, there's a place I have an itch to see."

Such an itch it was, that Tom had no qualms about tearing Lambsfoot from his bread and onions — which he was eating under the trees in the company of his mastiff — to ask about the old nun-house. "There must be something left, surely…"

The sexton sniffed. "Ay, there is. It ain't much to see, what the Leathersellers left."

"How do you get there?"

"Ah, that now…" Lambsfoot rubbed at his nose. "This side, that would be through the vestry."

And, it being plain that Tom wouldn't leave him alone, the sexton climbed to his feet, brushed crumbs off himself, and threw the last crust to the dog, which caught it in midair and swallowed without chewing.

"Come then, Yer Honour," Lambsfoot said. "Ye're like a bloodhound, eh?"

Pretending not to hear the snort from Skeres, Tom followed the sexton to the church, and to the vestry where, a few hours earlier, he'd been observing the severed hand. There seemed to be no other door at first, until Lambsfoot drew open a section of the wainscoting. So small it was that Tom had to bend his head under the lintel. It led to a roofless room, somewhat wider than the vestry, and missing a whole corner. When he looked back, Tom saw the outline of a larger and taller door in the wall's old brickwork. Where a piece of roof still stood, Lambsfoot's spade, sickle and rake were stacked, and past the missing corner rose a length of hip-high wall, supporting pairs of slender columns. The old cloister — or part of it, not unlike the one at St. Anthony's.

Skeres and Lambsfoot joined Tom, and the sexton waved around.

"They use it like a backyard, see?" He pointed to what had to be the kitchen door, and two rows of windows. By the door stood a squat wooden bench. "Goody Lovell wanted to make a herb garden here, but it would be a waste of good elbow-grease…"

For the place faced north, and buildings loomed over it on two sides. Little would grow there, beyond the coarsely mown grass around the cobbled centre where rainwater had pooled.

Beyond the roofless room, though, the open space made a bend and went on, towards the large hall with the mullioned windows Tom had mistaken for a church.

"The Leatherseller's Hall?" he asked.

"Ay, and their almshouses. And this way, there's a bit more of the nun-house, and where they tore down old St. Mary. There was a bricklayer as began to build there, using the old stones. Never went far."

Tom wasn't listening anymore. He went round the corner and found that the Leathersellers' wall also made a bend, leaving a rickety fence and a few bushes to close off St. Helen's ground. There were holes, a few just large enough for an active child — or a pig — and one or two rather bigger. Tom bent to push through the largest one, cursing when his sleeve snagged on a thorny branch. Beyond the fence the ground was littered with heaped stones, bricks and rubble, bushes gone wild, rotting planks, clumps of nettles, and the wheelless remains of a cart. A large piece of masonry stood tall — a buttressed corner of the old church, and part of a window.

"The Papey isn't all that far from here, is it?" Tom asked, as Lambsfoot came to stand at his elbow.

The sexton peered this way and that, as though the fact had never occurred to him before. "Why, no, it ain't," he admitted. "But there's no way out on the church side. And I sleep over the vestry — which is not saying much, for I sleep on my good ear — but I leave Sturdy out at night."

The mastiff… "Last night, too?"

"It rained too hard, last night, Yer Honour. Sturdy's no pup… Oy!" The sexton turned back to where Skeres had managed to ensnare himself between fence and bushes, and ran to help. "Wait — wait! Ye'll undo the fence!"

Tom forged ahead, towards the surviving buttress and the Leathersellers' wall, picking his way among the creepers and the coarse grass, feeling for holes under his boots. So last night there had been no watchdog — just when Faldo's pig was abroad and rooting out dead hands. Couldn't the beast have found a body buried around here, and then run with its booty from some noise or movement —

"Master!"

The bellow came from behind, accompanied by a crackling from above. Tom looked up in time to see the ruined windowsill crumbling down in a shower of stones and mortar.

He threw up an arm to shield his head, stepped away, and caught his heel. Footing lost, he crashed onto his back among the bricks and nettles, a larger stone hitting his shoulder hard as he fell.

"Mr. Tom!" Skeres dropped to his knees at Tom's side and dragged him up to sit.

There was rumbling and skidding behind the wall, and wet running steps.

"Catch him!" Tom choked out — and, scrambling in the mud, Skeres disappeared around the ruinous wall, right as Lambsfoot arrived at a limping run.

"Are ye hurt, Master?" The old man fussed, brushing mud from Tom's doublet as he climbed to his feet. "Why they don't tear down that thing, I'll never know. Kill someone, that it will."

Only, the wall hadn't crumbled by itself. There had been a flash of movement — an arm, perhaps, black against the bright sky. Someone had been there, dropping old masonry.

As soon as he was upright, Tom dashed around the buttress, following Skeres's steps.

There was more unchancy ground beyond, with St. Martin's graveyard on one side, and then a huddle of unkempt houses — the ill-famed tenements, no doubt — with two narrow slits to divide them. Of Skeres, of their quarry, there was no trace. Drawing his rapier, Tom chose the farthest alley — for, unless he was following by sight, Skeres was sure to have taken the closest — and ran splashing in the rain-swollen runnel. It was a short way and, when he spilt out into the street, there was nothing to be seen. The new houses, where the Papey had been, clutched against the city walls on one side, and the Bishopsgate stood tall on the other. People went about their business, giving no sign that any running fugitive had disturbed the crowd.

Tom stopped at the alley's mouth, catching his breath until Skeres trotted up to join him, dripping with sweat and puffing.

"Lost 'im," he panted.

Ay, well — so had Tom. "Did you get a good look at him?"

A sulky shake of the head. "'Eard 'im run like the wind, but 'e was too far ahead. Knew where 'e was going."

Hades and Tartarus take it — the chances were they'd just lost Isaac Finch's murderer. Although, what he was doing still at St. Helen's…

"Out to make lard of you, 'e was!" Skeres snarled. "Near cracked your 'ead!"

"Ay, well, he failed." Tom made to sheathe his rapier — only, his arm obeyed sluggishly, and a sharp pain shot from shoulder to wrist. He bit back the curse and tried to smooth out the wince — but Skeres was quick to catch it.

"Is that broken?" he inquired, and thought to offer his support by grasping Tom's battered shoulder, quite hard. "There! That's your sword arm gone," the Minotaur sentenced, when he earned a pained hiss.

Tom tried to roll his shoulder, and liked it very little — but he still managed to slide the rapier in place. Could he hope this meant no broken bones? Well, no use in loitering and wondering on a street corner, was there?

"'Twill pass. Let's go back," he ordered — and, for once and for a wonder, Skeres followed quietly.

There was no retracing the fugitive's steps — not in the tangled grasses that covered most of the ground. Still, as they made their way back, it became plain where the man had been hiding: the remnants of St. Mary still held part of a narrow spiral flight of stairs on what had been the inside. A few steps and a few more stumps led up — the way to a long gone matroneum, perhaps. The stone-thrower must have thought to hide in the black nook that remained — and from there... Awkward with his aching arm, Tom climbed up the shallow heap of rubble at the foot of the ruined stairs.

"Cuds-me, Master!" Skeres climbed after him, stomping enough to unsettle the mound.

By chance alone Tom didn't lose his footing again, but unthinkingly steadied himself with his bad hand, and hissed at the jolt of pain.

"Stand back," he ordered. "You're a plague!"

And see how reproachful the Minotaur looked as he stumbled in turn. "And you lack a maybug's wits, somewhiles!" he had the cheek to grouse.

There was reward: one of the steps was broken to a sharp edge, and what was that dark wetness coating the edge? Tom touched it.

"See?" He held up stained fingers. "Our friend gored himself a little."

It would have been beneath a rebuked Minotaur's dignity to show himself impressed, of course. "Serves 'im right!" he groused. "Shame 'e didn't break 'is neck."

A shame, ay — and a worse shame the fellow hadn't had the courtesy to drop a ring, or a note addressed to him! Still... Tom measured himself against the bloodied stone. A man at a run could have hit an arm against it.

"Well," he said, as he half climbed, half slid down the rubble. "We can look out for grazed wrists or elbows."

They fussed a good deal, back at St. Helen's, where Lambsfoot had already spread talk of how Isaac's gentleman had been all but crushed under a shower of stones.

Dr. Lewis, perhaps fearing what Mr. Secretary would have to say if his kinsman never returned home, looked most upset — and, while Skeres regaled the women with his tale of saving his master's life and chasing the murderer, the rector drew Tom into his study.

"Thank the Lord you are safe!" Dr. Lewis exclaimed — hands twitching as though he had to keep himself from brushing mud and mortar from Tom's doublet. "Whoever would...?"

Whoever would try to kill you?

"If this was anything to do with Finch's disappearance, Doctor, then it means I'm on the right path," Tom said — which didn't sound half reassuring.

It was no marvel that Dr. Lewis's voice pitched higher. "*If* it was, Mr. Walsingham? Could it be otherwise?"

Could it, indeed? Tom dropped into the chair that was offered, nursing his heavy arm close to his chest. He had no enemies of his own to want him dead, and even the sharpest creditors liked their debtors well alive. "I could have stumbled into some bit of thievery, or worse. You'll forgive me if I say that what lies north of here doesn't strike me as the pleasantest of neighbourhoods."

Being in no case to take much offence, poor Dr. Lewis shook his head in distress. "I won't deny there are a few unruly souls in the parish. And yet, thievery is one thing — but murder?"

That the rector wasn't wrong; that conspiracy — or the uncovering or it — was a much better reason for killing; that if this was the case, the murderer could only still hover around St. Helen's because he either had buried Finch there, or thought someone there knew more than they should — all of this Tom kept to himself.

Still, Dr. Lewis's imaginings must have followed the same path, and it was with much dismay that he asked, "Shall we all be killed in our beds?"

Much as Tom would have liked to reassure him, there were too many things he didn't know yet. "Might someone here have held back from me, Doctor?" he asked.

There was nothing but bafflement in the rector's tremulous wondering of why would anyone…?

Why, indeed? Because they had something to hide — perhaps something of great danger. Tom said none of this. Still, it was better to have St. Helen's on their collective guard.

"In your place, I'd have that fence repaired," he said. "And the sexton keeps his mastiff in the old cloister at night, doesn't he?"

He stood, and oh, how his cursed shoulder stung! He mustn't have hidden it well, because Dr. Lewis turned most solicitous.

"Before you go, Mr. Walsingham, my housekeeper makes a fine comfrey salve."

Tom's protestations were to no avail, and he found himself ushered to the kitchen, where Goodwife Lovell waited with a jar and a length of linen. Skeres sat in a corner, peering most calf-like through the open window. It was no surprise to see the window looked out on the half-cloister, from where the voices of Grace and her little cousin reached them, together with the canine huffs and scrabbling that revealed the presence of a pleased Sturdy.

"Please, Your Honour…" Goodwife Lovell motioned Tom to a stool, and had him unlace his doublet and shirt to bare a shoulder that was turning a most ugly purple.

The housekeeper clicked her tongue at the sight, took a dollop of salve from the jar, and spread it on Tom's bruises, rubbing with the cloth. It was most unpleasant, what with the housekeeper's heavy, insistent fingers, and the odour of comfrey, so like that of rotting flesh… At length Goodwife Lovell judged her ministrations done, and Tom could dress again, the buttons awkward for his left hand. With many thanks, and a last recommendation to Dr. Lewis, he tore Skeres from his lovelorn contemplation and left — with the impression of having had enough of St. Helen's to last the rest of his life.

Another servant might have warned his master that he had mud and grass bits strewn all over his person, and a tear in his sleeve. Another servant might have tried to redress the worst of the damage. But, Skeres being Skeres, Tom had the aspect of a Southwark beggar by the time a young lad ran up to him by the corner of Leadenhall. Pip Leman, middle son to Mylls's cook, and errand-boy at times, was flushed with the run and his own importance.

"Mr. Thomas," he began — but stopped short at the sight of Tom's state.

"What is it, Pip?" Tom grabbed the boy's arm and suffered more gawping, and a twitch of the nose — at the corpse-like stench of comfrey, surely. "Pip!"

The lad shook himself to attention and produced a note. "'Tis Mr. Berden, Sir. 'E's at the Castle. I was to bring it 'ome — but seeing as you're 'ere…"

F's at the Castle Tavern, Berden wrote, *together with T. — there for the netting, if the warrants can be had.*

Ballard and Tilney… And no, there was no question of the warrants, but — Fates be kind! — could they be there to leave word of the cursed bay horse?

Tom surveyed his mud-stained self, then Skeres, then their surroundings. There, across the street, was the church of St. Peter, and that's where he turned his steps, with the two servants following.

Once inside, he slipped into a side chapel, and began to undo his doublet, hissing as he slipped the sleeve off his bad shoulder. "Don't stand there like a gudgeon, Dolius," he hissed at the lowering Skeres. "Give me yours!"

The Minotaur disapproved. "'Aven't you 'ad enough that they tried to do you in?" he grumbled, and then turned to the baffled Pip. "Tried to murther 'im, they did!"

Oh, for God's sake… "Even if someone did, it was never Ballard himself."

Or Tilney, with his fine clothes, and his fastidious manner. It was hard to imagine Tilney scampering over ruins to drop quarried stones. Tom held out an impatient hand. "I just want to have a look at the Castle."

The very figure of unheeded reason, Skeres took off his russet doublet and thrust it at Tom. "I'm not telling 'Is Honour, if you get yourself murthered," he growled, and crossed his arms to watch as Tom gingerly put the thing on.

It was too big, and reeked of its owner on a hot day — but it would have to do. Tom unclasped the rapier from his girdle and handed it to Skeres, together with his hat. Finally, he snatched the cap from Skeres's head and donned it low on his brow.

"You go with Pip to Tower Hill," he ordered. "Tell Mr. Mylls I'm seeing Berden, and then go where you're supposed to be."

All the way across the street, Tom felt his servant's sullen glare on his back.

Berden's welcome, under the porch of the Royal Exchange next to the Castle Tavern, wasn't much cheerier — and less so when he heard there was no warrant.

"But what are we waiting for, Mr. Thomas?" The spy blew out his cheeks, restless eyes scanning through the crowd of merchants and idlers. "I know 'tis not for the likes of me to question — but…"

It was hard not to feel a touch of sympathy. If he hadn't known about the letter, wouldn't Tom himself be dancing with impatience by now?

He stepped where he could better see the Castle Tavern's door. "Where are they?"

"You're never going in there!" Berden exclaimed. "They've seen you, Master — they'll know —!"

"Is Savage there?"

"Ballard and Tilney."

"And they half-saw me once, briefly, and disguised. If they remember me at all — which I misdoubt — 'twill be as the servant who brought the letter. 'Tis you they mustn't see skulking around."

There was naught Berden could say to that. He backed away, deeper into the porch's crowded shadow, feigning a great lack of interest in the world in general.

"Have a care, though," he said. "They're all on tenterhooks — enough that Ballard sent me on a fool's errand. Ah — there they go!"

Berden backed away further, dragging Tom with him and flattening them both against a shop's window. From there, Tom half-saw two men cross the street, headed Cheapside-ward, deep in conversation. He glimpsed the taller one, in the black hat with the silver buttons, and the trim doublet — and then they were gone.

Only two men... "No Maude?" he asked.

Berden made to answer, and paused. "You know," he said slowly, "I think he wasn't there."

"Doesn't he always follow Ballard?"

"Ay..." A tilt of the head. "He'll be at Babington's house. I'm to meet them there later, with a pair of capons."

On tenterhooks or not, they never lost their appetite, these would-be martyrs. Ah, well. Let them have their supper — it might well be their last, if the letter was done.

Dismissing an unhappy Berden, Tom made his way to the Castle Tavern's stables. They weren't large, and at this time of the day a lonely groom went about his work in the cobbled yard. Wondering whether he was the one Mylls had put there, Tom inquired about Mr. Tilney's bay.

With a good-humoured grin that lacked a few teeth, the man shook his head. "Mr. Tilney, you say? He has two horses here — neither a bay... But see!" The man pointed behind Tom. "Ask him yourself."

Tom's shoulder stung like all the devils when he stiffened, and turned slowly. A man was coming across the inn's back door. A tall, slender man wearing a doublet of apricot-hued silk, with a tall hat, and a pearl in his ear: there — and not strolling Holborn-way with Ballard — stood Charles Tilney.

And bless all cheerful ostlers with hot water! "Mr. Tilney," the fellow called. "This lad here asks about a bay horse of yours. You want it stabled here, Your Honour?"

Tilney crossed the yard, a small frown on his narrow face.

Oh, for his discarded rapier...! Tom kept himself as still and stolid as he knew how. Then recognition flashed in Tilney's eyes, and the frown dissolved into a smile that wanted to be bland and was tight.

"Not yet," he called to the ostler. "Soon enough, though." And then he turned to Tom, clasping his shoulder. A quiver ran through the taut fingers, the corners of the smile, the low-pitched voice.

"Be of good cheer, lad: we'll send you home very soon."

They're all on tenterhooks, Berden had said. And whatever the others' hooks were, it was plain as day that Charles Tilney's patience was wearing thin enough to break.

CHAPTER 13

Tom would have much preferred to slip back to Seething Lane quiet and unnoticed. Skeres, however, had preceded him with his tall tales of murther and whatnot, so that Mrs Jeffreys was waiting with a clean shirt and a doublet, chattering of possets and more comfrey.

It took some doing to talk the housekeeper out of the medicaments, but Tom accepted the clothes and, after washing off the worst of the mud in the scullery yard, he threw the doublet over his arm and repaired to his writing room with a manchet, a piece of cheese, and a cup of ale. As compensation for the lack of a posset, Mrs Jeffreys had spread two spoonfuls of honey on the bread. Honey on a manchet: Frances's all-consoling remedy when she was a child.

But if he'd thought to sit a while in blessed solitude, to eat and think his thoughts, Tom was disappointed. No sooner had he lowered himself in his chair — an uncomfortable exercise for his battered shoulder — than there was a knock at the door, and Mylls and Phelippes filed in.

Mylls was in a scolding mood, and it was a rather testy exchange, until Tom told of his brush with Tilney. *Very soon...* Oh, how this mellowed the secretary, if only for a moment! For it meant they could set aside at least one of their worries, and they'd soon have the blessed letter.

"Unless..." Mylls was quick to darken again. "Unless he was looking to lead you astray, and they know you for what you are, and the letter is at Chartley already."

Lead him astray? Tom would have scoffed at the notion — but for one nagging uneasiness.

"Maude wasn't there," he said. "He never leaves Ballard's side, but he wasn't there."

Phelippes hunched forward. "Sent to Chartley?"

This Tom hadn't considered. It should have occurred to him, surely? "Or else sent on a fool's errand. Like Berden was."

Hardly a more sanguine prospect.

There was a spell of silence while each man contemplated chances, until Mylls sighed.

"Let's pray the letter wasn't sent," he said, as sternly as though this were all Tom's fault. "But Mr. Secretary will have to be told."

And he marched away, leaving behind a less than happy Phelippes.

Tom sat back, rubbing his shoulder. "I'll ride to Barn Elms first thing tomorrow. Whatever Tilney meant, there's the matter of the hand."

"You reckon 'tis Finch, then?"

Tom rehearsed the morning's findings in his sluggish mind. "Ambrose Lopes says 'tis from a corpse dead these three or four days. A body, it would seem, that wasn't buried in any proper place." He shook his head to stave off the objection he himself would have raised. "And I know, I know: none of this makes a sound tie to Finch — and yet, the pox scars are much like his." And one thing was certain: whatever Goodwife Lovell thought, none of this looked like retribution for petty theft.

Phelippes hummed. "And there's also that someone tried to kill you, or at least to scare you away."

Which in turn could have been for all sorts of different reasons. Oh, Jove, it was all so thin! A groan escaped Tom. "Ah, well — I'm for Barn Elms, tomorrow. Let Sir Francis make of it what he will."

"Not first thing, though," Phelippes said. "Unless you don't mind a long wait. His Honour wrote from Court this afternoon that he'll be sitting in Council all morning. Will they let you see him, do you think?"

No, they wouldn't — unless he brought very urgent tidings. Tom had memories of pacing to and fro in the Messengers' Antechamber, wondering if what he carried warranted an interruption of the Privy Council's work — and deciding that little in this world did.

"I'll leave later in the morning, then — and before that, I'll try to learn where all were who could have done mischief to Finch," he said. And perhaps a few more hours would let his shoulder settle before he rode.

And trust Phelippes to notice. "You rest now, Mr. Thomas," he said. "I'll have you called if there's need."

"Oh — and Phelippes, see if you can find where Maude is, will you? I don't know what I'd like less: that he's off to Chartley, or here and suspected."

The cypherer gave a grim nod. "Let's pray we haven't run out of time," he said — and was gone.

Pray, indeed — but Tom didn't. He sat alone, listening to the blackbirds' evening warble in the garden, eating left-handed, and turning this way and that all the pieces in his mind. He had always liked to think of them as bits of coloured glass — but they were as flimsy, this time, as shreds of gauze, refusing to keep a shape. And the ache in his shoulder, he found, was no help in thinking. Oh, what a soft, peevish fellow he'd become! Sir Francis was ever in pain — and did he let that stop him? Still, since Phelippes had promised to call if need be, perhaps…

Tom went to peer into the windowless passage. Nobody was there. Folding his doublet into a makeshift pillow, he lay down on the nearest bench. Only a little while, he told himself — and he fell asleep to dream of Goodwife Lovell, with her reddened eyes, dropping stones from the ruins of St. Mary Axe onto her brother, who huddled deep in a black chasm underneath.

Rob Poley, it seemed, had asked to see Mr. Walsingham and him alone — and, in Phelippes's considered opinion, Mr. Walsingham had better see him before Mr. Mylls either suffered a fit or throttled the man. All of this was said very glumly.

Oh, for God's sake! Couldn't Mylls and Poley — whom nobody had tried to kill that day — sort their megrims between them?

Tom hauled himself off his bench, and awkwardly donned his doublet. Oh, but his shoulder had grown stiff! The uncharitable thought crossed his mind that here was Mylls, making him pay for the other night.

"There — there he is!" was Mylls's testy salutation when Tom entered the scriveners' room — and Poley, who had been standing taut as a strung bow, spun on his heel. Even without candles, the twilight was still clear enough to see how turmoiled he was.

"So let Mr. Thomas hear you!" Mylls barked. "See how he likes your vagaries!" And with that he stomped off to his room in a fine taking.

"Mr. Mylls —" Tom called after him, stopping short when the door slammed shut after the enraged secretary.

"What have you done to him, Rob?"

Poley had been busy all the while, remaking his smiling mask, but the smile was a tad brittle. "He won't listen to me!"

"And I will," Tom said a little wearily, with dinner at the Pewter Pot in mind.

"You sent me to Barn Elms. And as like as not you know what His Honour told me."

Tom did indeed, from Sir Francis's letter — but he said nothing and waited.

"Push the boy, he said. Have him open himself, for there's a great deal more to the matter — and unless he's wholly honest..." Poley looked up. "Well, now the boy's ready to be. All he wants is to see Mr. Secretary, and to put himself at His Honour's mercy."

The scriveners' tables were all empty, now. Tom leant against the nearest one, covering a wince when he crossed his arms. "And what loosened his tongue like this?" he asked.

"What is it that loosens tongues? He's out of his wits with fright. He spoke with Ballard yesterday — and after that he was white as a sheet. That supper at the Rose... Ballard was there, and Savage, and the others. Master Anthony paid for it all, fed us all like he was fattening a flock of geese — and never touched a crust himself. He drank, though, and trembled whenever Ballard turned an eye on him."

"Ballard, yes." *Poley was there, then went away*, Gifford had said. Tom pitched his question to the mildest, coldest curiosity. "Two days you've known Ballard is back in London, and it never crossed your mind to send word?"

Back on guard, Poley showed nothing but the most innocent surprise. "You'd plenty of folks to tell you that. You know my orders. What was I to send word for, until I'd spoken to the boy?"

All of it likely, all of it plain-headed. Had it not been for *the boy*... "And now you have."

"Last night he drank more than was seemly. When the others went their ways, he was tippled. Sack and fear on an empty belly — 'tis enough to undo an ox, never mind Master Anthony! So I brought him to my lodgings, dragged him there half weeping, and put him to bed." Poley shook his head. "A long night, it was — and then all day he wouldn't move from my side. We walked, and spoke, and I talked myself hoarse, and he got sick twice, and I thought he'd have a fit — but the long and short of it is, he wants to see His Honour."

"Did he say what it is they're plotting?"

"He'll tell His Honour."

"But not you?"

"He wanted to — but I stopped him."

Stopped him! Tom stared in disbelief. "Now, let me understand, Rob. Chances are, Ballard is ready to make his move. Ballard's friend tries to unburden his guilty bosom — and you stop him?"

"Ay, ay — I did!" A brisk wave of the hand. "I said he must tell His Honour and none else, and he must do it at once, so the Queen will be merciful —"

Whatever Poley had expected, it must not have been Tom's burst of unamused laughter. "And this is what gave Mr. Mylls the vapours."

"You know what the boy did when I refused to hear more? He fell on my neck sobbing and called me his angel. Now he'll jump into the river if I say so!"

"But you didn't say so. On the contrary, you dried his tears, and promised … what? To gallop off to Mr. Secretary, and secure an audience?"

But he hadn't, had he? He could have hired a horse, and ridden off to Barn Elms. Instead he'd come to share his tale, to ask for a permission he could have done without. Was he seeking support for his notion? Or buying more time for Babington, while he played the zealous go-between?

Well, then — it was a game two could play.

"Very well," Tom said. "I'm for Barn Elms myself tomorrow. We ride together. If Ballard's about to act…"

There was that small smile again, the same Tom had seen at the Pewter Pot — the one that said, *fair enough*.

"The boy says they're not ready yet," Poley said.

Poley's lie, or Babington's, or Ballard's? Or it could be true — but then… "If they're not, what has him in terror?"

Poley opened his mouth and closed it — and rubbed his fingertips along the table edge in slow consideration. When he spoke, Tom was sure it wasn't what he'd been going to say. "Much as he likes to fancy himself a hero and a martyr, the boy's half dead with fear."

Fear of Ballard's murderous plans, of what that would mean for all who were embroiled in it, of what Ballard would do to one who stepped off the path. And at the same time, he was afraid of the Queen's retribution. All of which begged another question: what of the letter for the Queen of Scots? A shame the man best placed to find out couldn't be trusted with the question.

"And now he thinks you've gone to Mr. Secretary. I wish…" Tom huffed in feigned irritation. "What is he doing, Rob? When he's not throwing costly suppers or sobbing on your shoulder, what *does* Babington do?"

A foolish question by all reckonings, and Poley was too old a fox.

"He prays," was all he said. "Prays to the Lord for courage to be a martyr, and for the Queen's mercy in the same breath."

On this, the man was dismissed to find himself a pallet upstairs, and to be ready to ride late next morning.

When the door had closed behind Poley's back, Tom let himself slump against the table and kneaded his aching shoulder. The bitter jest was: would Babington still write his cursed letter now he was throwing himself on Sir Francis's mercy?

Tartarus take Poley, and Babington, and all! What Sir Francis would have to say to this bore no thinking.

CHAPTER 14

2nd of August

Physicians and midwives alike will sing the praises of poppy to ease sleep. Tom found, on waking early and much refreshed, that there was much to be said for good plain fatigue, in this respect. In spite of his many worries and his painful shoulder, he'd slept like a lamb through the night.

And if he awoke to find his whole arm black and purple, and so stiff that dressing was a chore, well, it would pass.

Neither poppy nor rest — nor, for that matter, time — would ever resolve a threat to the Queen, though, nor the matter of a man's death. This was why Tom set out to find Alderman Casey and inquire where he'd been the previous morning.

Or he would have set out, but he hadn't crossed the stables' threshold when Toby Chandler came running after him.

"Rouse Casey's here," the boy announced. "He says the deacon asks for Mr. Mylls."

Gifford! What did he want now? "Then send Rouse to Mr. Mylls."

"Mr. Mylls isn't at Tower Hill, Master," Toby said, trotting at Tom's elbow. "Rouse went there first."

"Then Mr. Phelippes?"

"He hasn't arrived yet."

Which was odd enough, Phelippes being the very pinnacle of timeliness, as a rule.

Ah, well. Tom went back to the house, to find Casey waiting in the hall, shifting his weight from foot to foot in a disquieted manner that boded ill.

"Is it Savage?" Tom asked.

Young Casey shook his head. "He won't say. He wants Mr. Mylls — but —"

"What of your master?"

Another shake of the red head. "Mr. Phelippes won't do. He wants Mr. Mylls."

And why not the Lord Chamberlain, while he was at it? "Does he? Then, he can go to Tower Hill and wait."

"He says it can't wait." Casey squirmed, his hands fisted in his cuffs. "And he won't come here. He's waiting at Paul's Walk. I don't know what it is, but he's half out of his wits."

And what if Savage was keeping his oath? "Well then, he'll content himself with me. You come along, Rouse."

And must the lad blink and gape, and scramble after Tom like one torn from his sleep?

Down to the river and the Water Gate was a quick walk. Tom hailed a wherry to carry them to the bridge. Even though they had to alight there, walk around the bridge and find another waterman to row them to Paul's Wharf, going by water was faster. Soon enough, Tom and a glumly quiet Casey were climbing up Bennet's Hill and entering old St. Paul.

After the rush and the early sun, the air was chilly inside, and felt chillier for the smell of damp stone. The fashionable time was still hours to come, so that, in the absence of gentlemen and those aspiring to be seen as such, the great nave was all but empty. Booksellers and stationers were setting up their stalls at the foot of the mighty pillars, and the first gossip-mongers strolled about in twos and threes, squinting against the morning light that cut in through the east windows. The noise would grow into a many-voiced clamour later; for now, it was sparse enough that the odd louder call reverberated under the soaring vaulted roof.

Paul's Walk — London's marketplace for books, notions and rumours, no matter how hard Crown, Council, and City tried to cleanse the temple. Not the most discreet of meeting places, in truth.

"There!" Casey pointed to a narrow figure in tawny velvet, hunched at a stall a little way down the nave, fingering a book.

"Wait here," Tom ordered. "Be ready to follow when he leaves."

Twice Gifford peered over his shoulder, and still didn't sight Tom until he was at his side. Then he startled, dropping the book.

Tom picked it up: a cheap quarto commentary of the Letters of Saint Paul. "Old habits die hard, Deacon?"

Gifford stiffened, face hardening in a mask that perhaps wanted to be of loathing — but came across as peevish. "What are you doing here?"

"Mr. Mylls wasn't there to obey your summons."

It seemed at first that Gifford would argue — but Phelippes had been right. It was stark fear that glittered in the black eyes as, grasping Tom's sleeve, he pushed him past the stall, into the grey quiet of the aisle.

Another of these play-like round glances, and then: "I must leave London."

Now, this was unexpected — although perhaps it shouldn't have been. But of all the witless things… "No."

"But I must! Don't you see?"

"I can't say that I do," Tom said. "Unless Savage is growing to misdoubt you?"

Gifford looked away — most likely reckoning what would be worse: to own himself suspected, or to remain in London. "I must be gone before he does. That would endanger Mr. Secretary's work —"

"Nothing would be more suspicious than having you disappear of a sudden."

"I'd give good reason to Savage, and he'll believe it, for he trusts me. He counts me as his friend."

It was almost too easy. "God pity him — but then, why should you fear he'll suspect you?"

Nobody liked being caught. Gifford gritted his teeth. "'Tis easy for you to mock — but you remember Savage from Rheims."

Oh, yes. Blunt, unsubtle, square-minded... "I thought you had him under your thumb?"

And see how Gifford gaped, wrong-footed into silence. It was a very short silence, though, and followed by enough childish arrogance to quash any twinge of pity Tom might have felt.

"This is useless," the man scoffed. "I'll speak to Mr. Secretary."

Mr. Secretary who happened to be, quite conveniently, out of London. "We'll advise him that you seek audience —"

"You must think me a fool! I'll write to Mr. Secretary myself. I'll appeal to him directly, and tell him how I'm treated by his men!"

Jove — but one could have sympathy for the exiles in Rome, kicking this petty churl out of their Seminary. "I'm for Barn Elms myself, later: I'll carry your letter. Or, if you'd rather, go to Tower Hill and have Mr. Mylls dispatch it — when he's back."

Gilbert Gifford stood there, taut and angry, weighing things in his mind — and, for once, held Tom's gaze. "I want your word," he ground out in the end. "Your word that you'll deliver my letter to Mr. Secretary himself."

"You have it."

And instead of being appeased, Gifford exclaimed, "Because you think Mr. Secretary will never grant leave!"

Oh, Lord give charity — for Tom was losing what little he had. Besides, their hissed conversation in the shadows was drawing curiosity. Heads turned and eyes peeked around a pillar. Slipping his arm under Gifford's, Tom drew him back towards the nave and the stalls.

"Write what you want to write," he said, "and I'll be gone."

Choosing a bookseller with a rather fine display of Latin poetry and histories — though not one of his habitual haunts — he asked the apprentice for paper, pen and ink.

At his shoulder, Gifford worked his jaw, sulking as the youth provided a couple of sheets, a quill, and a small inkpot. "What's the use, if I won't be allowed to leave?"

"Then don't write. It's all the same to me. Good day —"

"Wait!"

Before Tom could move a single step, Gifford leapt to grab paper and quill. So unsteady were his hands, that he would have knocked the inkpot on its head, if Tom hadn't snatched it out of harm's way.

Taking it back, the deacon bent to his task.

There wasn't much to do in the meantime, but to inspect the seller's wares — keeping a discreet watch.

"You know, Gifford," Tom murmured, when the man crumpled the first sheet of paper and grabbed the second. "One is brought to wonder what makes you so skittish, of a sudden."

Gifford snorted. "You wonder! You force me to risk my life and wonder?"

Oh, for God's sake! "If you must be a fool, be a quiet one!" Tom ordered.

"A fool —"

"You put your own life at stake when you ran off to Rome. And, in fair truth, it didn't make you much safer when you crossed back to the right side of the game."

Fates send nobody was watching them too closely, because Gifford all but sobbed. "Your uncle forced me!"

"Cousin," Tom corrected — more out of habit than anything. "Sir Francis is my father's cousin — but you should blame yourself, rather than him, and make your peace with the fact that we all risk our lives every day, in this game."

"Ay — and see what happened —" Gifford bit off the rest, and leant lower over his letter.

Tom left him to it for a heartbeat and picked up a nice octavo print of Sallust's *Bellum Catilinae*, before leaning against the stall as if to observe the man's writing over his shoulder.

"What happened to whom?" he asked under his breath. "To Isaac Finch?"

"Casey says he's been missing for days," said Gifford, looking up sharply. "You never think…?"

Tom held the man's stare. "Oh, I just wonder. For one thing, I wonder if you don't know Finch better than you say. Now, write."

While Gifford wrote, Tom leafed through the book — not that he should buy it. He'd sworn off buying books, which was less sad than one might think, with Sir Francis's library at his disposal. His mind wasn't on Sallust, though. Half of it was deciding Catiline, greedy for power and money, was not a good fit for Ballard after all, while the other half considered the deacon and Finch. Would a murderer seek Sir Francis's permission instead of just running? Perhaps, if he thought he could stave off suspicion…

You let your dislike of the man sway you, Mylls had chided — and perhaps he wasn't wrong, for the notion of Gifford as the culprit sat almost too easily on Tom's mind.

"It must be a great ease and comfort."

Tom blinked, and there Gifford stood, holding the folded letter, with a bitter twist to his mouth.

"What must be?"

"To have the trust of all." He shook his head. "Did you like Finch, Mr. Walsingham? Not a whit, I'll swear — but who'll even wonder if you killed him?"

To think Tom had been nursing qualms about this bad-minded ass! "To my credit, I've never betrayed anyone," he said.

Gilbert Gifford laughed — a sour, bleak little laugh. "Followed your conscience or your fear into what someone else will call betrayal — that's what you've never done. Although perhaps they'd think differently, back in Rheims."

And, pushing his letter between the pages of the Sallust, Gifford disappeared into the thickening crowd of book-buyers and gossip-mongers, leaving Tom speechless, angry, and with a sour taste in his mouth.

They left for Barn Elms late in the morning, Tom and Poley — and it wasn't long before Tom wished he'd thought to go by river. It was slower than a good horse — but, Jupiter above, how each cantering step shook his poor shoulder!

Soft, Tom Walsingham — that's what you are! he told himself again and again, and forged on. Once they left the marshy grounds just south of London, it was pleasant going, with the

Thames glittering on one side and the fields glowing in their harvest glory. There were harvesters at work, children who ran and called, shrill as the swallows above in the enamel sky, and there were linens strewn to dry on greens and hedges. There was a sweet breeze blowing from the river, and even the road, for once, was alive but not crowded, and neither dusty nor muddy. Ay, pleasant, cheerful going — for those who weren't trying to muster in their minds an array of doubtful facts, conjectures and half-findings for the perusal of Sir Francis Walsingham.

Tom slowed his mount's pace to wait while an empty cart turned off the road, into the path between two fields. A man about Tom's age drove it, while a boy and a girl of twelve or so walked at the one ox's head, guiding the huge beast ahead, and calling it their clever darling. At one point the cart lumbered, and the boy capered out of the way, nimble as a cat. The man and the girl laughed.

Before even a thought of simpler and easier lives could take shape in his head, Tom kneed his horse ahead, pushing past on the road's shoulder.

All the time Rob Poley followed in hunch-shouldered silence. He must have felt Tom's glance, though, for he looked back, one brow raised not so much in question as in anticipation of one.

And indeed Tom had a question — one he'd meant to ask, and half-forgotten, and now it swam to the surface like a carp in a pond. "You were with Babington yester-morning, weren't you, Rob?"

Poley squinted for a heartbeat. "Yester-morning? Ay."

"All morning?"

And let no one ever call Robert Poley a fool — for his face went blank. That he knew was no great surprise, considering the noise Skeres had raised in Seething Lane. Another might have protested, explained, even denied ever going near St. Helen's. Poley only brought his attention back to the road.

"I told you, Mr. Thomas: all day, the boy wouldn't move from my side," he said, and pointed to the treed lane on the right, the one that led to Barn Elms.

Sir Francis rose to take the packet, with a stiff briskness that spoke of back pains ignored.

Even as he broke the seal, he spared a searching glance for his young kinsman.

"Phelippes writes you had a misadventure, Thomas?" he asked. "Frances was much distressed to hear it."

Tom should have thanked him, and made little of his injury — but he was surprised into a smile. "She's still here? I thought her on her way to Flushing."

Sir Francis hummed as he sorted through his letters. "Spending a few last days with us and the child, before she leaves. You can reassure her of your health before you ride back." He lowered himself into his chair, selected a letter, and opened it. He read a few lines, before glancing up and waving a little impatiently. "Do sit, Thomas. You're never playing courier to amuse yourself, surely. Is it this matter of the hand?"

"In part, Sir, yes."

Tom sat and began his tale, as Sir Francis listened, close-faced. There was a brief silence when Tom was finished.

"It is your conviction that the hand belongs to Finch?" Mr. Secretary asked.

Tom had had a day, a night, and a ride from London to consider this thoroughly. "There is no way to be certain," he said. "But from what Ambrose Lopes says, and from my own

193

observation, I must assume Isaac Finch died when he went missing or soon after."

Finch would have been well content to see how Sir Francis's shoulders bowed under the near-certainty of his death.

"You did well to have young Lopes. I don't suppose he could tell if there were marks of torture?"

"Perhaps when he sees the whole body…"

"And, unless your mishap was mere chance, the body may well be in the whereabouts of your church. Are the wardsmen searching for it?"

It struck Tom of a sudden that he didn't know. "I reckon—"

"You must make sure." It was not often Sir Francis Walsingham showed his impatience more openly than in a hardening of the voice. That he drummed his fingertips on the table was an alarming sign.

"I think…" Tom cleared his throat. "If the body is at St. Helen's, we may hope Finch wasn't tortured. They wouldn't torture him there, and they wouldn't bring back the body after torturing him."

Sir Francis nodded. "More than once I told your father he should have sent you to the bar. Still, your logic remains hypothetical."

"Until we find the body, yes." Tom sighed. "I'll visit Constable Hallet."

"Good." Sir Francis leant forward, steepling his fingers. "I take it you have no news of the letter?"

"No, Sir — and yes."

Tom had not been looking forward to relating his encounter with Charles Tilney at the Castle Tavern; it was little wonder when Sir Francis frowned on hearing of it.

"It was a great risk to take, Thomas — but if Tilney promised to have the letter ready..."

But had he? Under his cousin's searching gaze, Tom found himself less certain than he would have liked. Tilney's taut manner, the quivering clasp... *We'll send you home very soon.* It had sounded like a promise — why, it had been — but a promise of what?

"*Did* he promise it?"

Oh, to have just one square answer for Sir Francis! But Tilney would never openly discuss rebellion before a strange ostler? Or would he?

"I don't know what else he might have been promising," was all he could say — and it sounded damnably lame to his own ears. Had he been standing, Tom would have shifted his weight. He kept himself from squirming in the chair — but not well enough that Sir Francis wouldn't notice.

"What else, Thomas?" he asked, with such weariness that Tom wished he didn't have Maude's absence to recount.

"Phelippes found that he was at supper afterward, so he didn't ride to Chartley. But if he aroused Ballard's suspicions..." Then, after being little use when he was trusted, Bernard Maude could do great damage when the trust was lost.

There was another of those long, tired sighs, and Sir Francis lowered his eyes to the letters on his table. "'Tis a most bitter jest: we know so much of this conspiracy, and yet so little —" He stopped short, picking up one of the letters, addressed in an unfamiliar hand. "What is this?"

Oh, yes — that one. "Gilbert Gifford. A supplication that he may leave London, I believe." Tom couldn't help himself. "And, likely, railings against myself."

Was it a flash of amusement in the dark eyes? "I fear he'll have more to rail against, for he may *not* leave London now. You can tell him — or, if you think it will carry more weight, I'll write." Sir Francis put Gifford's letter aside. "Is there anything else?"

There is that I've been doubting you, losing patience with your worries. "I've brought Poley with me, Sir. He comes with a most urgent request from Anthony Babington."

"Does he now?" A weary shake of the head.

"It seems that Babington is ready to speak," Tom ventured. "Of course, Poley doesn't know all that's at stake."

"No, no — he doesn't." Sir Francis straightened his back. "Fetch the fellow, will you, Thomas? And be so kind as to stay: you know him better than I do."

Four-and-twenty, seven years in the Service, and Mr. Secretary's own pupil, and still Tom hadn't the knack of hiding his pride at such a mark of trust and confidence. He bowed and hastened to obey, and Fates send Sir Francis hadn't caught too much of it.

He went to stand behind his cousin's chair as Poley bowed himself in and stated his errand. When there was no reaction from Sir Francis, Poley went ahead with his tale, as though he'd been asked.

"'Tis a wonder how fear works, Your Honour!" he exclaimed for a conclusion. "Now Master Babington is all zeal. Devoted to the public service — that's what he wanted me to say."

This time, Sir Francis tilted his head. "Is it?"

"Your Honour must not think…" Poley stepped closer to the table. "Father Ballard takes great pains in marking Master Babington as the leader of this treason — but he's not! Being a young fool, he's let Ballard drag him…"

"And now he won't be dragged anymore?"

"He's ready to drag back."

"May I see what he writes?" Sir Francis held out a hand for a letter that, Tom was sure, he knew didn't exist.

Not that Poley ever missed a beat. "He doesn't dare to write, Your Honour. He wants me to tell you this, as proof of his good faith: Ballard's out to start a rebellion. The Spanish Ambassador in Paris is behind Ballard's back, and also Paget, the chief agent of the Scots Queen."

All of which Sir Francis knew only too well. "I see," he said — and one who didn't know better would have thought his interest caught. "Still, he will have to put it all in writing, if he wants to serve Her Highness. You must tell him this most particularly."

Poley grimaced and shook his head, more earnest than Tom had ever seen him. "'Tis that... I've told Mr. Thomas: the boy's half mad with fear that Ballard will discover him. He begs to meet Your Honour, and then he'll tell all he knows."

There was a little silence, then Sir Francis reached out to take one of the quills carefully lined up at his side. "Very well," he said — and then he dropped the quill back in its place. "But I suppose, if he's so frightened, he won't want a letter from me. You will thank him on my behalf, Poley. You will tell him I'll be glad to see him here at Barn Elms."

Never in the years he'd known Poley had Tom wished so much that he knew what went on in the fellow's head. Could it be true, unforged relief that lit his face?

"Tomorrow, Your Honour?" he asked.

"The day after, I believe. When would that be, Thomas?"

"The fourth, Sir."

"Yes, no earlier than the fourth, for I'm to travel back to Richmond later today, and attend Her Highness." Sir Francis held up a forefinger. "But, Poley, meanwhile he must write down all he knows of the conspiracy. All he knows."

Poley shifted his weight. "Your Honour —"

"Tell him it will be difficult to accept his good faith unless he consents to put what he knows in writing."

For once, there was no smile on Rob Poley's face, no bland amiability. "Your Honour, Mr. Thomas saw them all: ask him. Ask him if the boy has cause to fear Ballard."

Tom stepped forward. In fair truth, he'd seen Babington just the once, and the man hadn't seemed to struggle in the throes of terror. Then again, there was no question that Ballard was dangerous.

"Babington could write at Poley's lodgings, Sir," Tom suggested. "And leave the papers there for safety. It will be but a day or two."

Of course, Sir Francis understood what was not said.

"Very good," he said. "Surely this will satisfy Mr. Babington, Poley?"

It was doubtful that Poley agreed — but there was no mistaking the finality of Mr. Secretary's pronouncement — or the dismissal it contained.

Knowing better than to pretend or to insist, Poley bowed low. "I'll ride back to London then, Your Honour," he said — and the guarded smile was back, if tighter.

Sir Francis watched him go and sat there for a few heartbeats, fingers drumming slowly.

"Can we trust him, Thomas?" he asked at length. "He hasn't been dishonest so far — and yet I'm loathe to open myself to him. I hadn't expected to hear him defend Babington so."

Unlike others in the Service, Tom didn't quite mistrust Rob Poley — and still wouldn't have thought the man capable of being loyal.

"I'm not sure he tells us all he knows, and at times he sounds so eager to save Babington."

"Unless it is himself that he's eager to save." Sir Francis twisted stiffly in his seat. "Could he be embroiled in this matter of Finch?"

"Yes — if Finch had caught him playing us false."

"But there's no telling..." Sir Francis hunched forward. "You know Mylls isn't quite convinced that Finch's disappearance has to do with Ballard and his cronies?"

"He's told me so, yes. More than once — but —"

"He writes that you have other suspects, people with more mundane reasons for wanting Finch dead. An alderman among them, I believe?"

Oh, pinch Mylls for a meddling coxcomb! "A deputy alderman, yes — but even he might be tied to the conspiracy. And even admitting that Mr. Mylls *could* be right, can we rule out the chance he's wrong, and the secrets at Chartley are uncovered? I doubt —"

"You doubt!" Sir Francis hit his palm on the table. "Well, I doubt too, Thomas. I doubt, and you don't know with what impatience I read each of your letters, always hoping to find that you've unravelled this devilish tangle — and all you ever have are questions, and suspicions, and more doubts!" Half choking on the last word, Mr. Secretary fell silent, breath harsh, shoulders hunched.

Tom stared, aghast. Never in his life had he seen Sir Francis lose his temper or swear. He raked his mind for an answer, and found it empty.

And then, thank Fates, someone knocked on the door.

Sir Francis had to clear his throat before he called to come in — and in walked Frances, carrying a sealed letter — a beam of sunlight in a kirtle of ochre silk.

"Your pardon, Father." She stopped short on the threshold, a frown creasing her white brow, her dark grey eyes going from her father to her cousin and back again. "A messenger came from Court. I thought you'd want to see it at once." She brought the letter to her father, and her frown deepened when Sir Francis's hand trembled a little as he took it from her.

"Tom, dear..." There was a question in Frances's gaze, one he didn't know how to answer.

Before he could, Sir Francis thrust the letter on the table, and they both startled.

With the slow, careful breath of one mastering himself, Mr. Secretary looked at his daughter and cousin, and whatever he saw made him check himself. "Don't worry yourselves, children. I'm summoned back at Court."

It was Frances's turn to flare in irritation. "Oh, Father! You just came from there!"

She sounded so much like her mother that Tom had to hide a smile, and Sir Francis sounded very mild as he answered, "It seems Her Highness needs me, my dear."

"Indeed, and because she does, she could allow you some consideration. Couldn't she, Tom?"

Sir Francis tutted. "Don't push your cousin to speak traitorously, my dear," he said. "If you would have one of those draughts of Dr. Lopes's sent in to me, though, it would be most kind." He seemed almost rueful when he turned to Tom. "And, Thomas, would you see to it that my boat is readied? I'll have letters and instructions for you, when you ride back later."

It was as polite a dismissal as one could wish for — and Tom and Frances hastened to obey.

Tom watched Frances as, at the kitchen door, she gave old Gawton instructions for her father's draught. Gawton knew all there was to know about the draught, Tom suspected, but Frances fussed a little — thinking perhaps it would be a long time before she could fuss over her father again.

She looked very grown, at nineteen: Lady Sidney these past two years, mother to a babe — and soon going to join her husband. Ay, she looked grown — and sad.

Still, once Gawton had bowed himself away, she found a smile for Tom, and took his arm.

"May I come with you?"

"Must my Lady Poppet ask?"

The way she lit up at the old childhood name lifted Tom's heart after Sir Francis's fulminations.

That Frances had heard at least some of it was plain: she kept peeking aslant at him as they walked together out of the herb garden, and along the path down to the river.

"You must not take it ill, Tom," she said at length, pressing his arm. "Father isn't well. I think he feels it all slipping from his grasp."

She stopped when she caught sight of the nurse strolling under the plum trees in the orchard, carrying the white bundle that was little Bess. Frances waved, and the nurse made the child raise a tiny red hand in greeting.

The hem of Frances's skirts gathered bits of grass as she resumed her walk. "My poor little Bess," she sighed. "I pray I can give her a brother soon. I've never felt so much the weight of being just a daughter."

Grace Finch's unhappiness echoed in Tom's mind. *Am I a son, that Father should tell me?* But Frances, surely…

"Your father loves you very much."

"He's so kind to me, and always has been — 'tis just that I'm not a son." She shook her head. "The last time I was at Court, I saw him watching the Cecils — my Lord Burleigh and that awful Robert —"

Tom huffed. "Robert Cecil — slippery as a lamprey!"

That drew a little smile out of Frances, but it was gone at once. "A lamprey who'll continue his father's work, while Father... He has no heir, Tom. I'm useless."

It was all Tom could do not to take her in his arms. "Never, Poppet! There will be Bessie's brothers — and meanwhile, he has your husband."

He cursed himself over the bitterness he'd let creep into his words — but he shouldn't have worried. Frances's little sob of a laugh was more bitter by far.

"My husband is too high-minded, I'll have you know, for a spymaster. He's not made to compromise his conscience." Repeating her father's words.

So Sidney had faults after all. Tom was ashamed of himself, and all the more because Frances watched him, full of understanding and unhappiness.

"I'd better see to that boat," he murmured.

When he made to go she caught his hand, and he stopped under the shade of the willows that swam in the breeze. The dappled sunlight played on her dark hair as she reached out to touch his cheek.

"Dear, dear Tom — I so wish it could have been you." She turned away, her voice breaking.

Tom held her slight, cold fingers more tightly. He'd never seen Frances weep, not even as a child. When he turned her around, her eyes glistened.

"You would have loved me, wouldn't you, Tom?" she whispered. "Loved me for myself, not just as Father's token?"

Damn Philip Sidney for hurting her! It burnt through him in one great gust of flame — anger first, sharp and brief, and then... Then he was lost.

Fool that he was, that he'd always been, never knowing his heart, and a worse fool now — for she was another man's wife, besides being Sir Francis's own daughter.

He never knew how he came to be holding her so tightly, the soft warmth of her against him, her scent of summer roses in his nostrils. And there was no *would have*. Past words, past thought, he leant over her upturned face, and kissed her.

She was a streak of light in his arms, a quiver of flame under his lips — until her fingers brushed his cheek, and she pushed him gently away.

He reached breathlessly for her, like one drowning, and she caught his hands.

"They call..." There was something in her gaze that Tom's swirling mind could not read. She stood on tiptoe to touch her lips to his. "Dear, dear love," she said, softer than the river breeze, and then, steadying herself: "I'll have Coley ready the boat."

With that she ran away, holding her skirts — a gleam of fleeing summer among the willows.

It was a dazed Tom who took a shuddering breath and stepped out of the shadows, blinking in the sun. He saw two men up by the herb garden's wall. Davies stood there, pointing; the other hurried down the path. It was Rouse Casey.

"Mr. Thomas!" he called from afar, waving as though Tom could have missed his approach. He almost broke into a run, and seemed ready to shout his tidings to the four winds.

Tom hastened to meet him, his summer warmth dissolving with each step. What now?

Casey skidded to a halt, drenched in sweat and twitching. "I've brought a letter from Mr. Phelippes," he panted. "His Honour wants to see you at once."

Tom's stomach clenched, and he ran up the path. Had they waited too long? Had Ballard and his men taken flight?

CHAPTER 15

We are all cozened in waiting for Babington's answer, Phelippes wrote. *He appointed today to deliver it, but rode out of town instead. Two things are to be conceived — either he has run away or else he has resolved to carry the answer himself to Lichfield, whence he thinks the letter came.*

All lost — all gone to ruin.

Mr. Secretary turned a questioning gaze on Rouse Casey.

"Ay, please, Your Honour..." The lad cleared his throat, squeezing his cap. "There was the bay horse brought to the Castle Tavern. 'Twas yesterday late, but we only found out this morning. And seeing as Mr. Thomas had ridden away, Mr. Phelippes sent me to Holborn, so as I'd fetch the letter." He swallowed. "The house was all shut up, and not a soul answering. Then a servant came out to say his master's out of town."

"But never for good, surely? Not if he left his servants?" Tom asked. "And where to?"

Casey shook his head, and couldn't have looked more forlorn if it had been his fault. "The man didn't know," he said.

"Not even when his master left?"

"Not much after cockcrow, he said. With nothing but his horse and a cloak-bag."

Right at that moment there was a knock, and Davies appeared — huge enough to fill the doorway, with a touch of glumness on his wooden countenance.

"Poley's been gone for nearly an hour, Master," he announced. "Gone back to London."

Of course. Of course — and under Mr. Secretary's own orders, no less.

Sir Francis sat back, exhaling through his nose.

"You'll ride back yourself, Casey. Davies will see to it that you have a fast horse. Tell Mr. Phelippes to find Poley — for he'll be in London by the time you arrive."

He waited until the two servants were gone before he murmured, "Unless, of course, Poley has gone to join Babington, wherever he fled to."

And whether he had or not... "What of Father Ballard, Sir?" Tom asked. "Because if Babington has run alone, it is one thing — but..."

Sir Francis motioned to the letter in Tom's hands. "Ballard was still in London yesterday. Phelippes was waiting to make certain when he wrote."

So Berden would be at Seething Lane by now, watching Phelippes with his pup-hound eyes as he gave his tidings: Ballard was in London, Ballard was gone... Either way, it ceased to matter whether the crows had had their suspicions from Finch or not.

"Of Finch we —" Tom stopped short. Petty, that was how it would sound after the earlier reprimand. Petty and callous, for Isaac Finch had been one of their own: what had become of him must still matter, surely.

But, for once, Sir Francis didn't see through Tom's uneasiness. He shook his head instead. "Finch, or Poley, or perhaps..." He made a weary gesture. "Or perhaps ourselves. I pray the letter didn't raise suspicion."

Not the letter, of course — not all of it, but the postscript that was to have trapped a queen in her own nets, and now might prove the undoing of them all. A day of prodigies indeed. Bleak and unsettling prodigies — when Frances wept, and Sir Francis looked so lost.

The room had a large bay window that opened on a stretch of park, and outside among the trees a wood pigeon cooed lazily. Had Frances come back from the river? Tom startled, with the impression that Sir Francis had spoken to him.

"I beg pardon, Sir…" And Hades curse all blushing fools! *I beg pardon, for I love your married daughter, and just kissed her, and reel under this revelation, that I love her more than I thought my heart could love.*

Sir Francis sat with his head tilted, waiting — and there was a strain of impatience in his voice. "I said I'm wondering, Thomas. You've met Anthony Babington: would you reckon him a man of active courage, who rides off under our noses to deliver a most dangerous letter to the Queen of Scots, or rather a weak-willed youth caught between two terrors, and running?"

Babington, ay. Tom took a deep breath, clearing his mind of all thoughts of ochre silk and soft, sun-dappled hair. He thought of Babington instead, past Poley's talk of fear, back to his own brief glimpse of the man — the long martyr's face, the boyish smile and, most of all, the ever shifting gaze.

Of all things, there was a gleam of amusement in Sir Francis's manner. "Phelippes seems to think he ran off to Lichfield, and is raring to follow him, with a pair of sturdy fellows."

The notion of short-sighted, puny Phelippes galloping to overtake a traitor on the roads tugged at the corners of Tom's mouth — but, in truth, Babington as this romance's villain didn't sit right with him.

"Run off to Lichfield… If he was ordered, perhaps." He thought of Ballard watching the younger men in the dark hall at Hern's Rent. "Had any one of the others gone —

Tichborne, Tilney, Savage — I'd think as Phelippes does. But Babington... In John Ballard's place, Sir, I'd be wary of letting young Babington out of my sight."

Of this he was assured — enough to hold Sir Francis's long, level gaze, until the great man gave a nod.

"A man is already galloping to warn our people at Lichfield and at Chartley — for we can't take chances — but I believe you're right. Or at least..." Sir Francis shook his head a little ruefully. "At least, I pray you are."

Once more, as he'd done at Greenwich, Tom wrote under Sir Francis's dictation. He wrote notes and instructions. This time, it was the arrest of Babington and Ballard both. Mylls must keep his pursuivants in readiness, and find one or two more men to make up the party — men who were both trustworthy and not in Sir Francis's pay. Phelippes must prepare the interrogation; Berden must draw a list of all the conspirators. Tom himself must see to it that none of the conspirators slipped through the net.

"But you must not act. Not yet. If you are right, Thomas, where is Babington now?"

But here, alas, was where all certainties ended.

"Never back to his place in Derbyshire, surely? Still, he has friends."

"So he does." Sir Francis pushed himself upright, his mouth tightening at the pain. "I fear I've made Her Highness wait too long. Ride back, Thomas — and think well on it. I'm sure we'd all sleep better for knowing where Anthony Babington is."

Frances was nowhere to be found. No one had seen her or knew where she was. Down by the river, perhaps, waving her father on his way. Or else... Tom found himself chilled to the marrow. She must be regretting already, mustn't she? The words, the kiss, whatever promise had been in them. But then, what promise? Of the two of them, Frances was the wiser, surely. Oh, she wouldn't be the first married woman to love another man, and her own damn fool of a husband wrote sonnet after fine sonnet to the very married Lady Rich. But, Good Lord, this was Frances! She was Sir Francis's daughter, and Tom was no Philip Sidney. What would the world say if she bestowed her favours on a penniless cousin? And worse, infinitely worse, what would Sir Francis say?

No: Frances was wise. She was leaving, and they needn't see each other again but in the most cousinly, distant manner.

Tom felt very cold and bereft. And then he entered the stables and found them empty — but for one slender figure in ochre silk. Oh, how his blood flared alive. Frances was waiting for him in the back, bright-eyed, lips quivering on the brink of a smile.

"They're all down at the river," she said. "But I've had the grooms saddle a horse for you."

Oh, curse wisdom! All wisdom burnt away as Tom closed the distance in two strides, and caught her in his arms. "I thought…"

Perhaps it was the tiniest laugh, perhaps a sob. "I'll be gone the day after tomorrow." She reached up to take his face between her hands.

Gone. Gone across the sea. Gone to her husband. The awful cold nipped at the edges, as Tom lost himself in the flame and kissed her again, and again, until his head spun, and he leant against the wall, drawing her to him.

Then a nicker broke through the fire, and a huge head butted against his aching arm. The tall grey gelding they'd saddled for him had had enough.

Frances burst into soft laughter, hiding her face against his shoulder — and, after a breathless moment, he joined in.

The horse's big rolling eyes were nothing short of disapproving.

"Killjoy!" Tom groused — and Frances laughed anew.

Tom looked down at her. All he could see was a dimple on her flushed cheek. Why must this be all they could have — so little, and so late?

And still too much, cold wisdom hissed, and it was unfair enough to drown in it.

"Ah, Poppet..." Tom stroked the dark locks that had escaped Frances's severe coil.

She straightened then, leaning a little away from him. "I was afraid you'd never call me that again, now."

Now that his little cousin had changed into the woman he loved — the woman he loved and could never have? "I'm so sorry," he murmured into her hair.

But Frances looked up, trembling a little and so serious. "Oh, don't be! I'm all alive with it. It's as though all must see it glimmering inside me, as though I were different from everyone else." She tilted her head, thoughtful of a sudden. "But perhaps I'm prideful to go with my other sins. Perhaps every woman carries a man in her heart, who's not the one chosen for her?"

She turned away, and began to twist and pin in place her disordered hair. With her arms raised, she stood straight like a lance, glowing in the gloom of the stables, and it tore at Tom's heart not to go to her.

"I must..." He hardly knew the hoarse whisper for his own. He must go before he betrayed Sir Francis's trust more than he had already, and he must go because treason and complot had no time for lovers. "One of our men was killed — and now—"

Frances put light fingers to his lips, for she was her father's daughter. "I'm not to know," she said. "You must go, and I must see Father away."

Still she lingered, watching as he led the horse to the yard and mounted. When he leant from the saddle to hold out a hand, she took it and made herself smile through her tears.

"I wonder if Father sees how like him you are." Her voice hitched. "Off with you, Tom Walsingham. Go and find the truth!"

She walked by the horse across the yard, until it occurred to Tom that, if she forgot to care who saw them from the house, then he must care in her place.

"My Lady Poppet, God guard you always!" he called, and spurred the horse, and never turned back — for, if he did, there was no earthly force that would keep him going.

Babington gone, Frances, Mr. Secretary ailing and uncertain… It was in something of a daze that Tom rode back to London, reaching Southwark and the bridge, and then Seething Lane, in the long summer twilight.

He'd half forgotten his battered arm with all that had passed at Barn Elms. When he leant from the saddle to use the knocker, he gasped at finding himself stiff with pain. Famished and tired, he dismounted in the yard and eyed the kitchen door. Could he fetch himself a bit of bread and cheese, or at least a sip of ale, before going in search of Phelippes?

The head groom put paid to the notion. "Mr. Phelippes asks that you find him at once, please, Master," the fellow said, and hastened back to where three horses were being saddled.

What else now? Hadn't this day been penance enough already?

There was no need to find Phelippes, as Tom ran into him at the back door.

The cypherer was all agog. "Babington is in Poley's garden!" he announced, forgetting himself enough to push Tom back towards the stables. "A boy came knocking at the door, told Tib Fisher, and then ran."

"And who sent the boy?"

"Tib asked, but the boy didn't tell. And I fear that, if we tarry…"

Young Casey and the groom led the three saddled horses into the yard, and Phelippes reached for the bridle of the smallest mare, with the squinting wariness of one who had no great liking for horses. And here was the man who'd wanted to gallop in hot pursuit, all the way to Lichfield!

But urgency, it seemed, made the little cypherer bold — and a touch reckless, perhaps?

Tom checked his rapier and parrying knife. "Are you well armed, Rouse?" he asked. The young man showed the dagger at his hip.

"Phelippes?"

Phelippes didn't like blades much more than he liked horses — but something in the colour of Tom's question gave him pause. Hand on the saddle's pommel, he turned. "You think we're walking into a trap?"

And Tom found he rather thought they were. "A stranger sent a spoken message, saying that what we want most waits in a dark garden. And yesterday someone tried to stone me."

Phelippes fretted. "But we can't dismiss the chance —"

"I'm not saying we do. Only … Rouse, run and fetch a dagger for Mr. Phelippes."

Almost before Tom had spoken, young Casey was gone at a low-headed run.

"What's with Rouse, Philippus?" Tom wondered, the old name slipping out of its own accord. "Have you bitten his head off?"

There was no answer, the cypherer being too busy hauling himself into the saddle. Tom ignored the grunting effort, and also the sour glance he earned by mounting in turn with unthinking ease.

Casey was back in a trice with a sturdy blade for Phelippes, and they were out in the street, and on their way to Holborn at a small trot.

They travelled out of Ludgate, down Fleet Hill, and stopped at the Horn Tavern, where they left their horses — for it wouldn't do to charge in like a cavalry troop. Then they walked into the quiet, dark Fetter Lane, where Poley had his lodgings, and the garden Babington liked so well.

The house was a pretty half-timbered thing, nestled just past the point where an arch straddled the lane — which made it convenient to watch. Behind it, the boughs of a few apple trees spilt over a tall fence. A pleasant place, when it wasn't all shuttered, quiet, and dark as a tomb, with no light, no curl of smoke from the brick chimney.

"A day of empty houses, is it, Rouse?" Tom fingered the hilt of his rapier.

At his shoulder, Phelippes stood hunched in fidgety silence. One didn't suspect Phelippes of swearing, not even under his breath — and yet, Tom would have wagered the cypherer's thoughts were less than holy.

Tom's own were, for sure. He didn't quite know what he'd expected to find — whether Babington at supper with his friends, or an ambuscade. Shapeless, wordless hope, it seemed, was stronger than any reason, for much as he mistrusted this mysterious warning, some part of his mind had been composing the note they could write to ease Sir Francis's mind. Instead, there was nothing. No Babington, no Poley, no black-cloaked plotters lying in ambush, not even a sense of threat… Or was there?

Busy scanning the darkening lane, trying to decide just how deserted it was, Tom was caught unawares when, of a sudden, Phelippes marched out of their shadowed shelter, straight for the door.

Oh, pinch the fellow — chained to his writing desk until yesterday, and now… Tom gave chase, and caught him by the arm a heartbeat before he knocked.

"What if anyone answers?" he hissed, very much wishing to shake the fool. "What if some nosy neighbour asks what we want?"

In the last dregs of the purple twilight, Phelippes hit a peevish fist on his hip. "I just…"

Just hoped to find that we're not cozened after all — that we still hold the upper hand.

Tom grimaced at the house. "Come, now." With Phelippes in tow, he slipped around the corner, into the black alley that ran along the garden's fence. It was a sturdy wooden affair, as tall as a man and well kept — but there was no such thing as a fence without a fissure large enough to peer through. Not that there was much to see — a play of purple shadows, bushes all still in the moonless evening. All was quiet but for a blackbird warbling its evensong among the trees.

"No one's here," Tom whispered.

There was an unconvinced tongue-clicking, and the muddy scrape of Phelippes's steps as he pushed deeper down the alley. Oh, but it was growing irksome, this new boldness of the man.

Then the blackbird beyond the fence fell silent — and the hair on Tom's neck stood on end. *Here goes the ambuscade.*

"Halt!" he called, drawing his rapier and stepping in front of Phelippes. "Who's there?"

In the darkness ahead, someone broke into a run. Having just scolded the cypherer for charging blindly, Tom gave chase. He sensed, more than he saw, something flying at him from the shadows, and raised his arm in time to stave it off. It caught him all the same, reeking of mould, too soft to hurt, but enough to make him step back into Phelippes.

"He's fleeing!" the cypherer shouted — and yes, a few yards ahead, a dark shape jumped to grab the fence's top, and hauled itself over it and into Poley's garden.

Shouting for Phelippes to fetch Casey, Tom sheathed his blade in awkward haste and leapt after their fleeing quarry, grabbing the top of the fence to haul himself up. Or he would have — but his bad shoulder didn't hold his weight, dropping him painfully into the mud.

Tom cursed in all the tongues he knew, climbing back to his feet with Phelippes's help.

"Where's Casey?" he gasped, as more running steps sounded from the side of Fetter Lane. With a hiss of pain, Tom fumbled for his hilt.

Then the newcomer called, "Master?"

Casey — Fates be thanked! Tom pushed the servant towards the fence.

"Jump over," he ordered. "There's a man there…"

Before he could explain, the lad was scrambling over the fence, jumping down to the other side with unimpeded agility.

Now to join him. The alley ended a dozen yards ahead, though, against the back of another house. Was there another access on the other side?

Tom's wonderings were cut short when a pair of shutters slammed open somewhere across the garden, and an unseen man shouted, "Thieves!"

All they lacked now…

"Rouse! Come away — quick!" Tom called.

The young man must have thought much the same, for in a trice he came clambering over the fence.

"He's gone," he panted. "Jumped out all the way across…"

Tom shushed him brusquely. "And where were you?" he growled — which was unfair, for he himself, and not Casey, had failed to catch these people, twice in two days. But then, as he'd asked Phelippes, what if he'd caught them?

Waving aside Casey's stammered explanations, he made them all huddle at the alley's darker end, waiting until they heard the window close, and quiet descended again. Could they hope that, after raising the cry, the good citizen had gone back to bed without alerting the Watch?

After a quiet while, Tom led his little troop out into Fetter Lane again. Nobody was there — and most certainly not the constables of Farringdon Without.

Was it worth leaving Rouse on watch? Doubtful as it was, the servant took station under the arch, where the shadows were of the deepest black, with stern orders to do nothing more than see if anyone came to the house.

That settled — for all the good it was going to do — Tom and Phelippes recovered their mounts from the Horn's stables, hired a linkboy, and set out for Seething Lane at a plodding pace.

After all the ado, Tom's shoulder ached most unpleasantly, suiting the even more unpleasant thoughts that whirled in his mind, and he brooded on them until Phelippes broke the silence.

"You were right," the cypherer muttered. "It was a trap, and I walked us all right into it."

"Was I?" The more he thought about it, the less Tom understood: what witless sort of intriguer lured into a trap the very Queen's men he was trying to elude? "If you think you understand what's happened tonight…"

The whites of the linkboy's eyes gleamed as he peeped warily, perhaps alarmed by the bitterness in his customers' exchange. Oh, wouldn't it be a fitting end to such a day, to scare away their torch-bearer and be left to grope their way home in the darkness, because they had to bicker and play faults?

Tom swallowed a sour itch to laugh. "Never you mind, Philippus. We'll get to the end of it."

Perhaps deciding there was no danger of a brawl, the linkboy picked up his pace, and Tom followed, letting the horse pick his way as he pleased.

CHAPTER 16

3rd of August

They were all there: Tom's brother Guildford, Poley, the arch-traitor John Ballard, Frances, Rouse Casey with his arms crossed, and a stern-faced Sir Francis. They all stood in a circle around a pile of stones. On it lay a swollen, faceless corpse that Ambrose Lopes poked this way and that, making black blood ooze from it. Most unfairly, nobody else appeared to be bothered by the stench. Why, Frances even had that sad smile on her lips as she wondered aloud whether every woman carried a man in her heart — and not the one chosen for her…

Tom wrenched himself awake, with his heart in his throat, blinking in the earliest grey light of dawn. He was in his bed, and the cadaverous stench was Mrs Jeffreys's comfrey salve, and Skeres's truckle was empty — and Frances…

Frances — oh, Jove. *Does every woman carry a man in her heart…?*

The pieces fell into place in one clicking rush. Of course! Of course Frances was right, and Grace Finch had lied!

Tom dressed in unlit haste, buttoning up his doublet left-handed as he clambered downstairs — to find people in the hall.

In the light of one candle, a yawning Fisher closed the door after letting in two men. One was Skeres; the other…

"Rob Poley!" Tom took the last three steps in one bound. "Where the devil have you been?"

"With Master Anthony, as His Honour said…"

All reason, he was!

"But where, pinch you? You were with him — and where is he?"

Poley spread his hands, the very picture of thankless effort. "In Bishopsgate Without, Master, not far from the Bedlam. He changed lodgings yesterday."

Tom laughed bitterly. Changed lodgings!

"Told you 'e'd be mad," Skeres rumbled.

"In Bishopsgate Without!" Tom looked at the Minotaur for confirmation — and earned a slow, tooth-sucking nod.

Poley was still playing helpless. "I don't know what bit him, Mr. Thomas. I'd left him at my place, and when I rode back there, I found a note saying to find him in this place."

"And you never thought —" But no, there would be time for this. First... "Fisher, have your son run to Leadenhall —"

"Mr. Phelippes is here, Master. Never went home last night."

"Then fetch him!"

A minute later they were all crowded in Tom's writing room — he, Phelippes at the table and taking notes, Poley, and Skeres.

"Can't stay," the Minotaur announced. "I was to fetch these at Rob's place, and run back." He dug out a pair of fine buckles of chased silver. The sort of small errand one used to try a new servant — or to have him out of the way.

"Run back then, and on the way stop at Berden's place. Tell him where they are."

And, once Skeres had clattered away, Tom turned to Poley.

"What about you, Rob? What are you supposed to do?"

"Give Skeres the buckles, and then errands for Master Anthony, for all Tichborne and Tilney know."

"And for what they don't know?"

Tom had a fair notion, and knew for certain the moment Poley hunched in that supplicant's manner he assumed when it came to Babington. "He wants me to see His Honour again—"

"You heard Mr. Secretary." Tom cut him short. "He's at Richmond."

Which wasn't a lie — but had been yesterday. Tom much misdoubted that Sir Francis meant to see Babington at all — on the morrow or any other day before he was in gaol.

And perhaps Babington suspected this, or at least Poley did.

"Then I'll go there — for look you, Master: 'tis a matter of time before fear breaks the boy."

"Isn't that what we want?"

"What if he breaks the wrong way, and goes to Ballard to confess the weakness of his soul?"

At the table the dry whisper of the quill stopped, and Phelippes looked up with bird-bright eyes.

"You were telling a different tale, yesterday," Tom said slowly.

And then something happened that Tom had never thought to see: anger flashed in Robert Poley's face — true and raw.

"Mr. Thomas, I was nigh on two years at Cambridge as a youth. A poor bursar, I was, but I know how the game's played. Still, rhetorics are one thing, and men's souls another. The boy's frenzied with consolation that Mr. Secretary will give him a way out. Last night, to make it sweeter, I said Her Highness herself might deign to see him."

There was a soft snort from the table.

Poley waved it away. "Ay — and you know how the young fool spent the night? Thinking about what he'd wear to attend the Queen. Why do you think he wanted the cursed buckles? I tell you: frenzied, he is — and frenzy's a rope that frays when you draw it too tight."

Tom resisted the urge to trade glances with the silent Phelippes. "Well, I don't know about Her Highness — but he's seeing Mr. Secretary on the morrow."

Which, being a lie — for some impediment was sure to come up before evening — did little to solve the quandary.

It was plain that Poley thought the same. He hung his head, pursing his lips. "He showed me a letter from the Queen of Scots."

A letter. Tom's stomach knotted. Was it even possible? Two, three, four days…? All the way there, smuggling the letter into Chartley, Mary Stuart's answer written and cyphered, and then…? "Did he?" A foolish part of his mind was proud of how prompt, how even it sounded. Too even, perhaps? Shouldn't he be keener to hear?

Thank Fates that Poley was too unquiet to catch on to Tom's indifferent playacting. "'Tis a copy he's made. A gift for Mr. Secretary, he said — and then Ballard and Savage arrived. They gave the boy a bad start, I tell you. He thrust the letter at me as he went to meet them. They went out to stroll in the garden, and there I was, alone with the letter."

"And you read it." Phelippes's attempt at Sir Francis's manner of not quite questioning was marred by the faintest hint of a squawk.

"I made notes, but he caught me —"

"You made notes?" cried Phelippes, just as Tom exclaimed, "He caught you!"

And, for once, Rob Poley had no glib answer. "He returned of a sudden, wanting back the letter, and I had no time to hide the paper. He didn't understand what it was at first…"

"Then it dawned on him, I'll wager." Oh Hell, and Tartarus, and Hades! Sir Francis was going to have them all flayed alive.

"I made little of it. I said he'd want a copy made for His Honour."

Phelippes groaned. "He never believed you?"

"Ay — when I tore it before his eyes. I said there was no need for it, for he himself would bring the letter —"

"And what did *he* say?"

"He just…" When Poley exhaled, long and slow, it was like air going out of a bladder. He seemed smaller when he ran a hand through his yellow hair and shook his head. "He said there's little in this world he wants more than to trust me."

Ah, well. If this was a fabrication, Tom couldn't, for the life of him, see the use of it. And if Skeres found no one in the rooms in Bishopsgate Without, they'd know soon enough. Unless, of course, Babington's friends knocked down the Minotaur, and…

"What was in it?" This was from Phelippes, quietly spoken. "You read the letter: what does Mary Stuart write?"

An excellent question — and it had Poley squaring his shoulders into something akin to his usual glibness.

"She writes…" He squinted at nothing. "She's glad of Master Anthony's support and good work. She thinks that unless they act soon, it will be too late to save England and the true religion. They must discuss troops, and places, and money, and weapons, and how to free her, and then tell all to Ambassador Mendoza in Paris. They must be secret about it." He shook his head. "'Tis a long letter, Master — but this much I remember: she wants to know how they'll go about the plan, and the six gentlemen who'll do it. And she wants the boy to burn the letter."

This time Tom did look at Phelippes, and found him tracing a fingertip on the table: a square missing the bottom side — *gallows*.

Not a new letter. This was the one they'd had for weeks now. The one that carried Phelippes's postscript. The one Tom himself had delivered to Babington.

Only, Poley was not to know. Not if there was the faintest suspicion that he was in league with Babington. Let him think the silent look between his betters was bred of awe.

Slowly, Tom turned back to the man. "Mr. Secretary must know of this before it's sprung on him tomorrow. Have a horse saddled, Rob — and once in Richmond, ask for Davies."

Another thought occurred to him after Poley had bowed himself out — a most important one, so he followed out into the passage. "Rob? Did Babington say anything about an answer?"

Poley had recovered enough to smile. "He's writing it," he said, and was gone.

Once back in his room, Tom closed the door and leant against it, shaking his head in disbelief. When he burst out laughing, the cypherer followed.

"They've no notion," Tom gasped at length. "Sir Francis must be told —" He stopped short. Phelippes was already folding a letter. All the time he'd been making notes for Mr. Secretary.

"I was answering this, when you called for me." Phelippes turned a letter so that Tom could read it. Sir Francis was fretting over Babington's disappearance, fearing the postscript may have done more mischief than good.

"At least on Babington we can reassure him," Tom said.

"And on the postscript." And on the postscript, indeed. But there was something else nagging at the back of Tom's mind — something in what Poley had said. "Wait, Philippus."

Phelippes stopped, the stick of sealing wax hovering in mid-air.

"He's writing an answer, Poley says. But if he's still writing, why all the charade with the bay horse, yesterday?"

Phelippes clicked his tongue, shaking his head in forlorn irritation.

'Tis a matter of time before fear breaks the boy, Poley had said. Had the boy's friends noticed too?

"Ask for the warrant," Tom sighed. "Before we lose them all *and* the answer." *Or worse happens*, he could not bring himself to say.

Phelippes was already unfolding the letter. "A warrant to search Babington's place?"

"And to arrest him. And Ballard. Babington's little flight, whatever it was that happened last night, the letter — I've a notion it all ties together, and we won't like the knot."

The mention of last night caused an exclamation. "Oh — now you speak of it!" Phelippes waved his quill. "After some prodding and much thinking, Tib Fisher has remembered this: last night's messenger stank of horse dung."

"A stable-hand?"

"At an inn stable, since he was working so late. So I've sent young Tib to visit inn-yards."

Oh, bless the fellow! "Do you ever sleep, Philippus?"

Looking pleased, the cypherer went back to his letter, and Tom watched him add the request for the warrants. Sir Francis wouldn't want to risk losing Babington again, surely, and there was a sense that the whole tangle was on the point of unravelling — or of tightening into disaster, if they drew the wrong thread.

"Let Mr. Mylls know, too, will you? I'm for St. Helen's," said Tom.

Phelippes blinked in the fleeting surprise of one who had all but forgotten Isaac Finch. "You have news?"

A notion, more likely, and a certainty of having been lied to. And an eased mind, that he needn't drop the matter yet. "I might," Tom replied. "All the more if Babington hasn't run."

Now to see if he was right.

Early as it still was, and overcast, the day was becoming damp and hot by the time Tom entered the churchyard of St. Helen's, making plans for how he'd corner Grace Finch. He'd look the silly girl in the eye, and he'd tell her how his cousin Lady Sidney — a most wise lady ... or perhaps he'd tell her nothing of the sort — for why would Lady Sidney discuss this particular subject with her cousin?

Shaking thoughts of Frances from his head — strolling towards the river among the willows, packing her trunks, saying her goodbyes — he dismounted among...

Among what, indeed? What was this crowd? Morning Prayer, surely — but the churchgoers stood around in fretful clutches, watching the still barred doors.

Leading his horse, Tom made his way around the church's corner, and there met Paynter, Mylls's watcher.

"Master!" the lad called in relieved surprise. "I was coming to fetch you, only I didn't want..." He peeked at the rectory door.

Of a sudden, the day didn't feel hot anymore.

"Where's Dr. Lewis?" Tom asked.

The lad had the sense to lower his voice. "Church." He jerked his head. "I think the sexton found her."

Her! Not Finch's body, then — but ... *her*? And here the gossips were drifting towards them, sharp and eager as ferrets.

Tom threw his bridle to Paynter. "Send these people on their way," he ordered. "I don't think there will be Prayer this morning."

The lad grimaced at the gathering numbers. "What do I tell 'em?"

"Just that there's no Prayer. And when you're done, take my horse and go to Wood Street. Ask for Dr. Lopes's house, and Master Ambrose Lopes, if he would join me here."

The door to the rectory was only latched. Tom let himself in through the empty house, and into the church.

He saw them at once, huddling together a few steps from the vestry door. There was Dr. Lewis, all hunched, and Goodwife Lovell on her knees, with her arms around little Peg, and old Lambsfoot with his hands thrust in his white hair. Even Pratte, when he turned on hearing Tom's steps, showed a grey and slack-jawed face.

"Master..." he called, hoarsely, and all turned — all but the housekeeper. And over her bent head and shaking shoulders, Tom saw Grace Finch.

She sat on the floor, propped against the wainscoting, with her hands in her lap. Her head was bent forward, her loose russet hair cascading down to hide her face.

"She's dead," Dr. Lewis stammered, face stiff in waxen disbelief.

There was little question of that. Still, Tom knelt to touch poor Grace's hand, and found it lukewarm and stiff.

Oh, yes — she was dead, and Sir Francis was right to despair of his kinsman, for not only had Tom failed to find Finch's murderer, but he'd let the murderer kill again. That this proved Tom right — for Grace had known more than she told, and played games of her own — was the coldest of cold comfort. If he'd seen it before, perhaps, if he'd come yesterday to confront the girl... But there had been no time, yesterday — what with chasing traitors, and foes, and uncertain friends, and shadows! Warning Dr. Lewis, leaving watchers — none of it had served.

Thoughts of a lovelorn Minotaur flashed through Tom's mind. Never again would Nick Skeres make calf eyes at Grace. Nobody ever would — and Tom couldn't rid himself of a cold fear that it was his fault.

Goodwife Lovell had aged years since he'd last seen her, poor woman, and it seemed cruel to question her. So he turned to the men.

"When was she found?"

Dr. Lewis looked at Lambsfoot, who stood at his elbow, his brown face twisted and tear-stained.

"Each morning I come down here to make things ready," the sexton said. "Didn't see her at first, poor child — it was still dark. I..." *Stumbled into her* — but he couldn't bring himself to say it aloud.

"She must have risen very early." Tom studied her attire — the loose hair, the bare feet, and, from what he saw, a kirtle slipped in haste over her shift. "You and your cousin share a bed, don't you, Peg?"

When Goodwife Lovell's arms tightened around her daughter, Peg sniffled but didn't shirk the question. Instead, she took a tremulous breath to steady herself.

"Did you hear Grace rise?"

The girl sniffed again, her little face twisting in thought. "I half awoke, and she was stirring."

"Was it still dark? Was it near morning?"

Peg shook her head and hid her face in her mother's shoulder.

Ah, well — it had been worth a try. Tom stood, looking at the adults. "And none of you heard her unbar the door?"

"The front door was still barred." Goodwife Lovell whispered, hoarse with tears.

Which was no great surprise. "She must have come through the kitchen, and the vestry."

"Rusty never barks at us." Peg's words were muffled — but Tom was more interested in Lambsfoot, who, at the mention of the vestry, had dropped his gaze to the marble floor.

"What of the church doors, Sexton?" Tom asked. "Were they all barred too?"

There was a shuffling silence, and a shake of the bent head.

"Sexton?" Dr. Lewis prodded — like one already knowing the answer.

Lambsfoot groaned low in his throat and tugged at his hair. "The vestry door…" He shook his head. "I forgot…"

There was an exclamation from Goodwife Lovell — which Tom ignored for the moment, as well as Pratte's tongue-clicking.

"You forgot to bar it, Sexton?" he asked instead.

"We never bar it." Dr. Lewis came to the rescue — not that it changed things very much. "We lock it at night —"

He was startled when Lambsfoot silenced him with a sharp gesture.

"'Tis no use, Your Worship. It all comes to the same: I forgot! And in the dead of night, there was something — I don't know what. Rusty, I thought, but I don't know. I came downstairs — and the door … 'twas just latched." The old voice petered out to a miserable whimper.

Now, this changed things. "Was anything else amiss?"

"Nothing that I saw, Your Honour. Nothing that I heard. The yard was quiet, but for Rusty, all awake. He came up to have his head scratched, and then I locked the door and went back to bed."

"Ay, and Grace dead inside!" Goodwife Lovell cried through her sobs. "She heard the noise too, didn't she, Master? And found the door open, and the murderer…"

Who could have killed her, and run before the sexton's arrival — but…

"And the dog never barked?" Tom asked — though he rather thought he knew why.

He went into the vestry, the rector, Lambsfoot and the clerk trooping after him. The little door between the cupboards swung open with the faintest squeak of its hinges. "'Twas not just drawn to, then? Latched?"

Poor Lambsfoot. "I thought I'd checked it, God help me!" He looked from Tom to Dr. Lewis. "I'm getting old, ain't I, Yer Worship? And there's such as would have me thrown out!" On this, he glared at Pratte — but right then a small, sullen voice sounded from the door.

"Uncle Isaac says Dr. Lewis pays Lambsfoot good wages, for all it's us doing all the work." Peg hugged the jamb, an accusing glare on her face that made her look older than her years.

"Now, Margaret!" Dr. Lewis must have set out for sternness and lost his way somewhere around dismay. "You know your uncle spoke in jest."

The child sniffed, unconvinced — and small wonder, for Tom failed to remember ever hearing even the smallest jest from Isaac Finch. And it was plain that Lambsfoot shared the impression: something to take into account.

For the moment, though, the question was if anyone could have found a way past the locked door. The lock seemed intact, showing no scratches on either side. Sometimes, according to Skeres (and one didn't want to know how the lad came by such knowledge) a lock that had been picked became hard to work.

"You have the key, Sexton?" Tom asked. Lambsfoot produced it, and Dr. Lewis sent him to fetch the other from the house.

"We have two," the rector explained. "Lambsfoot always keeps one, and the other is hardly ever used." Dr. Lewis leant close, shaking his head. "The poor man will always bear this weight, I fear — but, in truth, I blame myself: I should have made a habit of checking the door myself. Lambsfoot grows forgetful in his old age."

"'Tis not the first time he's forgotten a door," Pratte sniffed — another of those who wanted the old sexton away.

"And Finch jested about it?"

Dr. Lewis had a reproachful glance for his clerk. "It might have been in jest on Isaac's side — but Lambsfoot never laughed."

And why would he, if he thought it a threat to his livelihood? Which might have been a reason to grow angry enough that tempers would be lost.

Dr. Lewis must have followed the thread of Tom's thoughts, for he gave a gasp. "Mr. Walsingham — Lambsfoot would never...!"

Wouldn't he? Lambsfoot had reason to resent Finch — and was hale enough for his age. But strong enough to overwhelm the courier — either by design or accident — and then conceal the body so well that it still couldn't be found? And, most of all, why would Lambsfoot kill Grace? Had she discovered the sexton for a murderer?

There is no saying, Thomas, what a man will do in an extremity.

"I mean to find out," Tom said, both to the rector and himself. To begin with, he carefully stepped out of the door, intending to study the ground outside.

Both the roofless room's flagged floor and the cloister's old cobbles were well swept.

"We all ran to the church this way, when the sexton came to fetch us," said Dr. Lewis, observing the ground in turn — though there was little to see.

The grass was no great help either, being neither tall enough nor wet enough to show whether it had been trodden. Past the stretch that Lambsfoot kept roughly mown, the ground was as unkempt as it had been two days earlier, all the way to the Leathersellers' wall, and to the ruins of St. Mary Axe.

Dr. Lewis followed Tom like a shadow. "You think the murderer came this way?" he asked, round-eyed and breathless.

"One of my men was keeping watch on the other side, Doctor — so yes," Tom said — and stopped as Lambsfoot came bustling through the kitchen door.

"It ain't there, Yer Worship," he announced.

"The other key?" Tom was not greatly surprised.

"But…" Dr. Lewis's eyes bulged. "Did the murderer break into the house, then, and find the key? And poor Grace surprised him, and…?"

"Oh no, Doctor," Tom said. "I've a good notion of where your key is."

He went back to the church, where he found more people than he expected. Pratte and the returned Paynter stood aside, awkward and solemn, while Ambrose Lopes was down on one knee beside a sobbing Goodwife Lovell and her daughter, murmuring to them in comfort, as though he'd done nothing else all his life.

Lopes greeted Tom with a sombre nod.

"I'm glad you joined us, Master Lopes. Could you…"

Perhaps it was the hesitation that made Hannah Lovell turn on Tom so fiercely. "What do you want of her now?" she demanded, hoarse with tears, leaving little doubt about whom she blamed for her niece's death — and perhaps her brother's too.

"I…" Tom found himself floundering. "If Master Lopes can discern —"

"It won't bring her back, will it?"

And Fates be thanked for Ambrose Lopes, who clasped the distraught woman's arm. "Goodwife, you want your niece to have justice, so she can rest in peace, don't you? Mr. Walsingham will find her murderer — and your brother's too — but he needs me to know how this poor girl died. I promise you, I'll be as gentle and as respectful as I know."

For a moment the housekeeper watched the thin, serious face, and then, with a sob that shook her whole frame, she dissolved into tears again.

The rector bent over his housekeeper, murmuring about going to the house and taking poor Peg away. He turned a beseeching look on his clerk.

"I know it's imposing on Goodwife Pratte at such a moment — but I was wondering…?"

It took the clerk a blinking moment to grasp that comforting a woman was a woman's work. He broke into assurances that yes — yes — of course his wife would know her Christian duty.

And then Goodwife Lovell let herself be ushered to the vestry with Peg trailing behind.

Oh Jove.

Ambrose Lopes didn't bother to rise, scooting closer to the body and leaning low to observe. "Shall I?" he asked. On receiving Tom's heartfelt permission, he began by feeling poor Grace's hands and arms. "Her limbs are stiffening — but she's not cold yet," he announced. He raised the hem of her kirtle, to observe some reddish discoloration in her heel and calf. "And her blood is gathering downward. I'd say she must have been dead … oh, at least three hours."

"It seems that she rose in the middle of the night, dressed in haste, and then… Oh." Tom remembered suddenly. "Would you check if she has pockets?"

Lopes reached to pat Grace's skirts, fiddled a little, and extricated what Tom had known he'd find.

"The key!" Dr. Lewis exclaimed from the vestry door.

The key indeed — for Frances had been right. Tom found Lambsfoot huddling a little apart, under Paynter's stern watch.

"I think you needn't blame yourself, Sexton. You did lock the door." Provided he wasn't the murderer, of course. One wouldn't have thought it, reckoning by the way he choked on this, poor fellow.

Dr. Lewis exclaimed, more aghast than ever. "Foolish child! What did she do?"

"What I'm told many women do: carry a man in her heart — but not the one chosen for her."

Right then, Ambrose Lopes asked for a candle, and Lambsfoot scurried away to comply.

Tom knelt by the body again. "Have you found something?"

The medicus had lifted the curtain of russet curls, showing poor Grace's dead face, and a rivulet of dried blood that ran from her left ear and down her neck. He was in the process of feeling her skull with his fingers.

"Here," he said. "If you would help me, Mr. Walsingham…"

She was stiff and coldish, and moving her away from the wall felt most unpleasant — all the worse when Lopes tilted the body to lean against Tom's arm.

"Here, you see?" he insisted.

Being on the wrong side, Tom didn't see at all, until they laid the body on its side on the floor. Tom had the briefest time to be glad Peg and her mother weren't there to see, before Lambsfoot arrived with the stump of a fat wax candle.

Lopes took it and, raising the hair again, lit the place where the skin was broken, and even under the congealed blood the bone showed a dent, right at the base of Grace's skull. Ambrose pressed on it, and something yielded under his fingers.

"A nasty crack, more than enough to kill her," he said.

"Lord help us — how horrible!" White to the lips, Dr. Lewis stared over Lopes's head, eyes bright as glass. *I blame myself,* he'd said — which he should not, if Tom was right — but this didn't change the fact that Grace had been of the man's flock, of his own household.

"Dr. Lewis," Tom said, as gently as he knew, "Master Lopes has seen what he could, I believe. You may have her carried to the house, if you wish. My man, here, will help."

"Oh — yes, yes!" The rector startled out of his grisly contemplation. "I'll have Pratte send for the midwife — and…" *And for the Watch,* he didn't say, tilting his head uncertainly.

Ay, the Watch — and that half-wit Hallet again.

"And the Watch must be called," Tom began slowly.

"But first the midwife, I'd say? And before that…" Apparently seeing no urgency in summoning the wardsmen, Dr. Lewis directed Lambsfoot and Paynter to fetch the table from the trestle in the vestry, and a sheet. Let Bishopsgate Ward grouse as they liked.

Tom went back to Lopes and his sad charge. "Was she hit from behind? With what?"

There was a hum, a tilting of the head as Ambrose fingered the fracture again. "'Tis a hard place to hit, and unless she was bending very low it would need to have gone upwards. I'd say she fell against a sharp corner, rather." He straightened and looked around.

Tom did the same. There was no sharp corner in the immediate vicinity, for the wainscoting was plain, and the gravestones on the wall were too far up.

"This is not where she died," Lopes pronounced.

Where, then? Here in the church, surely? Tom stood and moved along the nave. "Would there be blood?"

"Most likely. Wounds to the head bleed, and there was some bleeding from the ear."

As the rector, Paynter and Lambsfoot moved away the body, Tom and Lopes began to search. They had no need of candles, it having grown light enough that, even though the day was lowering, morning poured through the huge east windows, bathing every corner in a cold grey light.

"That side first." Tom pointed towards the chancel and, past that, the one-armed transept. "Lambsfoot sleeps above the vestry."

"You're thinking of a lover?"

"A lover — or…" Even as he said it, Tom felt a piece shift inside his mind — a gleam of coloured glass. "Or one who would be."

They searched. After a little while, Paynter returned and was put to the same task. Tom had questions for him about last night's watch, and asked them as they explored the chancel.

Paynter had relieved his fellow before cockcrow, he said: the man had spent the night under the churchyard trees, taking a turn around the church now and then. He'd seen nothing, heard nothing.

Which meant little enough — for, even on a moonless night, a small flame, well shielded, would hardly show from outside.

As though in answer to Tom's thoughts, Lopes's voice wafted from the transept. "They must have had a candle, surely?"

Tom hastened to join the medicus, and found him on his hands and knees at the foot of a marble sepulchre that carried the carved effigies of a knight and his lady.

Lopes pointed to a thick, oily stain on the floor: the grease had congealed around a half-burnt wick. "Someone dropped a rush-light here — and I'd think…"

One on each side, they observed the tomb, whose effigies rested on a slab of grey marble. This slab's edges were worked into a frame, cut at a sharp, sloping angle.

And, on the frame's edge, Tom found a dark stain. It was dry to the touch, with the trail of drip down the sepulchre's side. Lopes drew a piece of linen from the pouch at his waist, and rubbed at the stain. It came away in thin, rust-coloured flakes. "Blood," he pronounced. "This is where she died."

"Could she have fallen on her own, and dragged herself to die where she was found?"

"And then sat herself like that?" Consideration passed across young Lopes's face for the briefest moment before he shook his head. "Most things can happen under the sky — but no: I'd say she didn't."

"So someone was with her when — either by design or accident — she fell."

It was easy to imagine: Grace with her key, letting herself in, and a man, through the vestry door, lighting a rushlight and scurrying across the aisle, fingers cupping the small flame. They'd stopped by the altar wall, whose windows looked out onto the street, where the watchman wouldn't go on his rounds, there being no doors. And then they'd talked, and the talk had soured into angry whispers, and the man had shoved Grace, who'd dropped the rushlight as she fell backwards, and...

"And why did he carry her there?"

Lopes frowned. "He may have thought to find help ... but why leave her there, then?"

"Indeed! Why carry her — and leave her there?" Tom asked — and was surprised when Paynter, who had trailed after him, half-forgotten, made a suggestion of his own.

"Didn't the sexton come down —?" The lad blushed scarlet when both Tom and Lopes turned his way. So there was thought under the bowl-like mop.

"So he did, Paynter," Tom said, and the lad's blush deepened. "And that's when our man fled, latching the door after himself — because he'd never meant to find help for Grace."

"And yet..." Lopes looked around, gauging distances. "Why not push the body here behind the tomb and go on his way?"

"Unless..." It was all quite neat in Tom's mind — the pattern clear for the first time in days — but he wanted to see whether Lopes reached the same conclusion.

He did. "Unless he had a place to hide it!"

"The same place where he's hidden Finch's body — since it's baffling us so well. So..." With Ambrose and Paynter on his heels, Tom strode around the knight's tomb and through the arch into the quire. He moved towards the vestry door, left arm sketching the act of carrying something heavy. "He shoulders poor Grace, makes his way in the dark…"

"Only —" Lopes waved a forefinger at the vestry door — "he hears noise of a sudden: the sexton's a-stir! So he drops…" He stopped abruptly and pointed at the place where the body had been.

"But she wasn't dropped, was she?" Tom said.

A slow shake of the head. "She was laid there with some care." Lopes looked at Tom. "*A lover, or one who would be.*"

Indeed. "And he'd already laid her down when he heard the sexton — and was feeling for something in the dark." Tom raised a palm, like a rhetorician closing his argument. "Some kind of catch, a hidden door — for I'll wager you both that our hiding place is accessed from this part of the church."

His audience of two stood agape — less convinced than Tom would have liked.

Lopes voiced his doubts. "You mean… Well, not a priest hole, surely?"

"A crypt, rather."

"There is no crypt here. When the hand was found, the constable had it brought away."

"And yet the old nunnery must have had one." *They had all sorts of hiding holes around the church*, Goodwife Lovell had said.

"Mr. Thomas!" Paynter called, jerking his chin at the closed doors. "There's folks —"

And at the same moment, Lambsfoot bustled in from the vestry.

"Master Pratte's had the constable fetched, Yer Honour," the old man said in great agitation. "And Dr. Lewis sent me to open the door."

Oh, pinch Pratte for a meddling fool! But at least the Watch had the grace to arrive when Tom had a solid argument ready.

"Then do as Dr. Lewis says," Tom ordered — and then he grabbed Paynter and pushed him out through the vestry and towards the ruins of St. Mary, with instructions both strict and urgent.

When he returned to the church, Lambsfoot had opened the door to admit Constable Hallet's disapproving presence.

"Good day, Constable," Tom called, with the manner of one who had every right to be where he was.

It was little wonder that Hallet's rotund face darkened. "Ay, g'day," the young man grunted. "I knew 'twould be Yer Honour again."

He stomped into the church, pleased as one finding maggots in his cheese.

In fair truth, Tom had meddled greatly with the fellow's duties and the Ward's prerogatives. For a mercy, he knew his Hallet by then, and Hallet's sluggish wits.

"You've seen the body, I'm sure?" Tom asked, all brisk business, just as the rector followed Hallet in — as narrow as the wardsman was stocky. "Have you a crypt here, Dr. Lewis?"

"A crypt? No — or rather..." The rector lit up at the question, just as Tom had hoped. "There used to be one in the old days, most certainly. If not a crypt in the proper sense, right under the church, then there must have been vaults under the monastery. But I fear that any access was lost when the old buildings were sold to the Leathersellers, I'd say — which was ... oh, some forty years ago."

Hallet stepped ahead, feet planted wide, with his fists on his hips. "What's with the vaults? What's it got to do with the dead girl?"

"A good question, Constable." Tom navigated around the bulky figure to stand in front of the wainscoting where poor

239

Grace's body had lain. "And one I hope to answer. What do you know of secret doors, Doctor?"

"A secret door!" Dr. Lewis exclaimed — tickled in spite of himself, and Lopes, who had stood aside like a very interested owl, moved to run a hand along the wooden moulding.

None of them had the first notion about secret doors — but Hallet, it turned out, knew a good deal. He joined Lopes in studying the wainscoting, feeling his way with skilled fingers. Not a blacksmith, then, but a joiner?

Don't be hasty in passing judgment, Thomas, nor in discounting anyone — for sometimes even the roughest churl may be possessed of good and useful traits.

And it seemed that Constable Hallet was meant to prove Sir Francis right, for he was the one to find the hidden catch where none appeared to exist, and he released it with a pleased grunt.

"Cunning little bit o' work!" he said, as he slid away a panel of wood, and then another, to reveal a dark recess.

"Why…!" Dr. Lewis exclaimed. "This is…"

Now let *this* be what it ought to be! Tom pushed past the constable and leant into the hole, into a cold, stale draught of old stone and dampness. And, lo and behold! It was more than a mere hole. A stone step, and then another descended into the darkness.

"Fetch a torch," Tom called over his shoulder. "There are stairs here."

A narrow set of stairs, starting inside the old wall's thickness, and leading down to the nuns' vaults.

Dr. Lewis crowded behind Tom, craning his neck to peer over his shoulder and down the dark pit.

"Why," he kept repeating in head-shaking wonder. "That it should have been here all the time — and no one knowing…"

"But someone did," Tom said, and then took not a torch, but a candle from the returned Lambsfoot. He entered the hole and began his descent, shielding the flame against the draught.

It was so narrow, at first, that it made Tom wonder. He had to stoop as he picked his way down the uneven steps, and still his shoulders brushed the damp walls. How could a man carry a corpse down such a hole? But no, he wouldn't carry it: he'd drag it behind himself — a most unpleasant notion.

But there were dark stains on the stone steps — and then, after the first short, cramped flight, the staircase turned on its left, and grew wider. In fact, it grew just wide enough that a man could carry a bulky weight.

Tom stopped, bending to light the way beneath him — and, hearing the scrape of uneven footsteps above, called, "Have a care!" to whoever was following, for he had no wish to be bumped and tumbled down the steep flight.

At the foot of it was a passage with sconces carved in its walls, and what might have once been the lower part of a window — the embrasure long filled with bricks and mortar.

"Mr. Walsingham?" A moment later, the rector and Hallet appeared from the stairs — the constable breathing hard, and carrying a smoking torch the way he'd brandish a cudgel.

"I believe we're under the vestry — or the roofless room, perhaps?" Dr. Lewis said, in such gleeful awe that Tom was sorely tempted to send him back upstairs.

"This won't be pleasant, if I'm right, Doctor. Wouldn't you let Constable Hallet and myself go ahead? Please, go back, and send Master Lopes down to me."

And, of all things on God's earth, the man looked disappointed! Didn't he understand, for all his gruesome imaginings, what it was the murderer had meant to do — and had done once before? What they were going to find?

"Ay, Yer Worship, back up 'ee go," Hallet began — and stopped when Lopes came to join them, and there was no need to fetch him anymore.

Ah, well, let the rector do as he pleased.

Tom forged ahead. There was a door with a pointed arch at the passage's end, hanging on one hinge. It creaked as it swung open, and a different air wafted through it from the darkness — enough of it that it made the flames dance. It was colder and dryer, and carried with it a sense of a much vaster space.

"What is it?"

Hallet's question, subdued as it was, stirred an echo from the gloom.

Well, there was no answering until they went through, was there? Sheltering the candle, Tom took a wary step across the threshold … and stumbled on a crumbling slope.

He dropped the candle, and cursed, and would have tumbled down if a hand like a vice hadn't caught his arm. He hissed in pain — for it was his bad arm — but managed to catch himself, partly on the stone moulding of the jamb, partly on the sleeve of a tottering Hallet, whose torch sizzled and crackled as it was swung about.

"God's beard — what's… Saving yer presence, Doctor. What's this stinkin' place?"

In the ruddy glancing of the torch, Tom found himself on a slope of rubble and dirt. He thought he glimpsed pillars, and more heaped ruin, and high above… "Steady that light, Constable — and we'll find out," he ordered.

When Hallet raised his torch, there it was in the wavering glow: a tall, long, half-ruined hall, with pointed arches interlacing high above it. Was this what Hell looked like? Beauty undone and ever bathed in a fiery glow? Tom pushed aside the wild thought.

"I think we've found the old nun's vaults," he said instead — which was much more reasonable, and still drew a gasp from Dr. Lewis.

"Stay where you are, Doctor. 'Tis hard going down here." Tom's order was a little firmer than was seemly — but the last thing he wanted was a maimed rector at the pile's foot. Recovering the body — if it was down there — was going to be hard enough.

With Hallet on his heels, Tom began to pick his unsteady way, rubble shifting and sliding under each step. There had been windows, high up where the vault's ribs sprang up from the pillars: when the nunnery was undone, the bricklayers must have thrown all the broken stones, ground bricks, and grit down those openings, and then blocked them. Not all, though, for daylight shone at the hall's far end. Had one of the windows broken open again over the years? And together with that faint grey light, there was a faint buzz — and something else.

At Tom's side, the constable was sniffing the air with a grimace.

"You were right, Constable," Tom said. "A stinking place indeed."

On he went across the cracked flags, stumbling over chunks of stone and planks of rotting wood — and with each step the stench grew thicker, and the buzzing stronger.

It wasn't long before Tom saw it, hard to mistake even in the uncertain light, even covered in flies. Under one of those blocked windows, from yet another heap of dirt, an arm protruded. A stump with the hand torn away.

"God's pity!" Hallet choked, loud enough that it echoed under the ancient vault.

"Have you found anything, Mr. Walsingham?" Lopes's question seemed to float from very far away.

"Yes — wait where you are." Tom turned to the slack-faced Hallet. "Go and light the way for Master Lopes, will you, Constable? See that he doesn't twist an ankle."

Hallet hurried away with the ruddy light — and Tom remained alone with the half buried remains of Isaac Finch.

CHAPTER 17

There was no doubt. Once Hallet's watchmen unburied the bloated corpse, and Ambrose Lopes had a good look, there was no doubt it was Finch — stabbed in the chest.

There was no doubt the murderer had dragged the body down here, so it wouldn't be found.

There was no doubt the man had meant to do the same with poor Grace — had not Lambsfoot come to disturb his evil work.

There was no doubt Faldo's pig had pushed through the partly open window — and, when one nimble watchman was sent climbing up, he couldn't go through the narrow breach, but saw enough to recognise the ruins of St. Mary Axe.

There was no doubt, then, of the facts. No doubt but one: who had caused them to happen the way they had — and, even of that, Tom had his fair suspicions.

Leaving Hallet and his men to the gruesome task of carrying up the body under Lopes's orders, he climbed back to the church, and was still on the narrow stairs when he heard the raised voices. Stepping out of the hole and into the clean air and the daylight, he spotted the three men all across the quire and the nave, by the still barred side door.

Paynter and none other than Nick Skeres stood like a pair of mastiffs on either side of a seething Deputy Alderman Casey.

A mournful Skeres spotted Tom as he crossed the church. "'Ere comes Mr. Thomas. Go cry to 'im, if you must."

John Casey turned, shoulders hunched and face a-scowl. He didn't cry in the least.

Would an innocent man protest at once? Not of a necessity — but Casey had been angry at both the dead, must have known about the vaults, and the question remained of why Finch had changed his mind about him. And there was nothing but Grace's word on that, and Grace was dead — but didn't her very death point to at least a grain of truth in her claim? Oh, Tartarus — the pieces were all there, if only they'd take any shape other than that of a snake biting its own tail!

It was with the uneasy sense of an unsound argument that Tom moved to meet his suspect, who looked more agitated than cowed.

"These two oafs say that Grace is dead," was his chin-jutting salutation. "Your Honour'll say I've killed her, too."

"These two oafs are right, Alderman. The poor girl was killed last night." *And you seem unmoved enough*, Tom would have added — but on hearing it, Casey changed like quicksilver.

He lost all colour, and slumped out of his anger. "Grace… Lord 'a mercy!" he breathed. "I wouldn't believe… But why — who…?"

"That's what I'd like to know." Tom never took his eyes off Casey's face as he pointed to the hole in the quire's wainscoting. "Who killed Grace Finch and her father — and hid Finch's body down there."

Faces speak as much as tongues, Thomas. Discern a man's secret heart through his transparent face.

Only, it was damnably hard to tell Casey's secret heart, as his face wavered from horror to surprise to anger to dismay.

"Isaac's body…!" he choked, and would have surged forward, but Skeres grabbed him hard by the arm.

Tom looked coldly at the writhing man. "You and Isaac Finch used to hide there as children. So when Finch grew to mistrust you, it was the easiest thing —"

"But why?" Casey strained in Skeres's grip. "You keep saying he mistrusted me... Why would he?"

"He said you made a noise at the Exchange once, on finding your son there."

"My son...?" Casey was thrown — or pretended well. "What about him? He's a bootless fool — always was and always will be. If I were his master —"

"Do you know who his master is?"

Casey was taken aback enough that he stopped struggling. "Why, a Mr. Phelippes —"

"Who, in turn, works for me."

This stopped Alderman Casey in his tracks. Whatever he knew of his son's work, he must have had an inkling of Finch's — if only through Dr. Lewis's dark hints — and surprise ran across his thin face and gave way to calculation. It might be that of a cornered traitor; it might be that of an innocent man, shrewd enough to see the net that entangled him. Either way, Casey thinned his mouth to a thoughtful line.

"I had supper with Alderman Massam at his house last night," he said with slow deliberation. "You can ask him: he lives close by Duke's Place."

"Did you sleep there?"

"I went home to sleep in my own bed."

"By curfew?"

"We'd many matters to discuss. Ward matters."

Of course — and the Watch wouldn't bother their own Deputy Alderman, no matter how late he chose to stroll through his own ward. Why, they'd steer well clear of him for fear of some reprimand. Tom tried to picture Aldgate Ward in his mind.

"Duke's Place..." he not quite asked.

"Aldgate Street," Skeres supplied. "Near Cree Church."

St. Katherine Cree — the place with the sunken floor. "Not so far that a man couldn't walk here to give a piece of his mind to his wayward betrothed." Tom paced around Casey. "Only, Grace wasn't alone when you arrived here, was she?"

Casey startled. It was a bare heartbeat, before he covered it with anger.

"You'd blacken a dead woman's name, so you can paint me as a murderer!" He tore half free of Skeres's hold. "For all of your fine manner —"

"Oy!" the Minotaur grabbed again and shook hard. "Mind your tongue, you murthering knave —"

"Skeres!"

The brusque call made the lad stop, nostrils quivering and heavy jowls flushed in blotches. He grunted when Tom shook his head — but there was this to be said for Nick Skeres: no matter how gracelessly, he obeyed orders. He unhanded Alderman Casey with a brisk little shove. "You thank Mr. Thomas that I don't trounce you!" he growled.

Young Paynter gawped in awe, and Casey tugged his collar straight, with anything but thanks on his mind.

"I think you've little cause for righteousness, Alderman," Tom said, and ordered Skeres to fetch Peg Lovell. "And her alone."

And why must Casey's reproach sting? It was foolish, really, to care what this fellow said, who might well prove to be a murderer and a traitor. *You'd blacken a dead woman's name…*

"And I would *not* blacken Grace Finch's name, Deputy Alderman," Tom found himself saying with greater vehemence than was seemly. "What I would — and will — do is to find the man who slew her and her father."

"By listening to a wayward child?" Casey retorted, as Skeres came charging in with young Peg and, besides, half of Bishopsgate.

"'Ere, Master," the lad announced, with a shrug that meant, *what would you have?* Tom hadn't truly expected Hannah Lovell to let her daughter be questioned alone, but must Dr. Lewis also join the company, and Constable Hallet, and Clerk Pratte for good measure?

Under Tom's glare, Skeres shrugged again. In fair truth, what could he have done, short of locking everyone out of the church?

Ah, well. There came little Peg, all tearful and hanging onto her mother's hand.

"Come here, Margaret Lovell," Tom called, using her full name as Dr. Lewis had done. A thing for grave circumstances, surely.

Peg didn't hesitate: she tripped to stand right in front of Tom, and even dropped a skewed hint of a curtsey.

"You loved Grace, didn't you, Peg?" Tom asked. "She was like a sister to you?"

Peg's chin trembled a little, but she thinned her mouth — much like her mother — and nodded.

"I've a few sisters of my own, and they used to keep each other's secrets, never letting us boys know, or anyone else. Not even our mother."

The quickest peek at Goodwife Lovell.

"And you've kept Grace's secrets most loyally, I'm sure — but now, because of these secrets, someone has done her great harm. And I must know, Peg: why did Grace steal in here last night?"

It was no marvel when the mousy little face crumpled, and Hannah Lovell threw an arm around the girl, glaring at Tom.

The foolish woman! What did she take him for? This was why Tom had wanted Peg alone to question — and not half the neighbourhood, and most of all not Peg's mother.

It was a good thing that, before he could say something unkind, Dr. Lewis intervened.

"Let Mr. Walsingham do his work, Mrs Lovell," he said, gentle but blessedly firm — and, for a mercy, the housekeeper subsided.

Also, for another mercy, little Peg shook free of her mother's embrace and, tearful but game, faced Tom again. "I thought…" She swallowed hard, pressing her fists to her stomach. "When she didn't come back to bed, I thought she'd run away with her sweetheart!"

Just as Frances had said, so Tom didn't join in with the chorus of gasps.

Goodwife Lovell, it was worth noting, while she cuffed the child's wrist and exclaimed with the others, seemed more appalled than surprised.

Peg turned on her mother and the rector. "Ay — her sweetheart!" she cried. "He's young, and he's handsome, and he came to see her in secret, and she only told *me*! We'd leave the vestry door unlocked for him — and…" She stood there, shoulders heaving with the enormity of it all.

"And she was going to run away with this man?" Tom prodded.

"Uncle Isaac wanted to give her to old Casey. She'd have died before she wed him!"

And so she had, poor Grace. The thought seemed to hit Peg at once, and, with a wail, she crumpled in her mother's arms.

Goodwife Lovell was weeping too, while Dr. Lewis stood transfixed in dismay. Paynter and Pratte gaped like groundlings at the play, and John Casey — oh, how he lowered! Like one who'd had his betrothed's cheating ways unmasked — or his own dark reasons unveiled.

"So, Grace wasn't alone, was she, Deputy Alderman?" Tom asked.

The man's face darkened — and there was no doubting he'd seen Grace with the one Peg called her sweetheart.

Killed her for it, though? After killing her father? Because in truth, it kept nagging at Tom's mind, this surfeit of reasons: that Casey might have killed Finch over whatever it was that Finch had found out, and then killed Grace because he'd found her in the company of another man. Did one do murder twice in a week, for disparate reasons?

"And what is it now?" Tom snapped at the insistent presence at his elbow.

It was Arthur Pratte, dancing from foot to foot in purse-lipped importance.

Tartarus take all meddlesome clerks! "Pratte, if this is about the coroner, or the Watch, or the midwife, I swear —"

"No, Your Honour, that is..." the clerk stammered. "They've brought the body round from the other side, from old St. Mary, that is, and Hallet's sent for the coroner — but..." He held up a pacifying hand. "'Tis Goodwife Pratte, Your Honour. She'd have a word, please, Your Honour."

Goodwife Pratte. It took Tom a heartbeat to grasp that the man was talking of his own wife. And what could *she* possibly want now? "It will have to wait."

Pratte would have yielded, most likely, if Dr. Lewis hadn't come to his rescue, leaning close to speak in Tom's ear.

"I think Goodwife Pratte saw *something* the night that Finch..." The rector tilted his head, brows raised. "She's waiting in the vestry."

But no, she wasn't waiting in the vestry at all. In the time it had taken the rector to plead her case, Goodwife Pratte had come to join her husband, and was ready with a curtsey.

It must be in the nature of things that meddlesome clerks would marry meddlesome women, but she was here now, and it would be quickest to hear her, and — it must be said — she seemed more staid than Pratte and Dr. Lewis put together.

She was a flaxen-haired young woman, Joan Pratte, with an air of good sense about her, and that serene placidity of new mothers. It was rather encouraging that her mien was sober, with none of her husband's importance. Also, she lost no time in small talk.

"I'm Joan Pratte, Your Honour," she said. "And the night Isaac Finch last came home, I couldn't sleep, so I walked about the house until late. I heard Finch when he came back. Never one to be quiet, he was — rest his soul. And somewhat later, I saw him together with a man in the churchyard —"

"From one of the windows upstairs, that is," Pratte hastened to put in, as though his wife had said something unseemly. "For she couldn't find rest — and so she went to stand by that window where one can see the rectory's door — not that we ever…"

This earned a curl of Hannah Lovell's lip, and would have earned worse, perhaps — but Tom had no time for unneighbourly squabbles.

"And did you know this man, Goodwife Pratte?" he asked. "Did you hear what they said?"

She shook her head. "They spoke low — but this I can say: they did not speak in friendship. Isaac Finch gave a shove to this other, who was a smallish fellow, and then they walked inside, and I saw no more of them."

Because they'd gone to the church, or at least the murderer had stabbed Finch out of sight, and then dragged the body into hiding. "A smallish fellow…" Tom stepped aside, so she could see John Casey. "Like him?"

"Why, no." Joan Pratte tilted her head in consideration. "A little like him — but not Alderman Casey."

"There!" Casey cried — and Skeres silenced him with an elbow to the ribs.

There, indeed. There went Tom's neat pattern, all to pieces. "Can you be sure, Goodwife?" he insisted. "It was a dark night."

"Finch had a rushlight, and one thing I saw well: the other man had as red a mop of hair as I ever saw."

Red hair.

There was a spell of stunned silence. Oh, they all knew a man a little like the mercer, but with a mop of red hair — and young — although hardly handsome.

Tom nodded gravely at Joan Pratte. "Thank you, Goodwife. We won't impose on you more than we have already."

And she would have said it was no imposition at all — but her husband, knowing an order when he heard it, no matter how it was couched, took her by the arm and steered her away.

Goodwife Lovell waited until they were gone and then, grey-faced, rounded on Casey.

"Always sweet on her, he was!" she cried. "But no! You and Isaac must have your way, and you old enough to be her father, and never mind her heart, or your son's heart — and now, see what he's done —"

"No!" screeched Peg. "It isn't him — it isn't Rouse! Rouse'd never hurt Grace!"

It was beginning to seem that she liked young Casey very much — well enough to call him handsome, perhaps. Would she lie for his sake?

"How would you know it wasn't him?" Tom questioned. "Did you ever see Grace's young man?"

"It wasn't Rouse. Rouse loved Grace, and she used to like him, too — but now she has her gentleman, and won't give Rouse the time of the day, no matter how he —" She stopped short, clapping a hand to her mouth — for she was not too young to see what she'd done.

"So," Tom said slowly, "Rouse must have been very angry with your Uncle Isaac. And with Grace, if he found her with her gentleman." He let it hang, waiting to see whether anyone would take him up on it.

"The child is right." Behold Alderman Casey, remembering himself for a father! "And you're right too, Master: I was here last night, late. When I left Massam, I ... walked here. I wanted to hear Grace say her tales to my face. 'Twas the wine doing my thinking. I came by old St. Mary, and as I drew near, I heard them: Grace and a man, cooing between them — and it wasn't my son."

"Did you see him?"

"'Twas near dark — but I heard them well, and I'd know my own son, wouldn't I? This one... Peg's telling the truth: he spoke like a gentleman."

"So you found your betrothed out at night with a strange gentleman. What did you do?"

"Do?"

"You must have done something. You never just hid there to listen, surely?"

"What would you have me do, Master?" Casey chewed each word as though it were gall. "An old man finding his betrothed with a young fellow! If I revealed myself, how could I ever marry her?"

"So you walked away?"

"Ay, like the fool I am — and once she was my wife, I'd see to it she'd never step out at night again! But I swear before God: the man who was with Grace wasn't my good-for-nothing of a son!"

Which could be true or not — and if it wasn't, perhaps these two deaths had nothing to do with Babington's mayhem. But then one of them, a Service man, had done murder twice.

Tom observed the small company. Casey looked older of a sudden, while Finch's sister and niece were staggering under it all. Dr. Lewis, poor gentle soul, had seen Pandora's box spill its evils in his own household, and even Paynter had lost much of his barleycorn placidness.

When he ordered Skeres to find Rouse Casey and bring him to Seething Lane, the Minotaur obeyed, but it was plain he didn't like it at all.

John Casey tried again. "Your Honour, I swear —"

"I've heard you, Deputy Alderman — and I'll hear your son. Now, come with me — for you're not in the clear. Far from it."

CHAPTER 18

Seething Lane lived up to its name that day. The whole house, from the stables to the writing rooms, boiled and stirred when Tom arrived, with messengers coming and going, and all the scriveners at frenzied work.

Amidst it all, having left Paynter to guard John Casey, Tom went to fetch Phelippes, and found him with a much-agitated Mylls.

"You tell him, Mr. Walsingham!" was the secretary's salutation, together with a wave at Phelippes. "Tell him what's the use of entering and searching houses, unless we know for certain that Ballard's there!"

"And in fact, we've neither searched nor entered, have we?" The cypherer wore his usual manner of worry — but there was a quiver to his nostrils, very much like tried patience. "We're keeping watch on the house in Bishopsgate Without, Mr. Thomas. Keeping watch is all."

"And Ballard isn't there, I take it?"

"They expect him, Berden writes." Mylls spread his hands with a bitter chuckle. "And don't they always expect him? I'm half minded to suspect the man doesn't exist."

The sharp, luminous smile, the black presence. "Oh, he does!" Unless he was an image conjured by the devil… Tom shook the fancy from his head. "And we'll take him, Mr. Mylls — as soon as we have the warrant."

"Ah, but that we do!" Mylls sat up in his seat, hands flat on the table. "And a royal proclamation."

Tom's heart took one deeper beat, the way it used to do when, as a small boy on horseback, he'd feel his mount's huge muscles bunch on the brink of gallop. After all the wait, the painstaking work, the questions, the qualms, the sleepless nights, the mistrusting…

"What of the letter?" he asked.

Phelippes winced. "His Honour agrees with you: better lose the answer than the man. Any moment now, Lord Howard should send the warrant."

Lord Howard — the Lord Admiral, and not Sir Francis himself. Tom thought of the forged postscript … and then thought of Ambassador Mendoza sitting in Paris, and of Spanish ships crossing the Channel. "*The warrant*, you say? Just one?"

Phelippes nodded, but it was Mylls who answered.

"Just Father Ballard, for now, as a seminary priest — and much good it's going to do us, for unless we know where the rogue is…" And off Mylls was, once again, on what must have been his litany of the day, judging by the quiet sigh on Phelippes's part.

Having heard it once, Tom felt no need to hear more. "But we're keeping watch for him, aren't we?" he asked of the cypherer.

"At Babington's places, the old and the new." Phelippes counted on his fingers. "At the Castle Tavern, and at Poley's garden — for all that Poley himself is with Babington."

"Making ready to meet Sir Francis?" Tom wasn't surprised to see Phelippes shake his head.

"Oh, but he isn't going. His Honour delayed the meeting to Saturday, and Poley's to keep Babington soothed and quiet."

"Poley! Poley's a knave — there's no trusting him," grumbled Mylls, and turned to glare at Tom. "The last I heard, Mr. Thomas, you were thinking he's killed Finch — and still we rely on him to watch Babington? Still we trust him?"

Oh, but they didn't, did they? Tom picked up a penknife from the table, turning it this way and that. They didn't trust Poley a whit. What they relied on was that he knew they didn't, and would therefore keep Babington trusting him. Such a bleak, straining game!

"We don't, Mr. Mylls. We never have." Tom dropped the knife, and met the secretary's mulish gaze. "But if it turns out he killed Finch, I'll be very surprised."

And so he told of his morning at St. Helen's. Of poor dead Grace, of Finch's body concealed in the forgotten vaults, of Deputy Alderman Casey, and, worst of all perhaps, of his son.

"Where is Rouse, Phelippes?" he wearily asked once he was done — and he saw he could boast of something not many achieved these days: he had disquieted Sir Francis Walsingham's chief cypherer.

It wasn't often that one saw bafflement in the pale eyes, but it was there — no matter how Phelippes, having sent for his servant, strove for impassibility. "That I should fail to see...!" He clicked his tongue. "I don't suppose that woman could have lied?"

Mylls gave a soft snort, but said nothing as Tom thought of Joan Pratte's round, placid countenance and her little sniff at the sight of John Casey.

"A prying tattler she may be, but it would take a great deal of maliciousness to tell such a lie. I can't imagine why she'd —"

A knock at the door broke the exchange: Rouse Casey answering the summons.

He stood in hunched wariness, his hands fisted in his cuffs. The arrant idiot!

Tom liked young Casey; he didn't want him to be twice a murderer — but he'd lied, hadn't he? And he was looking to do it again, reckoning by his hare-like, twitching alertness.

Now, being the lad's master, by rights Phelippes should have questioned him — but the cypherer waited in his corner, arms crossed and face stonelike. If he was waiting for his servant to crumble and confess his sins under the weight of such flinty silence, then Tom had no time for it.

"You told me you've known Finch all your life, Rouse," he said. "But not that you wooed his daughter."

The lad's Adam's apple bobbed up and down. "Grace has naught to do with it."

"You've always loved her, and she loved you — and Finch wouldn't hear of it, for he meant her for your father."

"Ay, my father!" Red anger washed up the lad's face. "No matter that she didn't want him... Not that she wanted me, either, but I'm not my father, and that was good enough!"

Such bitterness — against father and daughter both. "Is this what you told Finch, when you followed him to St. Helen's?"

Whatever else he was, Rouse Casey was no great deceiver — all starts, and twitches, and blinking gapes. "I never..." he tried, hoarsely.

"He let you into the house, and then into the church, where nobody would hear you argue."

"No!"

"We all know what Finch was like — and he had scant liking for you. Perhaps you didn't mean to kill him. Perhaps he shoved you, and —"

"No!" Young Casey turned wild-eyed to Phelippes. "I didn't kill him, Master — you know I didn't!"

The cypherer straightened. "I thought I knew you lack discretion," he said. "Now I find you have too much — keeping from me that you'd cause to hate Finch!"

"'Tis not that I hated him: I love his daughter —"

"And without him, her aunt would give her to you?" Tom's question earned a bitter snort.

"Her aunt! 'Tis Grace that won't have me — not anymore!"

Which closed the trap around the young fool, and made Isaac Finch's death a puny matter of thwarted love.

"Ay, that's the worst: 'twas all for nothing." Tom found himself angrier at the lad than he should have been. "Last night you left your post in Fetter Lane to see Grace, and found her in the company of another." For, whether Alderman Casey had lied or not, Peg hadn't, after all — and there had been not one, but two young men wooing Grace. "And when he went away… Tell me, Rouse: was it because she loved another man? Or because she'd made you a murderer for naught?"

Young Casey shook his head like one dazed. "What was…?"

"What does it matter?" Mylls burst out of his silence. "Lord forgive me — but we should give thanks it was this knave, and not one of Babington's fools! Does it matter why he killed the girl?"

There was a strangled groan from the lad, and all colour ebbed from his face, leaving him so ashen that the freckles stood out dark. "Grace…?" he stammered.

"Leaving her body where you did, she was found as soon as it was light."

"Sweet Jesu … Grace!" Casey grabbed at his hair with both hands, and his cuffs fell back, baring his wrists. The left was roughly bandaged, and under the bandage was the end of a scrape, angry red and starting to scab.

So.

Tom grabbed Casey's wrist, and pushed back the sleeve. "And this you did to yourself at old St. Mary Axe."

This served to undo the lad. He tugged free, stumbling backwards. "I swear to God, Mr. Thomas — I never meant…"

A hard swallow. "I wanted to see Grace. Then you and Nick came searching, and you were bound to think ill! I only had to run — but no, like a halfwit I hid up there in the ruins. We'd hole up there, Grace and I, when we were small."

"And you thought you'd do away with Mr. Thomas, too?" Mylls demanded.

"No!" Casey turned on the secretary like a cornered fox. "I bumped a loose stone as I climbed. I never meant —"

"To kill me?" Tom considered the beseeching young face. "No, I don't think you did. But I was going to find you up there in your perch. A stone would slow me down while you ran —"

"No!"

"You're right: to see you at St. Helen's was to think ill — and all the more after Finch's hand was found."

Could the lad go any paler? "Hand?"

"You didn't bury him deep enough, Rouse. Pigs are nasty beasts."

That was when the lad's knees deserted him, and he dropped onto the windowsill, ashen and sweaty. All marks of a guilty man, surely?

Tom moved to loom over him. "Did you learn of the vaults from your father?"

"Grace —" Casey stopped short as his mind caught up with his tongue.

"Another childhood secret — Grace's, and yours," Tom said. "Children always know the strangest things."

And anyone could see how close the lad was to tears, how ready he was to confess — anyone but Frank Mylls, who leapt out of his chair and went to shake him. "But Finch's daughter was too grown for hide and seek, eh? You'd killed her father for her sake, and there she was, playing secrets with another man!"

Which, of course, made Casey rally. "I didn't kill her father!" he cried. "And I didn't kill her!" He stumbled to his feet and pushed past Tom and Mylls to appeal to the silent Phelippes. "Master!"

Now, Phelippes was the sort to take pride in his cold head and colder heart — and yet there was a ruefulness in his long, measuring gaze. "You're not to leave this house, Casey," was all he said in the end. "Not until it's decided what's to be done with you."

Only when the discomfited lad was entrusted to a servant and gone, did Phelippes allow himself a troubled grimace. "I wouldn't have reckoned him for one to do murder."

And, in fair truth, Tom wouldn't have either — but then... "He was seen at St. Helen's the night Finch died, and he had cause. He was there in secret at least once more, and he knew that Grace Finch had another man."

"And it's plain he knew of the vaults," the cypherer sighed.

"Not to mention that he tried to stone Mr. Thomas." Of the three of them, Mylls seemed the least disturbed. "I'll say it again: what does it matter? Rest Finch's soul, and his daughter's, too — but it's a blessed consolation that it's naught to do with Babington."

It must nettle him that, instead of joining him in such congratulation, Phelippes pursed his lips, and Tom asked, "What of Rouse's father, though?"

Mylls shrugged. "This clears him, I'd think? The girl lied through her teeth, and that mess at the Exchange was no more than foolishness —"

And right then the door flew open, and Berden barged in without a by-your-leave.

"Have you gone mad, Berden?" Mylls barked.

Never had Tom seen the spy so far beside himself, short of breath and dishevelled.

"We're undone, Masters!" he choked.

Which had him surrounded at once, and pelted with questions of what, and how, and why.

Berden shook his head and wiped at his sweat-covered brow. "I was with Sheppard — you know him, Mr. Mylls: the gaol-keeper of the Clink. We come across this man, and both know him for a Jesuit... And doesn't Sheppard go all agog to arrest him?"

Oh, Jupiter... "You never did?" Tom asked.

Berden spread both arms, pup-hound eyes full of consternation. "But what was I to do? I told the dunce, but did he listen? All a-fire with it, he was, seizing a Jesuit traitor. Short of breaking Sheppard's head for him, what could I do?"

Not much, in truth — but still...

"His Honour won't like it," Mylls said. "Now Ballard will be warned."

Sheppard, Berden said, had had the priest brought to the Clink at once, with orders that nobody was to know.

But they all knew what prisons were like, and how well such orders would work.

Never be rash, Thomas, but learn to judge quickly, and quickly act on it when circumstance demands it.

In his mind, Tom bowed to his absent cousin — for if ever circumstance had demanded quick judgment... "Well now, that's one decision made," he said. "We take Ballard for now — as yet another seminary priest — as soon as we're able to. Do we know where Babington is, at least?"

"At the Exchange with a few others," Phelippes said. "I sent Skeres to join them."

"Tichborne, surely? And Tilney and Savage, I'll expect."

"Of Savage we don't know." Mylls's face knotted into a frown. "Gilbert Gifford is nowhere to be found."

Again! It should be no great surprise, perhaps — but pinch the lily-livered braggart, wandering off again, right when they needed him most! This time, Tom doubted they'd see him again soon. So now Ballard, wherever he was, would observe Jesuits snatched from the streets, and supposed friends vanished into thin air. "Berden!"

"Ay, Master." The spy straightened, wolfish of a sudden, smelling the prospect of acting at long last.

"Go keep an eye on them; follow wherever they go. The moment you see Ballard, send word."

Berden ran away.

"And when he sends word?" asked Mylls, as soon as the spy was gone. "When he sends word, and we have the warrant, what is it that we do? We're all Mr. Secretary's men. We'll uncover his hand…"

This, another of Mylls's oft repeated worries, had been easy to dismiss while they waited for the letter, for the warrants, for Ballard himself — but now it was a matter of hours, and indeed Mylls wasn't wrong. What was the use of having the warrant signed by the Lord Admiral, if it was a man of Mr. Secretary's doing the arrest?

Unless, of course… "What of Deputy Alderman Casey?"

Two pairs of eyes went very round at this.

"You never want to trust that man?" Phelippes gasped.

"I trust he'll want to curry favour — for himself, and for his son if he can."

For all of Phelippes's purse-lipped disapproval, there was the hint of a smile creasing Mylls's face, grim though it was. "My pursuivants, and the Lord Admiral's order, and a city man — 'tis not the worst of notions."

It could still go awry in a hundred ways, and they had a murderer in their own midst for good measure. Was gunnery like this? To load up ruin and slaughter, and wait in taut silence to set fire to it, praying it wouldn't go off in your own face?

Go and find the truth, Tom Walsingham. It was nearing eight when, surfeited with waiting and pacing the narrow confines of his room, Tom yielded to the echo of Frances's words and hied himself to Cornhill — not to the Exchange, not this late, but to the Castle Tavern — where Babington had likely herded his guests by then.

The tavern was full to its eaves, thanks be for that, and noisy with toasts to Drake's return — as though each Londoner were to share in the adventurer's treasure. It took some searching to find Berden sitting in a corner with a pipe.

"I didn't know you for a tobacco drinker," Tom saluted. "Infernal stuff."

Berden made a show of welcome. "They're up there, eating like geese at fattening." He waved his pipe towards the stairs, and an idle peek revealed to Tom a door on the first landing.

"Fortescue?"

A shake of the head. "Babington, Tichborne, Tilney, Savage, an Irish friend of theirs, Skeres, and Poley. Poley's come out once to fetch more wine — but otherwise..." Berden blew a ring of stinking blue smoke.

Now just let Ballard join them.

Tom settled to wait — but it was barely a blink before Berden kicked his boot under the table. "The Irishman."

And there he went — a dark-garbed figure descending the stairs at a brisk pace, and disappearing through the door to the stable-yard.

"Gone to fetch our good captain?" Tom asked.

"Heaven hear you, Mr. Thomas," Berden pronounced most piously, and beckoned a passing maid. The woman stopped, flushed and harried, asking what they lacked.

"Sack," said Berden who, it was worth noting, had been drinking plain ale in his own company.

The best part of an hour trickled by, slow as molasses, without Heaven hearing Tom at all — no doubt because, to while away the wait, he'd resorted to playing passe-dix for groats with Berden. Heaven might dislike gamblers, as Tom's mother had been fond of saying — but still it let Berden stop mid-throw, and jerk his chin at the stairs behind Tom's back. "Here they go," he murmured, and made a show of dropping his pipe and diving under the table to recover it.

"Gone," he murmured, reappearing. He picked up the dice and threw eleven.

"The devil's own luck, have you?" A little sourly, Tom pushed yet another coin across the table. There was a reason why he never played dice.

Berden chuckled. "I'm for home while it holds," he said, as he pocketed his winnings and the dice. "Will you walk with me a while?"

And what was the use of all the play-acting, Tom didn't know. Did Berden fear that someone in the laughing crowd was observing them, and would run to warn Babington and his friends?

No one must have, at any rate, for when the two Queen's men reached the street — blessedly cool and quiet after the taproom — the little company of six was walking down

Cornhill with all the heedlessness, if not the cheer, of well-fed men. They had a linkboy to light their way in the purple evening.

"You think they're meeting him?" Tom asked quietly.

Berden huffed as if to say *who knows?* Slipping his arm through Tom's, he steered them both after their quarry at a discreet distance.

Babington wasn't going home to Bishopsgate Without. He walked with the others all the way past Newgate and towards Holborn, and stopped to part ways at the mouth of Fetter Lane. There was a lantern burning at the corner, and between it and the linkboy's flame, Tom had a good view of the little group. He saw Babington pay the boy, and motion him to stay with the others.

"Robin knows his way in the dark like a cat," Babington said, throwing an arm around the shoulder of a smaller figure — and nobody laughed at this description of Rob Poley.

After an exchange of greetings, the two men plunged into the darkness of Fetter Lane, while the others continued along Holborn.

"Follow them," Tom whispered to Berden, and turned into the lane.

Ahead, he could hear Poley and Babington's steps, and their quiet conversation. Once he stumbled into a heap of rubbish and stopped, flattening himself against a shuttered door, ears straining. It sounded as though Babington and Poley never halted their steps.

It should have eased some misgivings; it did not.

Babington, Tom could believe heedless, for all that his fears should have made him otherwise — but Poley? Hadn't a snare awaited last night in these same shadows — witless as it seemed? For truly, one man alone, hidden in the dark, fleeing on being discovered...

And, of a sudden, it was like a spark from a tinderbox, throwing a blink of light on the glass pieces inside his mind. A snare, yes — but not for them. Someone else, whoever had sent the warning, was the prey: fed a lie to see whether it would trickle to Seething Lane! And so it had, and they'd taken the bait, and now their mysterious informer had laid himself open. Would they find another corpse — and not of Rouse Casey's doing this time?

A noise shook Tom out of his thoughts. Damn it to Hades — why couldn't he pay heed? He took a wary step out of hiding, in time to glimpse two shadows before Poley's lodgings. There was a faint clacking of lock and key, and then the shadows disappeared into the darkened house. There had been just the two of them — most surely. Ballard hadn't joined them, nor anyone else. There was still a chance that the priest would go to Tichborne and Tilney instead, or that he would arrive later in the night. Tom moved to the arch where Rouse Casey should have kept watch last night. He had a view of both Poley's door and the alley's black maw, close enough to hear if anyone climbed his way into the garden — though neither Captain Fortescue nor Father Ballard struck him as the sort to scramble up fences. The Catilines of this world, surely, walked up to the door in the middle of night, with their cloak thrown over a shoulder, and their proud head high?

A fanciful conceit, but one that wouldn't go away — together with that of the faceless informer, baited, uncovered, and now perhaps lying dead somewhere in the warm summer night.

CHAPTER 19

4th of August

Tom might as well have stayed at Fetter Lane, after all.

After spending an uncomfortable night in the street, watching a dark and silent house, he'd trudged back home at cockcrow, and fetched a bare hour of sleep before news came from Poley: Ballard was to come and see Babington, and could Poley himself have a word with Mr. Thomas?

"Never another trap, surely?" Phelippes mused, standing at the foot of Tom's bed, already dressed and as bright as Phelippes ever looked.

Did the man ever sleep? Tom rubbed drowsiness from his eyes, and propped himself on an elbow. "In plain daylight?" he asked around a yawn. "And to smoke out whom, this time?"

The cypherer shook his head. "I still wonder at the mystery of it. You're right, they weren't after us — but who is it that they were hunting? Gifford, perhaps? Or Maude. I'll say I itch to know."

This was how one knew Phelippes was in great agitation: not by a change in his fretful mien, not by any alteration of his whitish voice — but (and a rare occurrence it was) by the rambling of his speech.

"But, if it was either Maude or Gifford, why go to such trouble to hide from us?" Tom sat up, rubbing his shoulder, stiff after the damp and restless night. 'I reckon, it won't count for much after today."

Phelippes went away, with the stretched mouth of one chewing sour thoughts — the same taste of unanswered questions Tom disliked with all his might.

"Upstairs." Poley glanced over his shoulder towards the house as he closed the wicket. "Master Anthony's still a-bed."

"Is Maude here?" Tom asked, and Poley frowned.

"I've seen less of Maude, these last few days," he said.

And he'd hardly noticed, for he'd had much else on his mind, and Maude, if nothing else, knew how to make himself go unnoticed. At another moment, Tom would have asked how many days, but it didn't matter anymore.

Poley hastened Tom through the unkempt garden and towards the house, where a back door opened, shadowed by a bower of vines and white musk roses, thick enough to hide them, should anyone peer out of the windows upstairs.

Robert Poley had no smile this day. "His Honour says he must delay seeing Master Anthony until Saturday," he said.

Not that Tom had expected otherwise. "Must he," he said — neither question nor statement.

"He can't leave Court, for Her Highness is unwell, and he can't risk having Mr. Babington seen there..." Poley stopped, and took a long breath. "Mr. Thomas, I ask you: will His Honour see the boy?"

"You just told me yourself: the day after tomorrow." It was the oddest feeling, under the jaded gaze, of having disappointed Robert Poley, this most slippery of self-serving rogues. "But that's never why you sent for me?"

It might have been, though. Poley, who had been scuffing his boot at the broken corner of a flagstone, looked up. "Deacon Gifford says he crossed from France to join the plot — then changed his mind, went to His Honour with his tale, and was turned against his friends, and left his freedom…"

When Tom said nothing, Poley forged on. "The boy offers so much more! Ballard himself, the whole plot, Queen Mary's letters —"

"Has he written to her?" Tom cut through — and to Hades with caution.

"He says he has." Poley waved it aside. "And if that mealmouth Gifford was granted his freedom…"

Ay — but Gifford wasn't the leader of the plot, exchanging letters with Mary Stuart and Mendoza, sworn to overthrow the State and kill the Queen.

"Your boy already changed his mind from regicide to humble service. Can you swear he won't change it back again?"

A sharp exhalation, just this side of crossness. "Give him a way out — and he'll eat out of His Honour's hand until his dying day!"

And see Robert Poley, of all men, running out of patience. See the mask cracking, hear the voice rising. It was a heartbeat before he checked himself. He swallowed, gathering his composure the way he would the folds of a cloak. But he'd betrayed himself and knew it. Oh, he was many things, Rob Poley — but never slow at reading his fellow man.

And for a heartbeat, Tom felt sorry for Poley: one whose rare loyalty was as dangerous as his ill will… Oh, baggage! What business had he feeling sorry? Now just let John Casey with the pursuivants make haste.

Tom moved to the edge of the bower, squinting up at the house, gauging windows, doors, and staircases.

From the dappled green shadow Poley watched him in thoughtful wariness. "If you arrest Ballard here, I'm bound to fall under suspicion. Even Master Anthony can't help but doubt me — never mind the others."

And wasn't this a most startling change of tack! "You're forgetting yourself, Rob. Who says it's us arresting Ballard? Haven't you heard? The hunt for priests is up."

Could it be that the Jesuit's arrest had remained secret for half a day and a night? For a wonder, perhaps it had, reckoning by Poley's uncertain mien.

"Who —?" he asked.

"It doesn't matter — and, to ease your heart, you'll be arrested too, as a friend and comforter of traitors."

In no earthly way could Poley have missed the thrust — and yet only the faintest ripple crossed the man's face before he gave a snort. "And you think they'll believe that, Mr. Thomas? Would you, in their place?"

It was with a childish urge to unseat the mask again that Tom shrugged. "I wouldn't know: 'tis always a little hard to believe you, Rob — but I'm sure you can blame yourself for it."

Of all things in this world, Poley began to smile. It was a slow, skewed smile — and what lay behind it wasn't to be known, for right then, the sound of heavy boots thundered inside the house.

Tom made to draw his blade, but Poley pushed him back into the bower's shadows and went to stand on the threshold. Over his shoulder, a man could be glimpsed. He was for Holborn, he called, and the front door slammed behind him.

"Savage," Poley whispered. "Going to meet the others."

John Savage — the soldier, sworn to commit regicide.

"As long as he's not running to keep his oath. Does he mistrust you much?"

A stretch of the mouth. "All mistrust me, Mr. Thomas. All but Master Anthony."

All mistrust me. Not *All here*, not *They all* — but *All*. Was this it? Was this why Poley found in himself a vein of loyalty to Babington — because the young man trusted him, and more fool he?

It was the thought of a heartbeat, for someone else was coming down the stairs, and a deep voice called for Rob.

"Ay, Captain?" Poley called back, and hurried inside, drawing the door ajar behind him.

Ballard. Now, what if Ballard was minded to leave? Where were Casey and his men? Gripping his rapier's hilt, Tom sidled towards the door, straining to listen.

"Ah, Rob," Ballard sighed. "Does Mr. Anthony know?"

A sudden coldness scraped up Tom's spine. *Does he know we're being betrayed? That you're a Judas? That it's all over...?*

Beyond the door, Poley made no sound. Tilting his head in question, most likely. Creasing his brow. Smiling a little, even?

"I've long thought he put too much trust in you," Ballard said. "But then, so did I in Maude, it seems."

"Maude?" Poley asked — the very voice of bafflement.

"Lying is a grievous sin, Rob. Is Mr. Anthony lying, too?" And there was such sadness in the soft words, so much regret.

It jolted Tom. He could imagine very few things a man like Ballard knew how to regret. Drawing, he sprang inside — and a heartbeat later, the pursuivants and John Casey burst through the unbarred front door.

They all stopped cold, like carved pieces on the black and white chequered floor.

Ballard had a dagger pointed at Poley's chest. He blinked, wrong-footed just long enough that the pursuivants caught him by both arms and tore the blade from his grasp.

Poley stumbled away, backing against the newel post.

And perhaps, after all, Alderman Casey was less of a dolt than his son would have him, for he went to stand in the middle of the narrow hall, brandishing his sealed warrant.

"By the Lord Admiral's command," he proclaimed, "I'm to apprehend the priest John Ballard."

Acknowledge none of us that you might see, he'd been instructed, which he executed by looking around again — until Ballard, tall and straight in the pursuivants' hold, bowed his head. It was the smallest, proudest nod: Catiline facing defeat.

"Away," Casey ordered, and the pursuivants marched their prisoner to the door, where another, thick-chested fellow waited, carrying a cudgel over his shoulder.

Ballard went quietly. He gazed at Poley — who stood white-faced at the stairs' foot — and then at Tom.

Tom had to fight an urge to explain himself, to say he was no mercenary priest-catcher. It was a struggle to meet gaze with sober gaze — and let Sir Francis never know how hard it was.

And then Ballard's eyes hardened in recognition, and he stiffened, half turning towards the stairs — to warn Babington, no doubt. Without a word, the man on the door stepped forward and pushed the end of his cudgel high in the priest's stomach. Not a violent blow — just enough to wind Ballard into bent voicelessness, as Casey and his men dragged him away.

In the hollow silence, as Poley went to close and lock the door behind them, Tom sheathed his rapier, finding himself a little dazed. Could it be that the hunt was over, that they'd caught their foe — John Ballard, traitor, intriguer, and leader of men?

"Robin?" The young, quavering voice wafted down from upstairs. "Robin?"

A spasm twisted Robert Poley's face. "Hear him?" he asked in a harsh whisper. "A dangerous murderer! Going to off the Queen, they were! And Lord Leicester, and Mr. Secretary…"

"Go upstairs. Tell him you'll run to Mr. Secretary, then go to Richmond. They'll arrest you there."

Upstairs, the young fool kept wailing for Robin.

Gritting his teeth and gripping the railing, Poley began to climb the stairs. He stopped mid-flight, to look down on Tom.

"Think well, Mr. Thomas," he rasped in a voice unlike his own, "before you let yourself like or pity these fools."

All the way back to Seething Lane, Tom tried to push out of his mind the thought of a few fools he'd liked — if not pitied — in Rheims. It was a persistent thought, though, and it was still weighing on him, together with Poley's qualms and Ballard's proud nod, so that he and Phelippes made a grim pair by the time the story of the arrest had been related.

"And say what you will, Mr. Thomas," Phelippes groused for the third time in a row. "Say what you will, but I can't bring myself to trust Rouse's father, or those two pursuivants. And you know who the other man was? Berden's brother-in-law!"

They sat side by side in a quiet corner of the White Horse, two doors away from Sir Francis's house, sharing a dish of oysters and a flagon of Rhenish wine. The cypherer chewed on his mouthful and his worries, with a sour manner fit to curdle milk.

"Do you even like oysters, Philippus?" Tom snapped at length. "Why didn't you have something else?"

Phelippes sniffed, and skewered another oyster on the point of his knife.

Oh, Jupiter… Shouldn't they feel at least a measure of triumph? Hadn't they beheaded the conspiracy? But then, conspiracies were famously like hydras, and even witless, the other nine-and-ninety heads were bound to have teeth.

Tom leant both elbows on the table and groaned. "God, 'tis like being adrift mid-river."

The old habit to beg, half laughingly, his wincing friend's pardon stirred — and was stifled at once by ill humour.

Tom was glad to catch sight of Tib Fisher across the room, bouncing on tiptoe as he sought them. He beckoned, and the boy made his way to them.

"I've found him, Masters!" he announced and, when this was met with blank stares, "The stable-lad from the other night!"

Oh, yes — the night-time charade at Fetter Lane, forgotten in this morning's whirl.

Poor Tib, what a face of crestfallen reproach he had for Phelippes! "You told me to keep looking, Master."

"Ay, so I did." And there was a gleam in the cypherer's eyes that said he hadn't lost all interest in the riddle. "So this ostler — what did he have to say?"

"Didn't know the man as gave him the message — just that he was old. Lad's a cod-head, mucking out after horses all day."

What would "old" mean to a boy — especially when talking to another of his age? Tom had a rueful notion that he himself must seem half-old to the likes of Tib Fisher. "And where is it that he mucks out, your cod-head?"

"The Benbridge Inn."

Seeing that Tom didn't know the place, Phelippes explained, "That biggish place in Lyme Street, close by Neville House."

And how a fellow of such Puritan bent should know where each and every inn in London was...

"Lyme Street?" Tom sat up of a sudden, pieces shifting inside his head. "Doesn't it go to Fenchurch Street?"

With a disbelieving huff, Tom met Phelippes's eyes over the boy's head. Of course — of course! Although, what hare-brained game the man was playing...

"Well, at least he's still alive," said Phelippes.

"Ay — and you were right not to trust him!" Tom rose and dug a few pennies from his purse. "Where is it that they brought our friend?"

"Wood Street."

Tom added a penny for young Fisher. "Well done, Tib — have yourself a codling!" he said, clapping the lad's shoulder — and ran away.

For all its stately width, and its tall, handsome houses and its goldsmiths' fine shops, Cheapside was no pleasure walk on an early afternoon in August, when the meat had lain for many hours open to the heat and flies, and the mounds of leeks and fennels, and the baskets of mushrooms, plums and berries had had all morning to wilt away under the sun.

Amidst the noise of heckling, peddling, and frayed tempers, Tom kept watch by Queen Eleanor's three-storey marble cross, until he found his man, emerging from Wood Street.

There was an old woman, staring in reverence at the cross, muttering the *Ave Maria* — as the elderly still did sometimes — and John Casey started to chase her away. Then he saw Tom, and he forgot the poor crone, his face darkening.

"Well then, Master. I've done as I was told, and your man's in the Counter. What of my son?"

And wasn't this past belief! "What of him? You never think we'll forget what he did because you obeyed your orders?"

"He didn't —" He bit off the rest — hearing the anger in his own swelling voice, perhaps. For a while he breathed through his nose. "Please, Master," he muttered at length, and jerked his head towards Wood Street.

Tom followed him around the corner and under the trees of a small churchyard, shadowed even at that hour — a better place to discuss life and death than a market street. The air hung damp and stifling among the walls, and Casey stomped along the graves to the end of the one gravelled path, before turning back.

"My son's a dunce, Master," he rasped. "But he killed no one — and never, never Grace Finch!"

As though one were to take on trust the words of a suspect's father! Still, in this particular instance... "You know, Deputy Alderman — I've half a mind to believe you." The pieces arranged themselves in Tom's mind as he spoke. "You and Peg Lovell both. It wasn't Rouse you found talking with Grace. It was her gentleman sweetheart — the one who'd have supper in Fetter Lane."

The mercer had looked up in relief at first. At the mention of Fetter Lane, his face went the colour of wet chalk. He crumpled to sit on a gravestone — and ay, he *would* look old to a stable-boy.

"The idiot girl!" he groaned. "Having trysts with a gentleman — and a malefactor! They stood by the vestry door, and never saw me as I stepped close. I loved her, Mr. Walsingham — for all her crabbed ways, I loved her dearly — and here she was, chatting and giggling with this fine fellow, who was sure to ruin her. He said he had to go, for his friends awaited him at supper. She asked him to come back later — kitten that she was! And he said he didn't know, for his friend's garden was all the way in Fetter Lane. You should have heard how she begged and cajoled, and then he went away, and I…"

"And you thought you'd give him to us?"

Casey gave a slow shrug. "Isaac was so secretive when it came to his master. Once, years ago, I'd followed him awhile, to see where he went. I didn't know the place for Mr. Secretary's house, but Dr. Lewis always said Isaac did the Queen's work."

"So, on your way home, you picked an inn where you weren't known, and sent a stable lad to warn me."

"I couldn't risk that you'd think ill of Grace…"

"And you'd have your young rival removed. A cunning plan, Deputy Alderman — if it hadn't killed Grace."

Casey jumped to his feet, shaking from head to foot. "Killed her!"

"Didn't you wonder why the fellow would tell Grace where he was to meet his friends? He was trying her, putting her to the test. And, through no fault of her own, he found her unfaithful."

"But didn't you catch him at his supper?"

"There was no supper. It was a test, I tell you: we took the bait and went there, and found an empty house. But Grace's gentleman was lying in wait, and what must he think, but that Grace had betrayed him?"

John Casey wavered, dropped to sit again, and wept.

One could almost be sorry for this man who, in his jealousy, had unwittingly killed the woman he loved. And yet… "There's still one thing, Casey. How did you know the man for a malefactor?"

Another, deeper groan. "That day at the Exchange — when I happened on my son, he was watching a group of fine gentlemen, and then Isaac arrived. Rouse was very nettled that I made a noise, and Isaac didn't like it, either. I thought nothing of it, back then — but the other night I knew that young man for one of those my son watched, and I thought of Finch, and the Queen's work…"

"And you are sure?"

"I know no names, Your Honour — but he was one of them. The finest of them all."

Berden would know the names, having been at the Exchange with the younger Casey — and Berden, Phelippes said, was at Poley's lodgings.

Off Tom trotted to Fetter Lane, then, to find a grim Berden, busy searching the rooms together with Paynter.

"He's gone," the spy announced, spreading his arms in bafflement. "Babington's gone, and sink me if I know how."

Berden, it appeared, had been watching the door. He'd seen Poley leave soon after the arrest of Ballard, and waited for Babington to do the same. Only, Babington hadn't left — and, when enough time had gone by to make him uneasy, the spy had climbed into the garden, forced the lock on the back door, and entered to find the house deserted.

"You know me, Mr. Thomas: I'm not one to seek excuses, but I swear, the devil must have opened the earth for him —"

"Or he'll have gone through the garden while you watched the front." Tom looked around, taking in the sparsely furnished hall, the two doors, the staircase, and the noises of the search upstairs. "Have you found anything?"

Berden shook his head. "Haven't been here long," he admitted. "Curse it, Master — is it my fault that Mr. Mylls said to wait until he left, and follow?"

Guilt is a lovely maid, Tom's old nurse had used to say, *but one no man will wed.* "Ay, well, in your place I'd run to Bishopsgate Without, and send Paynter out to Holborn, just in case. Before you do, though: that day at the Exchange, when Casey's father all but upset your cart, who was there? Babington?"

"Ay — and..." Already halfway up the stairs, Berden stopped and scratched at his beard. "Who else now? Tilney, I'm sure. Tichborne — for you seldom see one without the other ... and one or two other hangers-on."

"Oy, Berden —" Paynter appeared at the head of the stairs, waving a sealed letter, and stopped on seeing Tom. "See what's here, Master."

"From Babington?" Tom took the stairs two steps at a time, snatching the letter. It was addressed to Poley.

Robin, Babington wrote, *Sollicitae non possunt curae mutare aranei stamina fusi. I am ready to endure whatsoever shall be inflicted...*

"Is that Latin?" Berden asked, peering over Tom's shoulder.

"There's no mending broken cobwebs," Tom translated absently, which made Berden snort.

Babington went on professing his honesty to Mr. Secretary, and his love for Poley himself. As for what had just happened...

I am the same as I always pretended. I pray God that you be and ever so remain towards me.

And Tom found himself unaccountably glad Poley had left without reading that the boy begged him to take care, lest he should be blamed for his friend's misfortunes.

Farewell sweet Robin, if as I take thee, true to me. If not, adieu, omnium bipedum nequissimus.

"Vilest of all two-footed creatures," Tom translated before Berden asked, and, folding the paper, slipped it inside his sleeve. "Are there no other letters? No writings?"

Paynter shook his head — which was little surprise. If he'd taken the time to write to Poley, Babington would never have left behind a letter to the Queen of Scots.

"Check again," Tom ordered. "And when you're done, find a place called Hern's Rent in Holborn. You come with me, Berden. We're for Bishopsgate Without."

CHAPTER 20

The rooms in Bishopsgate Without were just as empty — and just as well-appointed.

"A fine notion of martyrdom, he has," Berden grumbled, flicking the Flemish tapestry on Babington's writing table. "But then, he was counting on Spanish gold and a peer's life, I'll wager."

Tom tried to imagine the soft Babington eating cabbage and wearing worsted at the seminary in Rheims — and failed. "They're going to pay a stiff price for everything they counted on," he said. Provided they caught them, that was. He slammed shut the silver-studded lid of a very elegant, very empty coffer. Not that he'd hoped to find the cursed letter, but... "What's that?"

Someone was clattering about downstairs, not even trying to be quiet.

Drawing his rapier, Tom motioned Berden against the wall by the room's open door, and sidled to the stairs. If this was Babington returned... *I caught Babington, Sir — without a warrant, and being as much a man of yours as can be. I let Babington go, Sir. I had him within my reach and let him go.*

He peered over the railing — to see a stocky, curly-headed fellow, most definitely not Babington, muttering as he fingered the forced lock.

"Dolius!"

Nick Skeres jumped with a yelp — and glowered up reproachfully. "Near swallowed me own tongue, I did!"

Tom sheathed his blade as he descended the stairs, with Berden on his heels. "What are you doing here?"

"They sent me — Tilney and Tichborne. Savage says the Black Foskew is caught —"

"Where are they?"

"At a barber's shop, Shoreditch-way. Mr. Tichborne's 'urt 'is leg —"

"And Babington?"

"'E was there too, then came away, and Tilney sent me to fetch 'im back —"

To fetch him back! "You dolt! Come, both of you!"

Oh, they galloped — but by the time the three Queen's men barged through the barber's door, all that remained of the conspirators was a bowl of pink water, and a handful of blood-stained linens in a back room.

"They've gone," the barber stammered. "The moment their servant was gone, they ran."

"Cuds-me!" Skeres threw his hat on the floor. "Go after Mr. Anthony, says 'e — and what do I do? I go!"

Having no time for the Minotaur's disgust, Tom turned to the barber, a long-limbed fellow in a white apron. "Did you see which way they went?"

"I didn't see them go." The barber tugged at a well-oiled spade-beard. "I went to fetch a cordial for the injured gentleman, and when I came back..." He spread both hands at the empty, disordered room.

Jove fulminate ... but whom, in truth? A knot of conspirators fleeing for their lives? A frightened barber? The much crestfallen Minotaur?

More crestfallen, in fact, than was his thoughtless wont.

"I'm a want-wit, Master!" the lad muttered. "I should've —"

Should have done what, in the face of the plotters' plain distrust?

And, if a guilt-ridden Skeres weren't prodigy enough, behold Berden, coming to the rescue. "They were never letting you go, Nick. They'll mistrust their own mothers now."

So they weren't, and so they would — and now…

Were they running to hide again? Leaving London? Putting their plan into action? Tilney, Babington…

Skeres and Berden shuffled and strained like hounds on the leash, waiting for orders — and beyond them, through the door to the front room, Tom caught the eye of the barber's apprentice boy, peering aslant as he washed a customer's hair in a basin.

And children knew all sorts of things, didn't they?

When Tom beckoned, the customer was left with a dripping head, as the apprentice obeyed the summons in a bound.

Eager as he seemed, it was no matter of conscience to him, so Tom took a ha'penny from his purse.

"There were two gentlemen earlier. Did you hear what they spoke about?"

"Ay, Your Honour!" With a sideways glance at his fretful master, the boy stepped closer. "I came in to fetch the soiled towels, and they chased me away — but I heard them. The one as was injured said they should all go their ways, and the other took it in snuff. *I'm not waiting while Savage buys fine clothes* — that's what he said."

Tom raised a brow at Skeres, who nodded.

"'Tis 'im as came to fetch us in 'Olborn, and said 'e'd seen what 'e'd seen, and brought us 'ere to find … you know. Said 'e was goin' to…" Skeres made a great show of brow-raising and head-tilting — his subtlety in not mentioning regicide.

"Only they'd never let 'im close, 'e said, not attired like 'e was. So 'is friend gave 'im money and a ring, and 'e ran like an 'are."

Ran to buy Court apparel — for one didn't murder queens in workaday clothes. But Tilney wasn't going to wait. And apprentice boys were lying, greedy miscreants, ever up to mischief — but this was too precise for an invention.

When Tom produced a second ha'penny and asked if there was anything else, the boy bounced on his toes, ferrety face glowing with importance.

"One of them said: *If not her...* just as he slammed the door. But, Your Honour, that's what he said: *If not her...*"

And then they ran! Tom threw the coins to the boy, and ran himself, with Skeres and Berden following.

"Go to Seething Lane, Berden," he ordered, as he jumped in the saddle. "Tell Phelippes and Mr. Mylls. Savage must be found — and Babington."

"And what about the other two? God knows where they are now."

"Oh, but we know where they're going." *If not her...*

Tom spurred his horse and took off at the briskest canter Bishopsgate Street would allow, with the Minotaur behind him.

Nobody ever crossed the bridge in a hurry.

The quickest way was a wherry across the river to Southwark, where there was no lack of horses to hire — and that's what Tom and Skeres did. At the George Inn, Sir Francis's authority let them have horses ahead of all others. As the two mounts were readied, Tom asked the inn folk about two gentlemen such and such, but wasn't surprised when no one remembered either pearl earrings or injured legs.

"They would be fools to stop here. Tilney's a Court man — he'll have some inkling of how Sir Francis works."

And there were half a dozen inns along the street — and wherever the fugitives had hired their horses, they were bound to be gone by then. Better to follow, as soon as the horses were ready, and take the road, cantering on the way to Richmond. They were clearing the last of Southwark when Skeres cried out and reined in his horse.

"What's with you?" Tom shouted.

Skeres pointed to a house right off the road, with a stretch of ground beside it, where a child was walking two saddled horses.

"'Tis their 'orses there!" he called, his own nag dancing under him. "They came by the bridge!"

Tom dithered, wondering at the two horses — a fine grey and a sorrel. Too easy — too easy. "Are you sure?"

"Am I sure!" Skeres slapped his own thigh. "Tilney's Spanish mare, and Tichborne's good old Grizzel. I saddled 'em meself!"

Tom threw himself off the saddle, and ran up to the house to pound on the door until a woman came to open it warily.

Tom wished he had a searching warrant — and made up for the lack with sternness. "In the Queen's name, I must search this house."

The woman tried to protest that her husband was from home, but Tom pushed past her into a neat little kitchen. "Now, Master!" she squawked, hoarse with fear but brave enough to stand her ground — for all the world, in her yellow bodice, a fowl before a fox. "My husband —"

The room had another door and a steep flight of stairs — no path for a man with a hurt leg. Still…

"Upstairs," he ordered to Skeres, and went himself for the back door. Over the woman's shrilling, he threw it open —

and there, reclining on a bench with his leg up and his round-cheeked face twisted in pain, lay Chidiock Tichborne.

Pale blue eyes opened to squint at Tom, far too bright and red-rimmed. The man was feverish — and he was weeping.

Also, he seemed to be alone.

"Where's Tilney?" Tom demanded.

Tichborne's sweaty face crumpled — whether in anguish or in pain it was hard to tell.

"Do what you must," he gasped as he tried to sit up. "I'm a poor sinner — but the Lord knows his own."

Which wasn't likely to favour heretics and traitors — but Tom wasn't going to belabour the point. "I trust he will," he said. "Tilney, now."

Tichborne stared back. This was the man who, according to Skeres, had begged Babington to abandon their design — but it didn't mean he would betray his friends. Instead, a pained smile lit his pale face. "*Pater noster, qui es in cælis...*" he chanted, arms trembling under him as he propped himself on his elbows. "*Sanctificetur nomen tuum. Adveniat regnum tuum...*"

Traitorous Church Latin — but then, what had he to lose?

He stopped when the door slammed open, and Skeres hurled in. "There ain't —" the Minotaur began, and froze at the sight of the injured man.

Tichborne gaped in turn. "You..." he mouthed, and fell back on the bench.

Skeres, Tom was ready to swear, had never once considered that the man he'd watched would come to know him as a treacherous foe, and shook his head like a harried dog. When he spoke, it was with a truculence that didn't fool Tom. Did it fool Tichborne? "Goodwife 'ere says they 'ad three 'orses, and left two behind."

Of course — of course: it *was* too easy!

Tichborne's smile twisted — a white mask of pain and exaltation.

Tom leant over him. "You may think it's not over — but you're wrong!"

And, leaving Skeres to arrest the man, in a trice he was on horseback and galloping off.

To think the last time Tom had ridden this way, he'd thought himself in the depths of confusion. Now Sir Francis's displeasure, the tangle of Finch's death — all of it seemed so puny against the urgency of catching the traitor in time. Even Frances — found and lost in the same breath — seemed no more than a silvered dream, as far beyond his reach as the moon. *Go and find the truth*, she'd said. *Go and find the truth* — it pulsed in Tom's mind with each hoofbeat on the way to Richmond. He knew the truth now — or most of it — and much good it would do him or anyone else, unless he overtook his man.

On he forged, galloping and cantering in turn, lest the hired horse betray him, shouting to make way in the Queen's name, cursing at carters, raising a storm of dust, half-blind with it at times, and at times with the river's glare. Never had the way to Richmond seemed longer — and never shorter, for each mile Tom rode with no trace of a fleeing horseman ahead brought him nearer to the fearful chance of being too late.

How much advantage had his foe? How much time had Tom lost, questioning barbers, and finding Tichborne, instead of giving chase?

And at last the turrets of Richmond Palace came in sight, huddling together like a surrounded troop, with their onion domes, and the weather vanes glistening like tongues of fire in the afternoon shimmer.

The lathered horse stumbled up to the great gateway, where the guards ran to meet this urgent newcomer, to bar his way, to grab his bridles. Tom flung himself out of the saddle, fumbling in his sleeve for Sir Francis's seal.

"I must see Mr. Secretary at once!" he gasped.

An officer came running from the gatehouse, and thank Fates it was an acquaintance.

"I won't ask what's afoot," the fellow said, as he led the way under the great arch. "A man of yours just came in on a half-dead horse, asking for Mr. Secretary —"

A man of theirs! *If not her…* "Where is he?" Tom grabbed the officer's arm. "Where did he go?"

"Why, the antechamber…"

Tom didn't stop to hear the rest, breaking into a run across the great courtyard and tearing past scatters of palace folk.

The messengers' antechamber was misnamed — it was an antechamber to nothing but long waits. Half a dozen men sat there on the benches along the walls, none of them the one Tom sought — which was no surprise. A household sergeant in chain of office hurried in Tom's way, and even the seal only half lessened his displeasure. "At least you have the grace to show it," he sniffed. "Unlike some Pensioners…"

Lord God — too late!

Half dizzy with it, Tom grabbed the man. "And you let him through? Where did he go?"

"He's a Gentleman Pensioner, I tell you —"

"Devil take you — where?"

Nobody must ever have shouted at this fellow before. "Mr. Secretary's taking the air…" Jowls quivering in cowed outrage, he pointed westward — where the great gardens lay.

"Send the guards," Tom called — and ran.

Out to the great court, he ran, all the way across it, and through the arch, into the walled garden that alone was as large as the moated grounds at Scadbury. He skidded to a halt on the thin gravel. The tortuous knotted beds, the dark-leaved topiary, the hedges winding in tangles... Parties of gaudy courtiers strolled the snakish paths, or rested in the galleries around — but no Sir Francis, and no —

Oh, Lord guard thoughtless fools — this wasn't where Sir Francis would take the air. Too open to the sun, and no trees...

Off at a run again Tom went, heart in his mouth, down to the great orchard.

No open ground here, no easy view. Plum trees, and pears, and medlars, apples and quinces — each sort tight in its own small, square wood, the too-sweet scent of ripe plums thick in the river air. Where now?

Gripping his rapier's hilt, hunched low, Tom stole among the trees — boots quiet on the soft soil.

Was that a shuffling far ahead? Out of the shadows Tom darted, into the next clump of trees. The paths were larger here, the gravel coarser, made for barrows rather than fine pinked shoes. Tom leant against a tree, the bark rough against his cheek, and strained his ears in the warm, still air. More plums — *the Queen loves plums*, Lady Ursula's words echoed in Tom's mind from some long-ago summer day. A thrush's fretful song, the buzz of wasps gorging on the swollen fruit, a cackle of laughter beyond the wall — and...

There it was — a flash of light-coloured cloth!

Tom drew, spun around, and leapt past a trunk, then another...

And he stumbled into a basket, sending the overripe plums a-spill. The basket's owner, a gardener's lad with his shirt sleeves rolled up and his hands stained, gawped at the armed stranger, mouth so full that the juice ran down his chin in bloodlike beads. And Fates be thanked for that forbidden plum — or the boy would have shouted instead of gurgling in fright. Tom gestured him silent.

Vague thoughts of showing the seal — as though the boy would know it — scattered away at a crush of running feet. Swinging around, Tom glimpsed a shadow flitting across a larger path, and into the depths of the orchard.

"Halt!" he shouted, and threw himself in pursuit.

There — amidst the trees, a dozen steps ahead…

"In the Queen's name, Charles Tilney — halt!" Tom called, all caution thrown to the winds.

It had been a whirl of pale grey; as Tom barged among the trees, it resolved into the tall figure of Tilney, with blade drawn and teeth bared. *The finest of them all*, although he didn't look it now.

Eyes running over Tom, the traitor lowered the rapier and changed his carriage to the utmost haughtiness. "And by what power, fellow?" he questioned. "I'm of Her Highness's Gentlemen Pensioners."

"And you wander armed in Her Highness's orchards?"

Tilney jerked his chin at Tom's naked blade — all the time moving his own in glittering figures of eight. "So do you."

"I didn't lie my way in, though."

"Oh, not in here." Contempt burnt in Tilney's knowing eyes. "Where's the blue coat, servant-lad?"

Boys playing at secrets, Skeres had called them. Boys, not above childish taunts. "And I'm neither a traitor nor a murderer."

The wicked point twirled faster. "Your sort are quick to speak of treason, when it comes to those who'd save England."

"'Tis a strange way to save England — by letting in the Spanish *tercios*. Or by murdering guileless young women?"

Ah, this now — *this* drew blood. See how the fine face contorted! "She wasn't guileless! But then, daughter to a Queen's man…"

"Now, that's one thing I wonder: how came you to know of Isaac Finch?"

A shrug. "I saw him once at Placentia, back before I left the Court. He was with a yeoman, seeking Mr. Secretary…"

"So you followed him back to St. Helen's."

"Not that time, no. 'Twas only ten days ago or so that I saw him again in London. God's gift, so I might spy what Walsingham was up to."

"And you found Grace, ready to fall for a handsome gentleman, to tell him of her father's comings and goings."

"All I ever learnt from her was that her father didn't just ride to Court. She said he'd be away for days, at times — and that set me a-wonder. I'd go to her, and woo her. I said we'd run away — next time her father was gone long enough… Perhaps I could follow him."

A shiver ran down Tom's spine. All of it chance — and yet so close to uncovering the work at Chartley. "But he caught you."

The traitor waved his rapier, as if throwing something aside. "I stumbled into him as I sought Grace. My first thought was to run — but he'd seen me. What if he knew me, what if…" He ran the back of his hand across his mouth.

And it struck Tom as though he'd seen it: Catiline's anger, his disappointment… "Ballard would never forgive you, would he? You had to kill Finch."

Tilney's eyes hardened. "Oh, never look so prim!" he scoffed, raising his blade. "You'd have done the same in my place. Why, you'd kill me now, if you could." And, sudden as a snake, he thrust.

And, for all he'd been expecting it, Tom had to work at parrying. Tilney was taller, his rapier longer, and he had desperation hardening his arm. The violence of it ran up Tom's still aching arm, even as he stepped out of harm's way.

"I will, if I have to," he called, more boldly than he felt. "Although I'd rather catch you —"

And here he had to leap back again, and circle before he could try a pass of his own.

Tilney came in under Tom's blade — and gave a grim smile. "Or else I'll kill *you*," he taunted. "I've no qualms, Queen's man — be sure."

They circled each other among the trees. Where in Hades were the guards? "And where will you hide my body? There's no Grace to show you a secret vault here."

Anger leant force to Tilney's fresh thrust — and made it rougher. "You think I wanted to kill her?"

"If you had qualms, they didn't stop you."

"She had misgivings." Tilney leapt forward and locked blades again. "She feared her father had been killed — and the place was always a-swarm with your people. I had to make sure."

"So you told her of a supper at Poley's house." Tom found himself rather breathless as he disengaged and lunged.

Be it the words or the thrust, Tilney was thrown enough to step unguardedly aside.

"'Tis you, then!" he cried, circling to come in on Tom's bad side. "Grace told you!"

Tom circled away. "She told no one, Tilney. Someone else was eavesdropping and advised me. Grace never betrayed —"

With a cry of rage, Tilney stomped in, batting Tom's blade aside in a rough *botte-de-paysan*, so fierce that Tom reeled, to find a boot hooked under his calf. He lost his footing and fell heavily on his sword-arm. There he lay on his back for a heartbeat, all wind knocked out of him, arm filled with pain as he felt for his dropped rapier, blinking up at Tilney.

"You see, I'll kill you!" The glittering point lowered towards Tom's chest. "Then I'll kill Walsingham — and if I do nothing else, I'll have rid England of a devil."

At the very last moment Tom rolled out from under the murderous blade. At the same time, he grabbed a handful of dirt and rotting plum — and threw it.

When Tilney raised his left arm to shield his face, Tom dragged himself to his knees, careening into his foe.

Down into a heap they went, Tilney smashing into the nearest tree. He was dazed enough for Tom to knock the rapier from his hand, and pin him where he was with a knee to the chest — right as the sound of booted steps and calling voices reached them.

"In the Queen's name!" the voices called.

The guards, at last.

The fallen man tensed under Tom's knee, and he tightened his hold.

"'Tis done, Tilney," he gasped, with all the sternness he could manage. "And all for naught."

And then the guards were on them, red-liveried and loud, dragging them both to their feet, snatching their weapons from the ground — and one of them, no guard at all, cried, "Mr. Tom!"— and of a sudden Tilney tore himself from the guards, and stood tall and proud.

"Take this murderer!" he cried. "Parsons, you know me: I'm Tilney, of Her Highness's Gentlemen Pensioners!"

There was mayhem — Tilney shouting, the guards hesitating, the officer called Parsons staring in round-mouthed confusion, the Minotaur bellowing and shoving, and Tom cursing the traitor's impudence.

"Peace, you all!" The rumbling command stopped all in their tracks, and the guards parted before Davies like a sea of red and gold. All knew Sir Francis's Welshman, all heeded him as he pointed at Tilney. "By Mr. Secretary's orders, Mr. Parsons: take this man and shut him up securely."

Poor Parsons! So eagerly he jumped to obey, seizing Tilney and barking at his men to assist him when they'd done so already. In the grasp of the guards, still Tilney turned back, the rotten plum staining his sleeve and face, the colour of drying blood.

"You're a lying dog, Nick Skeres," he sobbed. "And Maude betrayed the Captain — and Poley, and this one carrying the letter. Was it all but deceit?"

The cry hung in the damp air as Charles Tilney was dragged away.

And when the traitor had disappeared among the trees, Tom let himself slide down to sit propped against the nearest tree, rubbing at his maltreated shoulder. *I've found the truth, Frances — and stopped a murderer's hand.*

"Are you much 'urt, Master?" The rumble was soft enough that it took some thought before Tom knew it for Nick Skeres's.

"What are you doing here? Didn't I leave you with Tichborne?"

The lad shrugged and looked away. "And leave you alone to stop that murtherer? Anyway, I'd no warrant to keep Mr. Tichborne, and 'e was too 'urt to take with me."

And much good you did, trampling here when all was done. The wave of annoyance was so sluggish that Tom let it go. After all, Tichborne was injured and alone.

"Never mind, Dolius," he sighed. "Even if he runs, he won't run far."

Then Davies returned, with something on his wooden face that might have been a frown. "Are you well, Mr. Thomas? Master's safe — but he's been called away to Her Highness. He says the man must be arrested quietly. You'd better see to that, if you're well."

It was the longest speech Tom had ever heard from the Welshman. And, as if that weren't astonishing enough, when Tom nodded, and said he'd see to it at once, the nod was returned, and the frown dissolved into something akin to approval.

Yes, these were days for prodigies.

CHAPTER 21

5th of August

Tom Walsingham waited in the royal park, as he'd been told to do.

Carpets lay spread under a cluster of old oaks, an empty seat waited, piled with velvet cushions, two female players plucked at their lutes, and a dozen servants scurried about under the stern direction of a Pensioner in a red sash, and a white-clad lady.

Having been instructed to be at hand but not underfoot, Tom stood aside and waited. He'd been waiting for nigh on two hours, dressed in a fine suit of dark green satin that was not his. Sir Francis had had it fetched from Barn Elms for him — an epitome of sober elegance, with its buttons of chased silver, the fine lawn collar, and the matching ribbon in the high-crowned hat. It was very fine indeed, and Tom hated it. He couldn't rid himself of the thought of Anthony Babington, for one thing — fussing over his best clothes for a royal audience that would never be. And for another, Tom rather suspected the green suit belonged to Philip Sidney, left behind after some visit with his father-in-law. Attired in the clothes of Frances's husband — of all things! And one couldn't be presented to the Queen in his riding leathers, stained with dust and rotten plums — but, devil take it, Philip Sidney's cursed suit pricked at Tom's conscience like a shirt of Nessus. And then there was the cry of that other wearer of silks, Charles Tilney, echoing again and again in his mind: *was it all but deceit?*

Of a sudden the fuss sharpened into an image of earthly perfection, as most of the servants retreated out of sight and the players started a sprightly tune, and the attendants disposed themselves. Even the breeze picked up to stir the branches, and sweeten the sultry air. The sun alone was lacking, concealed above a canopy of grey clouds.

Shouldn't it shine on Elizabeth Regina, as she appeared among the trees, a glory of lemon-coloured damask amidst her scarlet guards, the bevy of white ladies-in-waiting and a black-robed man on either side of her?

She leant — hunched, almost, on the arm of Sir Francis, and her physician, Ambrose Lopes's father, walked on her other side. They led the Queen to the gilt seat under the oaks, and Tom bowed with the others as she sat a little stiffly.

All the time she kept up an unsmiling conversation with Sir Francis, and turned towards Tom when Mr. Secretary beckoned to him.

For the first time in his life, Tom approached his queen and made his best bow, learnt and perfected at the French court.

"This is my kinsman, Your Highness," Sir Francis said. "Another Walsingham — young Thomas, a son to my late cousin, Sir Thomas Walsingham of Scadbury, now brother and heir to the current Sir Edmund."

There was the shortest pause, then, "Your kinsman may rise," said the Queen.

Tom rose, finding himself under the scrutiny of his sovereign. Dark brown eyes glittered, knowing and birdlike, in a wizened face, whose lines no thickness of paint could conceal. And it struck Tom that it was right that the sun shouldn't shine — for the throne was yet in danger, and Mary Stuart still weaving treason, and the dupes of England's enemies still roaming free — and the Queen, wrapped in her splendour, was a frail old woman leaning on the arm of a frail old man.

Oh, Lord. A notion seized Tom that the keen gaze must see through him, see his treasonous worries, see even the clothes on his back for those of the courtly Sidney.

And then the Queen beckoned him closer — a flick of bejewelled fingers.

When Tom obeyed, Elizabeth leant forward, close enough to murmur for his ears and Sir Francis's alone.

"You spared us all a grievous harm, lad," she said, eyes darting to her Secretary of State. "We would recompense your courage — but what happened must be kept most secret. Will you be content with the gratitude of your Queen, Thomas Walsingham?"

And Tom found himself dazed into speechlessness. "Yes — yes, Your Highness," was all he knew to stammer as he bowed again. Tongue-tied fool.

It earned him a pat of the Queen's feather fan on the shoulder, and a tight-lipped smile.

Then Sir Francis was begging leave, and bowing them both out of the august presence, leading his dazzled kinsman by the elbow.

Your Highness's gratitude is a prize for which I'd willingly die... This would have been an answer, showing at least a grain of wit, if it had just occurred a heartbeat earlier.

As they moved away, the music thinned to a silvery strain. Tom turned back to see the Queen sitting very erect. With the dappled shadows playing on her upturned face, she looked young again — no: she looked ageless, the way a Queen should be.

"She'll remember you, if nothing else. But, Thomas…" Sir Francis pressed Tom's elbow. "I believe I've been unfair to you."

Tom stopped in his tracks under an oak. "Never, Sir! I've been slow in understanding, I —" But it wasn't the fulmination at Barn Elms that Sir Francis meant, was it?

"You were right from the beginning about Finch's death, and you understood in time to save my life, I believe — for which you have my thanks. It will sound as though I'm loath to die in the service of God, the Queen, and England — but there's so much left to do. We need to bring to justice Babington and his cronies, for one thing — and, if we can at all, the Queen of Scots with them." He gave a sigh, heavy with fatigue. "You are a man of good wits and courage, Thomas — and most loyal."

Loyal — oh, Jove! Guilt churned inside Tom like vinegar. "I…" *I love your daughter more than I should ever dare; I've doubted your wisdom, I…* "I thank you, Sir."

Sir Francis's eyes turned very sad. "Perhaps it never was right to demand more of you."

Such a struggle it was not to flinch — and Tom wasn't sure he'd succeeded. Did Sir Francis understand how deep a stab his words were? Yes — for Sir Francis Walsingham never spoke without careful purpose, and there was no mistaking the regret in his manner.

Tom had to force the whisper through a throat that was tight of a sudden. "I'm sorry, Sir…"

And to this Mr. Secretary replied as his daughter had. "Don't be. I'm forcing the Queen's hand, picking what truth to show her, dragging some of it before her by means of falsehood, so she'll sanction Mary Stuart's death. I'm selling my soul, I'm sure." He reached to detach an oak-apple from the tree, and threw it to the ground, crushing it under his foot. "I understand that you should doubt, that you should be dismayed, and it touches me that you'll remain steadfast in spite of it. It touches me deeply — but…" He took another oak-apple, and turned it in his palm. "I grow old, Thomas — and much as I pray there will be time for Sir Philip to learn ruthlessness…"

My husband is not made to compromise his conscience, Frances had said, as though she spoke of a fall from grace. She had been wrong on this — disappointment seeing what it wanted to see. Or perhaps it was childish jealousy — Tom's own — that heard what it wished to hear.

The second oak-apple followed the first to the ground and to destruction. "Phelippes is single-minded," Sir Francis mused — not at all absently. "Philip will need him against the Mendozas and the Guises of this world — and, in fair truth, against the Queen's wayward mind. And he will need you."

Provided I *can learn to compromise my conscience*. Tom stifled the thought as soon as it flared alive — or tried to — the less painful reason for it being, it didn't matter truly. No matter what Frances regretted, it had never been a question of Tom succeeding in Mr. Secretary's place, against the Mendozas and the Guises of this world. He'd always known it. Whereas Sidney…

"I'm sorry, Sir," he said again — a little more the master of his voice. "There are few things in my life I've wanted more than your approval."

"Oh, but that you have, child — and my full trust with it. What I hope is that I still keep yours."

The breeze was stiffening, thick with the river and distant rain. Tom thought of Ballard, leading men to their doom for the sake of faith; he thought of Poley's bifronted loyalty to Babington; he thought of Finch, who hadn't failed his duty, after all; he thought of the fugitive Gifford, twice a traitor out of conscience and out of fear; he thought of Sidney in Flushing, of Frances going to join her husband, and of the day they would come back; and he thought of the man in front of him, freely sacrificing his soul and asking no more of him — far less, in fact — than he asked of himself, and never for his own sake.

I wonder if Father sees how like him you are, Frances had said.

Tom bowed a soldier's bow. "You have my trust, Sir," he said. "And my loyalty, and my obedience, as long as you will want them."

HISTORICAL NOTES

The messengers came and apprehended Ballard, which (being done in my lodging, a place where Ballard had not often been before; and for that Mr. Thomas Walsingham was immediately departed from me, in their sight, before the pursuivants came) would be imputed, said Babington, directly to my charge.

This is how Robert Poley described Ballard's arrest — and his worries concerning it — in his lengthy report about the plot. So we know that Tom Walsingham was there on the morning of the 4th of August, receiving from Poley "such speeches as Mr. Secretary had commanded [him] the previous day". And I must begin this note by confessing that no, I didn't have the heart to send away my hero "before the pursuivants came". In my defence, Poley had been known to be selective with the truth before, so I don't feel overly guilty in letting Tom share in the action. What Poley's report tells us with certainty, is that young Thomas was involved to some extent in the undoing of the Babington Plot — which, if you ask me, would be better named after Ballard.

A Suffolk Catholic with a Cambridge degree, John Ballard fled to Rheims, where he was ordained as a priest in 1581. Unlike many of his fellows, he wasn't content with preaching and celebrating Mass. He wanted Elizabeth dead and England conquered back to Catholicism, and with this aim in mind he tirelessly shuttled between Rome and Paris, recruiting and scheming: the Papal court, the Spanish ambassador Bernardino de Mendoza, Mary Stuart's agents, the English Catholics... He kept telling the latter that Rome and Madrid were ready to act the moment England rose up against Elizabeth, and everyone else that England was ready to rise the moment Rome and Madrid acted. One imagines him as a charismatic, eloquent man. It seems that the wily Mendoza was a tad wary — but everyone else listened in rapt fascination.

Then in 1584 Father Ballard landed in England — very secretly, of course — for a campaign of clandestine Masses and exorcisms. Perhaps we, in our sceptical twenty-first century, don't entirely grasp the impact of such a thing, but the English Catholics were swept off their collective feet. Again, Ballard was quite the performer: commoners and gentry crowded his meetings, and among the others was a rather excitable young gentleman called Anthony Babington. It took Mendoza to resist Ballard's charm; young, hot-headed and prone to hero-worship, Babington fell completely under his spell.

He was sorely disappointed when Ballard left for the Continent again to resume his travels and campaigning: the Pope in Rome, Mendoza and Mary's men in Paris... The game never changed much: to everyone Ballard told what he wished were the truth — what he was convinced would become the truth with some nudging and pushing.

In 1586 he was back in England, charged with the preparation of a Catholic insurrection. They were in earnest, this time, and Ballard lost no time gathering a following of wildly high-flown young men — first and foremost Babington. To avoid suspicion and to move freely about, he adopted the alias of Captain Fortescue, a silk-wearing soldier known to his acquaintances as Black Foskew for his swarthy complexion and a penchant for black finery.

Still, neither a good actor nor a fiery zealot make necessarily for a good conspirator. Captain Fortescue never suspected that his traveling companion, Bernard Maude, was a Queen's man — if perhaps not a dreadfully effective one. And Babington's confidant, Robin Poley? Another agent. Moreover, when it dawned on him that Ballard's plans included the small matter of murdering the Queen, Babington grew nervous, and unwary, and loose-tongued.

Not that it would have made much difference. The plot was doomed from the start, and if it got as far as it did, it was because Sir Francis Walsingham was using it to seal Mary Stuart's fate. And indeed, Ballard had instructions to secure the support of the Scots Queen who, uncharacteristically wary at first, ended up compromising herself in full. As soon as Walsingham had Mary's incriminating letter in his hands, the game was up.

Ballard, as we have seen, was caught first, but soon Babington and the others joined their leader. They were all tortured — although there was precious little left to uncover by then. Within days, Ballard, Babington and four others were hanged, drawn and quartered — the whole process so horrific that it shocked even the usually bloodthirsty London crowds.

Whatever the fate of Ballard, Babington and their fellow conspirators, the fact remained that Sir Francis had won: at this point Mary Stuart was compromised in the most indisputable manner. What Sir Francis did with it … ah well, this you will find out in Tom's next adventure.

In addition to Ballard, Babington and Poley, Tichborne, Tilney, Berden, Francis Mylls, the Caseys father and son, Dr. Lewis, Ambrose Lopes, and even young Paynter are real historical characters — although I've taken a few liberties in portraying some of them. And, speaking of liberties, I also took that of delaying Frances's departure for Flushing. Actually, the very young Lady Sidney went to join her husband in the Low Countries in June. I kept her at home at Barn Elms for a few weeks longer — for purely selfish and narrative reasons.

And one last thing: what of the postscript to Mary Stuart's letter? Historians don't agree on the matter: some claim it was a forgery done by Phelippes at Sir Francis's behest, and some that, on the whole, the letter was damning enough without the postscript. From a strictly historical point of view, I rather agree with this second theory: Sir Francis simply didn't need the postscript badly enough to have it forged, and risk alerting the plotters. On the other hand, though, the forgery made for a better story — so I put it in the book, much to poor Tom's dismay.

A NOTE TO THE READER

Dear Reader,

Thank you for reading *A Deadly Complot*. I hope you enjoyed it. Whether this was your first Tom Walsingham mystery, or you've been following Tom for some time, I'd love to know how you picture him in your mind.

Tom's adventures are told from his point of view, so there is little description of him — certainly less than there is for the other characters. I have, of course, a face for him in my mind, just as I have for each of the characters I put on the page. For some, the better-known historical characters, there are surviving portraits, and often more than one. These include Queen Elizabeth I, Sir Francis Walsingham, Lady Ursula Walsingham, Frances, Lady Sidney, Sir Philip Sidney, Lord Leicester, Sir Walter Mildmay, and the Cecils — both father and son. Of others we have descriptions: Mary Stuart wrote in a letter a detailed (and not very flattering) portrait of Phelippes the cypherer — pockmarks and all; a spy named Charles Sledd lets us know across four and a half centuries that Cardinal Allen had a reddish beard, and his nails curved upwards; Father Ballard's elegant black clothes and soldierly manners were striking enough to make an impression on his enemies — perhaps not the wisest choice for a conspirator.

And then there are the men and women of whom no visual trace remains — Tom Walsingham among them. For each of them, as with the fictional characters, I have to make up a face, a presence, a gaze. I often wish I could sketch them — but, alas, I cannot draw, and so I resort to using different methods. Sometimes a character just comes to life in my mind, complete with freckles and voice timbre; sometimes I find them among period portraits, re-enactment pictures, or films. (Do you remember Rafe Lyggon in book three, *Death in Rheims*? Well, in my mind he looks just like Patrick McGoohan in the 1971 film *Mary, Queen of Scots*.) And then sometimes I just borrow the face of an acquaintance or a friend — like I did with Ambrose Lopes in this book.

So, how do you imagine Tom — or any other character? I'd love to hear from you — about this or Tom's adventures generally —through my **website** or via Twitter — where I tweet under the handle **@laClarina**. Meanwhile, if you enjoyed *A Deadly Complot*, I would truly appreciate it if you'd drop by **Amazon** and **Goodreads** to post a review, and let other readers know that you enjoyed this novel.

Thank you — and we'll meet again in the next Tom Walsingham book!

C. P. Giuliani

Sapere Books is an exciting new publisher of brilliant fiction and popular history.

To find out more about our latest releases and our monthly bargain books visit our website: **saperebooks.com**

Printed in Great Britain
by Amazon

53917281R00175